D0051052

THE DOG

THE DOG

Joseph O'Neill

PANTHEON BOOKS, NEW YORK

Copyright © 2014 by Joseph O'Neill

All rights reserved. Published in the United States by Pantheon Books, a division of Random House LLC, New York, and in Canada by Random House of Canada Limited, Toronto, Penguin Random House companies.

Pantheon Books and colophon are registered trademarks of Random House LLC.

Library of Congress Cataloging-in-Publication Data
O'Neill, Joseph, [date]
The dog / Joseph O'Neill.
pages   cm
ISBN 978-0-307-37823-1 (hard cover : alk. paper).
ISBN 978-1-101-87004-4 (e-book).
I. Title.
PR6065.N435D64 2014   823'.914—dc23   2013045030

www.pantheonbooks.com

Jacket design by Oliver Munday

Printed in the United States of America
First Edition
2   4   6   8   9   7   5   3   1

TO M, P, O, AND G

Here's the smell of the blood still: all the perfumes of Arabia will not sweeten this little hand.

—Shakespeare, *Macbeth*

I feel as a chessman must feel when the opponent says of it: That piece cannot be moved.

—Kierkegaard, *Either/Or*

THE DOG

PERHAPS BECAUSE OF MY GROWING SENSE of the inefficiency of life lived on land and in air, of my growing sense that the accumulation of experience amounts, when all is said and done and pondered, simply to extra weight, so that one ends up dragging oneself around as if imprisoned in one of those Winnie the Pooh suits of explorers of the deep, I took up diving. As might be expected, this decision initially aggravated the problem of inefficiency. There was the bungling associated with a new endeavor, and there was the exhaustion brought on by overwatching the films of Jacques Cousteau. And yet, once I'd completed advanced scuba training and a Fish Identification Course and I began to dive properly and in fact at every opportunity, I learned that the undersea world may be nearly a pure substitute for the world from which one enters it. I cannot help pointing out that this substitution has the effect of limiting what might be termed the biographical import of life—the momentousness to which one's every drawing of breath seems damned. To be, almost without metaphor, a fish in water: what liberation.

I loved to dive at Musandam. Without fail my buddy was Ollie Christakos, who is from Cootamundra, Australia. One morning, out by one of the islands, we followed a wall at a depth of forty feet. At the tip of the island were strong currents, and once we had passed through these I looked up and saw an immense moth, it seemed for a moment, hurrying in the open water above. It was a remarkable thing, and I turned to alert Ollie. He was preoccupied. He was pointing beneath us, farther down the wall, into green and purple abyssal water. I looked: there was nothing there. With very uncharacteristic agitation, Ollie kept pointing, and again I looked and saw nothing. On the speedboat, I told him about the eagle ray. He stated that he'd spotted something a lot better than an eagle ray and that very frankly he was a little bit disappointed I wasn't able to verify it. Ollie said, "I saw the Man from Atlantis."

This was how I first heard of Ted Wilson—as the Man from Atlantis. The nickname derived from the seventies TV drama of that name. It starred Patrick Duffy as the lone survivor from a ruined underwater civilization, who becomes involved in various adventures in which he puts to good use his inordinate aquatic powers. From my childhood I retained only this memory of *Man from Atlantis*: its amphibious hero propelled himself through the liquid element not with his arms, which remained at his sides, but by a forceful undulation of his trunk and legs. It was not suggested by anybody that Wilson was a superman. But it was said that Wilson spent more time below the surface of water than above, that he always went out alone, and that his preference was for dives, including night-time dives, way too risky for a solo diver. It was said that he wore a wet suit the coloring of which—olive green with faint swirls of pale green, dark green, and yellow—made him all but invisible in and around the reefs, where, of course, hide-and-seek is the mortal way of things. Among the more fanatical local divers an underwater sighting of Wilson was grounds for sending an e-mail to interested parties setting out all relevant details of the event, and some jester briefly put up a webpage with a chart on which corroborated sightings would be represented by a grinning emoticon and uncorroborated ones by an emoticon with an iffy expression. Whatever. People will do anything to keep busy. Who knows if the chart, which in my opinion constituted a hounding, had any factual basis: it is perhaps needless to bring up that the Man from Atlantis and his motives gave rise to a lot of speculation and mere opinion, and that accordingly it is difficult, especially in light of the other things that were said about him, to be confident about the actual rather than the fabulous extent of Wilson's undersea life; but there seems no question he spent unusual amounts of time underwater.

I must be careful, here, to separate myself distinctly from the milling of this man, Wilson, by rumor. It's one thing to offer intrusive conjecture about a person's recreational activities, another thing to place a person into a machine for grinding by crushing. This happened to Ted Wilson. He was discussed into dust. That's Dubai, I suppose—a country of buzz. Maybe the secrecy of the Ruler precludes any other state of affairs, and maybe not. There is no question that spreading everywhere in the emirate are opacities that, since we are on the subject, call to my mind submarine depths. And so the place makes gossips of us whether we like it or not, and makes us susceptible to gullibility and false shrewdness. I'm not sure there is a good way to counteract this; it may even be that there arrives a moment when the veteran of the never-ending struggle for solid facts perversely becomes greener than ever. Not long ago, I heard a story about a Tasmanian tiger for sale in Satwa and half-believed it.

Ted Wilson, it turned out, had an apartment in The Situation—the apartment building where I live. His place was on the twentieth floor, two above mine. Our interaction consisted of hellos in the elevator. Then, plunging or rising, we would study the Egyptian hieroglyphs inscribed on the stainless steel sides of the car. These encounters reduced almost to nothing my curiosity about him. Wilson was a man in his forties of average height and weight, with a mostly bald head. He had the kind of face that seems to me purely Anglo-Saxon, that is, drained of all color and features, and perhaps in reaction to this drainage he was, as I noticed, a man who fiddled at growing gray-blond goatees, beards, mustaches, sideburns. There was no sign of gills or webbed fingers.

The striking thing about him was his American accent. Few

Americans move here, the usual explanation being that we must pay federal taxes on worldwide income and will benefit relatively little from the fiscal advantages the United Arab Emirates offers its denizens. This theory is, I think, only partly right. A further fraction of the answer must be that the typical American candidate for expatriation to the Gulf, who might without disparagement be described as the mediocre office worker, has little instinct for emigration. To put it another way, a person usually needs a special incentive to be here—or, perhaps more accurately, to not be elsewhere—and surely this is all the more true for the American who, rather than trying his luck in California or Texas or New York, chooses to come to this strange desert metropolis. Either way, fortune will play its expected role. I suppose I say all this from experience.

In early 2007, in a New York City cloakroom, I ran into a college friend, Edmond Batros. I hadn't thought about Eddie in years, and of course it was difficult to equate without shock this thirty-seven-year-old with his counterpart in memory. Whereas in college he'd been a chubby Lebanese kid who seemed dumbstruck by a pint of beer and whom everyone felt a little sorry for, grown-up Eddie gave every sign—pink shirt unbuttoned to the breastbone, suntan, glimmering female companion, twenty-buck tip to the coat-check girl—of being a brazenly contented man of the world. If he hadn't approached me and identified himself, I wouldn't have known him. We hugged, and there was a to-do about the wonderful improbability of it all. Eddie was only briefly in town and we agreed to meet the next day for dinner at Asia de Cuba. It was there, by the supposedly holographic waterfall, that we reminisced about the year we lived in a Dublin house occupied by college students who had in common only that we were not Irish: aside from me and Eddie, there was a Belgian and an Englishman and a Greek. Eddie and I were not by any stretch great pals but we had as an adventitious link the French language: I spoke it because of my francophone Swiss mother, Eddie because he'd grown up in that multilingual Lebanese way, speaking fluent if slightly alien versions of French, English, and Arabic. In Ireland we'd mutter asides to each other in French and feel that this betokened something important. I had no idea his family was worth hundreds of millions of dollars.

Now he ordered one drink after another. Like a couple of old actuaries, we could not avoid surveying the various outcomes that long-lost friends or near-friends had met with. Eddie, with his Facebook account, was much more up to speed than I. From him I learned that one poor soul had had two autistic children, and that another had intentionally fallen into traffic from an overpass near Dublin airport. As he talked, I was confronted with a strangely painful idiosyncratic memory—how, during the rugby season, a vast, chaotic crowd periodically filled the street on which our house was situated and, seemingly by a miracle of arithmetic, went without residue into the stadium at the top of the road, a fateful mass subtraction that would make me think, with my youngster's lavish melancholy, of our species' brave collective merriness in the face of death. Out of the stadium came from time to time the famous Irish refrain

> *Alive, alive-o*
> *Alive, alive-o.*

Obviously, I did not share this flashback with Eddie.

He removed a pair of sunglasses from his breast pocket and very ceremoniously put them on.

"You've got to be kidding me," I said. The young Eddie had ridiculously worn these very shades at all times, even indoors. He was one of those guys for whom *Top Gun* was a big movie.

Eddie said, "Oh yes, I'm still rocking the Aviators." He said, "Remember that standoff with the statistics professor?"

I remembered. This man had forbidden Eddie from wearing shades to his lectures. The interdiction had crushed Eddie. His shades were fitted with lenses for his myopia; having to wear regular spectacles would have destroyed him. I advised him, "He can fuck himself. You do your thing. It's a free world."

"He's a total bastard. He'll throw me out of the class."

I said, "Let him! You want to wear shades, wear shades. What's he saying—he gets to decide what you wear? Eddie, sometimes you've got to draw a line in the sand."

Line in the sand? What was I talking about? What did I know about lines in the sand?

Young Eddie declared, *"Je vous ai compris!"* He persisted in wearing his sunglasses. The lecturer did nothing about it.

"That was a real lesson," Eddie told me at Asia de Cuba. "Fight them on the beaches. Fight them on the landing grounds." Removing the Ray-Bans—he preserved them as a talisman now, and had a collection of hundreds of tinted bifocals for day-to-day use; on his travels he personally hand-carried his shades in a customized photographer's briefcase—Eddie told me that he'd taken over from his father the running of various Batros enterprises. In return I told him a little about my own situation. Either I was more revealing than I'd thought or Eddie Batros was now something of a psychologist, because soon afterward he wrote to me with a job offer. He stated that he'd wanted for some time to appoint a Batros family trustee ("to keep an eye on our holdings, trusts, investment portfolios, etc.") but had not found a qualified person who both was ready to move to Dubai (where the Batros Group and indeed some Batros family members were nominally headquartered) and enjoyed, as such a person by definition had to, the family's "limitless trust." "Hoping against hope," as he put it, he wondered if I might be open to considering the position. His e-mail asserted,

I know of no more honest man than you.

There was no reasonable basis for this statement, but I was moved by it—for a moment I wept a little, in fact. I wrote back expressing my interest. Eddie answered,

OK. You will have to meet Sandro then decide. He will get in touch with you soon.

Sandro was the older of the two Batros brothers. I'd never met him.

Right away I came up with a plan. The plan was to fly New York-[Dubai]. This is to say, I had no interest in Dubai qua Dubai. My interest was in getting out of New York. If Eddie's job had been in Djibouti, the plan would have been to fly New York-[Djibouti].

OF COURSE DJIBOUTI POPS into my head for a reason. The French Foreign Legion has long maintained a presence there, and among the earliest and most reprehensibly innocent manifestations of my wish to flee New York was a fascination with the *Légion étrangère*. The men without a past! They suddenly struck me as marvelous, these white-kepi-wearing internationals whose predecessors fought famously, as my online searches revealed, at Magenta and at Puebla and at Dien Bien Phu, at Kolwezi and Bir Hakeim, at Aisne and Narvik and Fort Bamboo. *Vous, légionnaires, vous êtes soldats pour mourir, et je vous envoie où l'on meurt.* Unless the Wikipedia page misled, such were the exhortations that might drive into battle a fellow originating from any corner of the world yet beholden not at all to the compulsory systems of obligation of his native land. On the contrary, the legionnaire was bound only by the sincere comradeship into which he had voluntarily and humbly entered, a brotherly commitment captured with moving straightforwardness by his Code of Honor. I wanted to jump on a plane to Paris and sign up.

Though laughter would seem called for, I look back with astonishment and concern at this would-be soldier. How could this man, who had committed no crime and was guilty, to the best of my knowledge and belief, of not much more than the hurtfulness built into a human life—how could he find himself drawn to this absurd association of desperadoes and runaways? I remember how I yearned for a remote solitary fate causing shame and inconvenience to no one, for a life neither in the right nor in the wrong. Then along came Eddie Batros.

As the weeks passed and I heard nothing more from either Eddie or his brother and daily fought off the impulse to text Eddie for an update, it seemed that every five minutes brought mention of my new destination—Dubai. "God, I could be in my swimming pool in Dubai by now," groaned an English flight attendant during a runway holdup. The Albanian manager of my local hardware store said to somebody, "They got a hotel at the bottom of the sea. They got millionaires, billionaires. Beckham lives there, Brad Pitt lives there, every day you got Lamborghinis crashing into other Lamborghinis, every day you got sunshine, the gas is basically free, they got no taxes, it's heaven on earth." Dubai was suddenly everywhere, even in the office. A team from Capital Markets went over there for a two-day consultation that dragged on for ten days, and the whole thing turned into such a billing blowout that Karen from Administration was forced to look into it. The traveling partners, Dzeko and Olsenburger, reported that the quantum of fees and disbursements had to be seen in the relevant factual matrix, namely that the client had put up the team in a seven-star hotel in two-thousand-USD-a-night duplex suites offering a twelve-pillow pillow menu, a forty-two-inch plasma television set in a massive gold leaf frame, a rain room, a butler service, and Hermès shower gel and shampoo and unguents. Also significant, for the purpose of establishing an appropriate billing benchmark, was the client's frankly carefree concierging of the hotel's Rolls-Royce chauffeur service and its further concierging, on more than one occasion, of the hotel helicopter service. Moreover, excessive billing reasonableness by the firm might be perceived as verging on underbilling, a practice evidently inconsistent, in the eyes of this client, with a law firm of world-class standing. Afterward, getting hammered over cocktails, Dzeko more informally stated that these oil Arabs—he didn't want to generalize, there were other kinds of Arabs of course—these particular oil Arabs either had no understanding of how money worked, no idea about profit or value, or else knew all about it but just didn't give a shit and took a sick fucking pleasure in seeing these Westerners running around like pigs, snorting up cash on their hands and knees.

Dzeko was what we called a shovelhead, the kind of lawyer whose enormous industriousness is on the same intellectual plane as a ditchdigger's, so it was surprising to hear him come out with these speculations. But Dubai had called forth his inner theorist. Such was the provocative power of the brand, which was never more powerful, of course, than in 2007. In the middle of one of those agitated and sometimes frightening bouts of Googling with which, in those days, I would pass away my evenings, I finally entered "dubai" in the search box rather than, say, "fertility + aging" or "psychopathy" or "narcissism" or "huge + breasts" or "tread + softly + dreams."

I couldn't believe my eyes, in part because I was not actually meant to believe my eyes or was meant to believe them in a special way, because many of the image results were not photographs of real Dubai but, rather, of renderings of a Dubai that was under construction or as yet conceptual. In any case I was left with the impression of a fantastic actual and/or soon-to-be city, an abracadabrapolis in which buildings flopped against each other and skyscrapers looked wobbly or were rumpled or might be twice as tall and slender as the Empire State Building, a city whose coastline featured bizarre man-made peninsulas as well as those already-famous artificial islets known as The World, so named because they were grouped to suggest, to a bird's eye, a physical map of the world; a city where huge stilts rose out of the earth and disappeared like Jack's beanstalk, three hundred meters up, into a synthetic cloud. Apparently the cloud contained, or would in due course contain, a platform with a park and other amenities.

The marketing strategists obviously were counting on me, the electronic traveler, to spread the word—Dubai! But if it's possible to have a proper-noun antonym of Marco Polo, my name would be that antonym. To me, this wonderland was the same as any other human place: it boiled down to a bunch of rooms. I had a theory or two about rooms. They were still fresh in my mind, those evenings when Jenn would pace in circles in our Gramercy Park one-bedroom in order to dramatize the one-bedroom's long-term impracticality and reinforce the analysis she was offering, namely that all would be well if she and I, first, mentally let go of our apartment, the historic and rent-stabilized location of our love; second, acknowledged that it made sense to buy a place that would more readily accommodate the kid or kids who, in contradiction to her earlier feelings on the matter, Jenn now definitely felt ready to try to have; and accordingly, third, that all would be well as soon as we got ourselves a place with *more rooms*. I must have said little. I certainly failed to mention the following insight: if you cannot identify a single room in the world entry into which will make you joyful—if you cannot point to a particular actual or imagined room, among the billions of rooms in the world, and state truthfully, Inside *that* room I will find joy—well, then you have found a useful measure of where you stand in the matter of joy. And in the matter of rooms, too.

One way to sum up the stupidity of this phase of my life, a phase I'm afraid is ongoing, would be to call it the phase of insights.

During my first internet encounter with Dubai I had a vision (a thing of a split second) of myself, somehow disembodied, hurrying from tall building to tall building and from floor to floor and from room to room, endlessly making haste through one space after another and never finding good cause to stay or even pause. I associated this ghostly hurrier with one of those computer worms, created by the Israeli and/or American security agencies, whose function is to pass without trace from one computer to another, searching and searching until it finds what it seeks—whereupon it does damage. As a corrective to this unpleasant notion, perhaps, I developed an intensely enjoyable daydream of marooning myself on one of the outer islands of The World, say a fragment of "Scandinavia" or "Greenland," and living in a no-frills if comfortable almost-carbon-neutral cabin, alone except perhaps for a pet dog (one of those breeds that specialize in running into and out of water), a palm tree or two, and the odd visiting bird. I went through a period of islomania the symptoms of which included discovering the word "islomania," Googling "bee + loud + glade" and "islands + stream + Bee + Gees," and going to sleep every night listening to "La Isla Bonita."

Eventually I caved—I called Eddie for an update.

He told me everything was still on track but that the time line was kind of wavy on account mainly of Sandro's scheduling issues but that bottom line everything was A-OK. "Listen, I'm so sorry about this, I feel terrible, I'm going to take care of this right away, it's total bullshit." He apologized at such length, incriminated himself so excessively, that I began to feel a puzzled guilt. Had I missed something? Had Eddie done something wrong? He had not; and, knowing Eddie as I now do, I can see this was probably a tactical mea culpa and he was just handling me the way one handles any problem. I'm not suggesting Eddie has a lowly nature; I just think he's not above preferring business objectives to personal ones. (He subsequently admitted this to me, indeed insisted on it. He said (on the phone), "There's something we need to be clear on. I'm not going to nickel-and-dime you. You're going to get a sweet deal. Draft your own contract; do your worst. But you sign that dotted line, you're playing with the big boys. Same thing between me and my brother and my father: no favors. No mulligans. No quarter asked or given." Eddie laughed a little, and I laughed a little, too, in part at the thought of my grown-up old friend raising the Jolly Roger of business. "Got it," I said. "Absolutely.")

"No worries," I said to him. "These things always take time." I was being sincere. I didn't hold the delay against Eddie. He wasn't to know that the passage of time was unusually painful for me, that my circumstances at work were unbearable now that Jenn and I had separated and had to spend our days dodging each other at the office and being downright tortured by the other's nearness.

(From what I gathered, in addition to the core pain of the ending of our partnership, Jenn was suffering horribly from "humiliation" that was never keener than when she was at work, surrounded by the co-workers in whose eyes she felt herself unbearably lowered. I began to investigate this important question of humiliation, which I didn't fully understand (even though I, too, found it almost intolerable to show my face at the office and there be subjected, as I detected or imagined, to unsympathetic evaluation by certain parties). It seemed to me that there had to be, in this day and age, a substantiated, widely accepted understanding of such an ancient mental state. I took it upon myself to visit websites dedicated to modern psychological advances and to drop in on discussion sites where, with an efficacy previously unavailable in the history of human endeavor, one might receive the benefit of the wisdom, experience, and learning of a self-created global network or community of those most personally and ideally interested in humiliation, and in this way stand on the shoulders of a giant and, it followed, enjoy an unprecedented panorama of the subject. I cannot say that it turned out as I'd hoped. It would have been hard to uncover a more vicious and inflammatory collec-

tion of opiners and inveighers than this group of communitarians, who, perhaps distorted by a bitter private familiarity with
humiliation and/or by the barbarism in their natures, applied
themselves to the verbal burning down of every attempt at
reasoning and constructiveness. Frankly, it was grotesque and
frightening to behold. Apparently the torch of knowledge, con-
served through the ages by monks and scholars and brought to
brilliance by the noblest spirits of modernity, now was in the
hands of an irresistible horde of arsonists.)

In late March, I received a call from a woman speaking
on behalf of Sandro Batros. She wanted to postpone the get-
together until the morrow, Sunday.

"How do you mean, 'the get-together'?" I said.

"I'm transferring you now," she said.

I heard Sandro say how much he was looking forward to at
last meeting his little brother's friend. He said, "Listen, just a
heads-up, I'm fat. Fat as in really big. Maybe Eddie told you. I
just wanted to let you know. No surprises. Cards on the table."

Next thing, the assistant was telling me the appointment had
been rescheduled to 10:00 a.m. at Sandro's suite at Claridge's
hotel.

I said, "Claridge's in London?" I heard no reply. I said, "I'm
in New York. I'm in the U.S.A."

"OK," she said after a long pause, very absorbed by something.

I hung up, caught a plane to London, and took a taxi from
Heathrow to Mayfair. I cannot extinguish from memory the
terrifying racing red numbers of the meter. At 9:07 a.m., I
arrived at Claridge's. I recall clearly that the taxi came to halt
behind a Bentley. I presented myself at the Claridge's front desk
at 9:08. The receptionist told me that Mr. Batros had checked
out. She pointed back at the entrance. There he goes, she said,
and we watched the hotel Bentley pull away.

Sandro's assistant didn't return my calls. Neither did Eddie.

My return flight was not till the evening. What to do? It was a miserable, rainy day, and a walk was out of the question. Moreover this was London, a city I've never taken to, maybe because to visit the place even for a short time is to be turned upside down like a piggy bank and shaken until one is emptied of one's last little coin. I got the Tube back to Heathrow.

Looking up from my newspaper in the departure lounge, I saw two French-speaking little girls sneaking around histrionically as they tried to attach a paper fish to their father's jacket. The mother was in on the prank and the father was, too, although he was pretending not to notice. Something old-fashioned about the scene made me check the date on my newspaper. It was April 1, 2007.

So long as I have adequate legroom, I like flying long haul. The trip back to New York was spent contentedly enough: watching Bourne movies, which for some reason I never tire of; drinking little bottles of red wine from Argentina; and mentally composing a series of phantasmal e-mails to Eddie Batros. Successively deploying modes of outrage, good humor, coldness, ruefulness, and businesslike brevity, I let him know again and again about the London debacle and its inevitable consequence, namely, that I was withdrawing myself from consideration for the Dubai opening.

MORE THAN EVER, I am in the habit of formulating e-mails that have no counterpart in fact. For example, currently I am ideating (among others) the following:

> *Eddie—I think we should have a talk about Alain. I completely understand that the boy needs help, but quite frankly I cannot be his babysitter. Could you please inform Sandro that he will have to make a different arrangement?*

And:

> *Sandro—Please confirm that, contrary to what I'm told by Gustav in Geneva, I am authorized to pay MM. Trigueros and Salzer-Levi for their work on the Divonne apartment. Mme. Spindler, the cleaner, is also indisputably owed money. Or is it our position that they are bound by contractual obligations and we are not?*

And:

> *Sandro—You cannot involve me in your yachting arrangements so long as you require me knowingly to make false representations to the crew. This is professionally and personally intolerable. Now I am instructed (so I understand) to inform Silvio that mooring costs at Bodrum are his responsibility, when such is not, has never been, nor could ever be, the case. My response to you therefore is: (1) I will not say anything of the kind to Silvio; (2) this is the last straw; and (3) the first sentence hereof is repeated.*

And:

> *Sandro—In answer to this morning's directive ("Make it happen"), I can only repeat that it is currently impossible to purchase Maltese citizenship for your cousins. Maltese law does not yet permit it, and I do not control the Parliament of Malta. I am ruled by the facts of the world.*

The reason I don't physically send, or even type, these e-mails is that it would be pointless. The Batros brothers are not to be influenced, never mind corrected. Even if they were, it would not be by e-mail and, even if by e-mail, then not by me. When I first took this job, I'd often write them tactfully making points A and B or floating X or running Y up the flagpole or, finally, forcefully advising Z, and the consequence in all cases was nil. It's unsettling to be in a position where the performance of actions ceases to have the effect of making one an actor. This is a problem for all of us working on planet Batrosia, as we term it, and I'm sure I'm not the only Batrosian who, in reaction, composes phantom communiqués.

Arguably it is a little mad to covertly inhabit a bodiless universe of candor and reception. But surely real lunacy would be to pitch selfhood's tent in the world of exteriors. Let me turn the proposition around: only a lunatic would fail to distinguish between himself and his representative self. This banal distinction may be most obvious in the workplace, where invariably one must avail oneself of an even-tempered, abnormally industrious dummy stand-in who, precisely because it is a dummy, makes life easier for all the others, who are themselves present, which is to say, represented, by dummies of their own. A strange feature of the whole Jenn thing was that when the news of our breakup got out—i.e., when Jenn got out her version of her news; I kept my facts to myself—some people at the office, and I don't think this is paranoia, emerged from their dummy entities. I'd be walking down a corridor in my basically upbeat office persona when it would become clear, from the hostile look I'd get from a passing colleague, that the normal dummy-to-dummy footing had been replaced by an unfriendly person-to-person relation—or woman-to-man, as I reluctantly came to believe. I had been educated to accept the factual, moral, and legal invalidity of pretty much every constructed gender differentiation—and yet there existed, I think I discovered, a secret feminine jurisdiction authorizing the condemnation of men in respect of wrongs only men could commit! More than once my arrival in a room was followed by the sudden scattering of women and the stifling of their laughter, and wherever I went, it seemed to me, I was given to understand, from significant silences and mocking gestures of friendliness, that I'd been seen through—seen through all the way into my odious male nucleus. This subtle invasion of my being was my punishment. Meanwhile the men stayed in their shells—in hiding, was my impression. Though one time, in the restroom, there was a fellow who wordlessly slapped me on the back with a certain amount of sympathy.

It was ironic, this eerie coming-to-life of my colleagues, because Jenn and I had been undone by the reverse development: at some point our bona fide human interaction had been thoroughly replaced by a course of dealing involving only our body doubles. The figure that gripped me, when I began to think about what was happening to us, was that we had been transformed into zombies controlled, it could only be, by evolution's sorcery. Which is to say, the question of children having been (so we thought) answered—we couldn't reproduce without complicated medical intervention and so decided not to—our being together became a matter of outwardness, so that whether we dined wittily with friends or, in bed, felt for the other's body, we might as well have been jerking lifelessly down Broadway, flesh dropping from our faces, triggering panic; and by the time we, or rather Jenn, changed her/our mind about the baby, it was too late. In this sense, it came as a relief when it came to pass, late in the fall of 2006, that Jenn took sole possession of the rent-stabilized Gramercy one-bedroom, and, after a brief crisis of relocation, I moved into a luxury rental with a view of Lincoln Tunnel traffic. This move, which involved some extraordinarily painful and exhausting and unbelievable scenes, at least brought what might be called spatial realism to our situation.

It was to this apartment of reality that I returned from the trip made in vain to London. I'd concluded that the most powerful statement I could make to the brothers Batros was to make no statement. Certainly it would have been self-contradictory to say to them that I had nothing more to say to them. Moreover, I was under no obligation of communication and indeed had just been so fucked over by them that it was hard to see what proper basis there might be for future communication on any subject. The salient point: I had no option but to put an end to my Dubai scheming—a suppression that cannot have been without side effects. It was around this time that, every evening after work, I tried to run from my building's lobby to my luxury rental on the eighteenth floor. My intention must have been to become fitter, feel more competent, clear my mind, etc.

I used the emergency stairway. To begin with, I could only run up to the third floor and would in effect creep up the rest of the way. Though I improved quickly, the going was always very hard after ten floors or so, and in order to push myself, I suppose, I fell into the habit of imagining that I was a firefighter and that a fire raged on the eighteenth floor and two young sisters were trapped up there in the smoke and the flames. The problem with this motivational fantasy was that it placed excessive demands on my real-world athletic capacities, so that by the time I finally reached my luxury rental I'd be in a state of very real distress because I was too late to save the two little girls, images of whose futile struggle for survival would pass through my mind in horrible flashes as I made my desperate, sweating ascent. A shower and a Bud Light would just about wash away this upset, but I doubt it was a coincidence that during this period I found myself brooding on the story of the Subway Samaritan—the New York construction worker who had, back in January, jumped in the path of an oncoming subway train to rescue a man who, in the course of a seizure, had fallen onto the tracks. Specifically, the Subway Samaritan had pushed the Fallen Traveler into the trench between the tracks and lain on top of him while the screeching train passed overhead.

I deeply envied this man, though not on account of the

money and benefits in kind that immediately rained down on him. (The Subway Samaritan, who had acted for the benefit of a stranger, himself became the beneficiary of the largesse and assistance of parties personally unknown to him, including Donald Trump (ten thousand USD check); Chrysler (gift of a Jeep Patriot); the Gap (five thousand USD gift card); Playboy Enterprises, Inc. (free lifetime subscription to *Playboy* magazine (the Samaritan had worn a beanie with a Playboy Bunny logo during the rescue)); the New York Film Academy (five thousand USD in acting scholarships for the Samaritan's six- and eight-year-old daughters (the Fallen Traveler was a student at the Film Academy)); the Walt Disney World Resort (all-expenses-paid family trip to Disney World, plus Mickey Mouse ears for the girls, plus tickets to *The Lion King*); the New Jersey Nets (free season ticket); Beyoncé (complimentary backstage passes and tickets to a Beyoncé concert); Jason Kidd (signed Jason Kidd shirt); Progressive (gratis two years of Progressive auto insurance); and the Metropolitan Transportation Authority (one-year supply of MetroCards).) Nor was it the case that I envied the Samaritan his sudden celebrity and public glory: he could keep his Bronze Medallion from the city of New York and his appearances on *Letterman* and *Ellen,* and he was certainly welcome to his guest appearance at the State of the Union Address of George W. Bush, at which, bearing the title "the Hero of Harlem" (like Lenny Skutnik, "the Hero of the Potomac," before him), he was the object of congressional and presidential admiration and congratulation. No, my envy belonged to a less material though maybe no less indefensible plane: I coveted the Samaritan's newly earned and surely undisputed privilege to walk into a room—an everyday room containing everyday persons—and be there received as your presumably decent human being presumably doing a pretty decent job of doing his best to do the right thing in what is, however you look at it, a difficult world.

But no—that privilege was disputed! It came to my notice that *even the Subway Samaritan* could not escape criticism from the online community, some members of which apparently didn't "buy" the whole "story," and suspected something "fishy" was going on, and noted that at the time of the incident this man was escorting his daughters to "their" (i.e., their mother's (i.e., not the Samaritan's)) home; had inexplicably and recklessly preferred the interests of a "total" stranger to those of his daughters; and (reading between the lines of even respectable threads) was a lowly African-American man and thus prima facie a parental failure and a person of hidden or soon-to-be-revealed criminality. I remember one electronic bystander invoking what he called the Stalin principle. That is, he rhetorically asked if Stalin would be a good guy just because he'd once helped a little old lady to cross a road. More clever than this small-minded chorus, and more menacing to one's simple admiration of and gratitude for a brave and worthy deed, were those who questioned the whole "heroism industry," who suggested that this kind of uncalled-for and disproportionately self-sacrificial intervention was ethically invalid because it could hardly be said that good people habitually did or should do likewise, and that moreover it was stupid retroactively to treat as virtuous an obviously reckless act that could very easily have had the consequence of depriving two children of their father. Another commenter even proposed that there was no point in looking for moral lessons in the behavior of some unthinking instinctual (black) man whose actions, in their randomness and spontaneity and irrationality, were essentially akin to the motiveless pushing of persons onto the tracks that also occurred in the New York subway.

I was like, Who died and made these people pope?

One day, I ran the stairs in the morning. This was how I discovered that I wasn't the only runner in my building. There was another, named Don Sanchez. He was a physically and psychologically well-organized-, everything-in-order-, sanely-wry-professional-looking guy who wore sweat-wicking Under Armour shirts made from recycled plastic bottles. He had moved into our building not out of any fondness for his particular luxury rental but because, as he explained to me one day, he loved the high-quality run offered by the brand-new stairway, which had great handrails, bright yellow-edged steps, and good lighting. Don told me, laughing, that he could no longer imagine living a life that did not include "vertical athletics." He had run the Empire State Building and dreamed of running Taipei 101 and Swissôtel The Stamford in Singapore. He ran with musical ladybugs in his ears. He was much faster and stronger than I, and quickly and easily made it to the top, twenty-sixth, floor. The little girls in my blazing luxury rental would always be saved if it were Don Sanchez coming to their rescue. I quit running in the evenings and instead woke at dawn to run with Don: falling quickly behind as he skipped up two steps at a time, I was able to trot steadily onward in the knowledge that all would end well for the endangered children. So reassuring was Don that I invited him down to my place for a drink. That was not a success. I had very few lamps in my luxury rental and only a few items of furniture, and what with the long shadows and the darkness it was as if I had contrived to place us in one of those grim, I want to say Swedish, movies my poor parents often co-watched, duplicating in the arrangement of their respective chairs the arrangement of silence, gloom, and human separateness offered by the television. I confided various things to Don. He, in turn, disclosed that every year or three, he'd come across a staircase that would really grab him and, other things being equal, he'd relocate to the building in question in order to run in it. He shared his physiological theories. He imparted his views on the different demands made by perpendicular and horizontal mobility, writing down for my benefit some relevant mathematical calculations. After a couple of somehow frightening evenings over the course of which each of us was, there can be little doubt, impressed more and more powerfully by the mental illness of the other, we restricted our friendship to the stairs.

By a meaningless accident, my current abode is also on the eighteenth floor, but of course it would be unheard of and frowned on and simply impermissible to race up and down the stairway at The Situation. The last thing The Situation needs is middle-aged guys running around and sweating hard in public and grunting and looking weird and signaling their pain and undermining our Ethos and putting under even more stress our already very stressed price-per-square-foot value.

THERE ARE PLENTY OF high-rises here in the Marina district, but for valuation purposes the owners of apartments at The Situation—the Uncompromising Few, as TheSituation.com names us—need be concerned with only two comparators: The Aspiration, inhabited by the Dreamers of New Dreams, and The Statement, home of the Pioneers of Luxury™. We are all each other's Joneses. Because by design we exclusively occupy Privilege Bay—an elite creek or inlet of the planet's largest man-made lagoon—and, more important, because all three residential propositions have agreed on an Excellence Ethos (the tenets of which are published on our respective websites), our troika competes internally for the favor of an ultra-discerning micro-market of property investors—those who wish to reach The Far Side of Aspiration, in the terminology of TheAspiration.com. In principle, we three residential propositions proceed consultatively. In practice, it is like the three-way shoot-out in *The Good, the Bad and the Ugly,* and each will do whatever it takes to gain an advantage for itself, and each reacts like lightning to the slightest move made by another. When the cardio machines in the gym at The Aspiration were upgraded, those in The Situation and The Statement were at once replaced or renewed; same story when The Situation unilaterally began to offer complimentary sparkling water to visitors waiting in the lobby, and when The Statement without warning piped therapeutic aromas into its reception area. There is increasingly good if unexpected evidence that our rivalry has in effect been collaborative, in that it has functioned as a joining of forces against the great, strange waves that have attacked the Dubai property market. True, we have taken a massive hit, or haircut; but we float on. In our respective determination to not be outdone by the other two, we have, almost accidentally on purpose, cooperatively kept high our standards and morale and built up the frail composite brand conjured and encapsulated by the collective name we have given ourselves: the Privileged Three. I think of this brand as our little lifeboat. I think also of the bittersweet song I learned as a child from my mother:

> *Il était un petit navire*
> *Qui n'avait ja-ja-jamais navigué.*

That is, it may be that the same-boat strategy is no longer a good one. Soon, it may be every man for himself and dog-eat-dog and the horror of the *Medusa*.

Why? Because something weird is happening in the last vacant lot on Privilege Bay. This is the lot formerly dedicated to the Astrominium, which was destined be the world's tallest residential building (at just over half a kilometer) and offer the Ultimate Height of Luxury to the Ultimate Demographic. Those of us who acquired apartments in the Privileged Three did so on the footing (reflected in the purchase price) that we would in due course live next door to the Astrominium and that our residential propositions would draw value and kudos and identity from our huge neighbor even as they kowtowed to it.

Then—the *crise financière*. Soon after, the Astrominium site gave us the spectacle of the world's largest man-made hole in the ground, its colossal dimensions made vivid by the abandoned orange digger at the bottom of the chasm. I spent many hours looking at this digger from my apartment window, my mind turning always to the idea of a lost lobster. A few months ago, the digger disappeared; and a very peculiar thing occurred. If I happen to look out my window—if "window" is the best noun for the immense glass wall that comprises the exterior perimeter of my apartment—I can see a new concrete platform on the sand, and on the platform there has risen a small concrete structure, about the size of a cottage, consisting of a concrete X that leans onto a cuboid concrete frame. Is it a sculpture? A monument? Is it the first part of an Astrominium-like edifice? More work apparently lies in store, because there's a bulldozer on site and a large pile of black dirt partially covered by tarpaulin. There's also a portable toilet. The indistinctness of what's going on is only deepened by the activity I've seen down there. Basically, from time to time a dozen management types in suits and dishdashas stand around and have a grinning conversation. Not one of them pays any attention to the structure. Then they leave. I keep waiting for construction crews to come in and take the project—which I have called Project X—forward to the next stage; it never happens. The structure remains inscrutable as Stonehenge. Nor is www.Astrominium.com any help: all we get is the assertion, by now more than two years old, that the "building" of a "building" will "soon" be under way. This doesn't sound even linguistically right. It is unclear to me how the creation of a residential proposition suitable for Privilege Bay can be described as "building" a "building."

I've got to find out what's going on. If the Astrominium plot isn't developed soon, and in accordance with the Excellence Ethos, the Privileged Three are sunk.

I do what I pretty much always do in Dubai when I need to know something. I ask Ali.

That's a Dubai joke—"ask Ali." When I first arrived here, I was given a couple of how-to books. The first was a how-to-work-with-Arabs guide titled *Don't They Know It's Friday?* The second was *Ask Ali*, on the cover of which the eponymous Ali, a cartoon individual in a dishdash, leans toward the reader, the back of his hand concealing his mouth, and mutters, "Psst . . ." I permit myself a good laugh about the premise of *Ask Ali*, which is that, in order to learn about life in Dubai, you should follow a hissing informant to a hole-and-corner rendezvous where only things that are already matters of public knowledge will be disclosed to you on a hush-hush basis. Thus Ali will whisper in your ear about the local climate (hot), voltage (220), and body language:

> Whenever you see two [Middle Eastern] people speaking loudly or pointing at each other, relax and remember they are probably just chitchatting and having a good time.

I found my Ali, if I may be so possessive, soon after I moved into The Situation. I needed someone to fix me up with a personal VPN. A virtual private network, more than one expat had assured me, was the best and safest way to access Skype and other websites blocked by the U.A.E. authorities. (Here the eyebrows of the expat would rise. Their import was not lost on me. I was really quite excited about re-connecting with the porn sites that, in my last U.S.A. years, had given me what felt like near-essential sustenance, presumably with Jenn's blessing, because she (who had once accused me of expecting her to be my "concubine") was clearly counting on me (as I was on her) to be ninety-seven or ninety-eight percent sexually self-sufficient, and must have understood that self-sufficiency of this kind would very possibly involve recourse to dirty movies. Even if she wasn't—even if Jenn was under the illusion that sexuality, like water left standing in a pot for years, somehow disappears over time—then surreptitiously making use of porn was clearly preferable to "going outside the relationship" and creating a serious risk of emotional injury to Jenn and/or the third party. (There remained, of course, the problem of the welfare of the erotic performers. Any anxiety I might have felt on their behalf was eliminated almost completely by my preference for what seemed to be husband-and-wife porno acts (often mask-wearing or otherwise incognito) who gave the impression, accepted by me as bona fide, of offering up their intimate doings for moneymaking reasons, certainly, but on a voluntary and fun and expressly "amateur" basis. In fact, if I felt guilty it was on account of my decision to not subscribe to these sites but instead to jerk off as a freeloader and so take the benefit of the product without doing the decent thing of compensating the entertainers for their valuable if hobbyistic efforts. I did not lose sleep over this wrong, it must be admitted, if it was a wrong, which isn't admitted. (Ideally, I should have found a way to content myself exclusively with cartoon porn, which is quite sophisticated in this day and age of digital technology, and in principle enables the viewer to erotically fuel him/herself without any question arising of humans being harmed in the course of the filming. But what can I say? I'm a flesh-and-blood kind of person, and I'm really not turned on by the animation of certain scientifically impossible and/or violent scenarios, e.g., the rapture of human women by reptilian extra-planetary creatures, or the rape of cartoon women by cartoon rapists.)))

At any rate, someone was recommended to me for the purpose of installing an illegal internet connection in my apartment. To my surprise, this person, Ali, was an Emirati—a surprise because Emiratis (so I had been given to understand) were protected from the socio-economic factors that incentivize a person to undertake relatively menial work or, for that matter, to exert him- or herself in order to make a living, the upshot of which protection (according to expat lore) was a nation afflicted thoroughly by a peculiarly cheerful form of Bartlebyism. In substantiation of this stereotype, the only U.A.E. national I could claim to know, Mahmud, who officially functions as the "local service agent" of Batros Family Office (Dubai) Ltd. and bears technical responsibility for the getting of licenses, visas, labor cards, etc., was never to be found or, if to be found, failed to turn up for meetings or, if he did, turned up at his own convenience and in his own sweet time and to no effect. Mahmud was put on the payroll by Sandro Batros on account of his professed *wasta*—his clout with the Emirati authorities. To this day Mahmud, who is always good-natured and pleased about things, has yet to procure a single useful piece of paper. His workload consists, as far as I can tell, of accepting his Batros emoluments and hanging out with his pals at the Armani Caffè in Dubai Mall. I have spotted him there several times. He never fails to greet me jovially. Invariably he and his friends pointedly disregard a nearby group of standoffish Emirati young women who have not covered their pretty faces and whose head-to-toe black is offset by red or electric blue trimming. In order to make a powerful impression on the women they're ignoring, the young men always talk gravely on the phone and urgently input their handhelds: each has placed two or three gadgets on the table. They work hard to generate for themselves a strong aura of possibility, as if the day were growing in excitement and they were in communication with some more interesting and important elsewhere and this interlude at the Armani Caffè was merely a parenthetical or trivial portion of some enormous indiscernible adventure. Whether in fact there exists such an exciting, adventurous elsewhere—this remains an open question. The question is especially open in Dubai, land of signs to nowhere: I have several times followed, in my car, signboards that direct you to roads that have yet to be built. Your journey fizzles out in sand. (The sand is natural. This is the desert. Disintegrated rock secretly underlies everything. It's almost nauseating to see the sand wherever the effort to cover it has not yet succeeded.) What's more, because of the velocity and immensity of the infrastructural operations, such roads as have been built are subject to sudden closure or transformation, and even old hands and taxi drivers are always getting lost and turned around. The U-turn is a huge maneuver here—and maybe not just because of the chaotic construction projects. Rumor has it that, in order to promote official control of the population, the traffic planning has been modeled on the oppressive urban development that apparently typified parts of Eastern Europe in the communist days, and it is no coincidence, say these rumorers, that cross streets and turnoffs are strangely few and the driver who has missed his or her exit (very easily done) has nowhere to go but straight on, sometimes for a kilometer or more, until another interchange or roundabout finally permits a turning back, the total effect being a city in large part traversable only by peninsular, cul-de-sac-like routes of benefit mostly to the security forces, for whom life is much simpler if everyone is corralled into a near-maze from which there is no quick escape.

A clarification: I'm not seizing on this stuff as a gotcha. It isn't some great telling symbol of the shallowness and witlessness and nefariousness and wrongheadedness of the statelet. I do not align myself with the disparagers. I'll always remember a certain Western visitor who ominously murmured to himself, for my benefit, My name is Ozymandias, King of Kings—as if the poem were at his fingertips and the dude had not fortuitously run into it while browsing online for some bullshit reason; as if he habitually carried on with himself a quote-filled conversation steeped in the riches of Western civilization and by patrimonial cultural magic bore in his marrow the traces of Sophocles and Erasmus and the School of Salamanca. Oh, how these bozos make me laugh.

As for Mahmud: who can blame him? Sometimes I feel

like high-fiving the guy. Here is someone who accepts without anguish his good fortune. Here is the hero for our times.

But Ali was the opposite of a Bartleby—a Jeeves. He turned up punctually; did the humble work he was asked to do; charged a reasonable fee; spoke good functional English. All of this was estimable. Outstanding was that he took it upon himself to fix the remote control problem I was having with the ceiling fan and also, as I discovered after he'd left, to swap the bathtub faucet characters so that faucet C no longer gave forth cold water, nor F hot.

Fittingly, it was while taking my first bath drawn with alphabetic correctness that I had my one solid-gold Dubai brainwave: I decided to hire Ali full-time, as my personal assistant. He has proven himself the perfect man for the job, which may be described as follows: to assist me with the challenge of day-to-day life in Dubai consisting of one goddamned glitch after another. (For example, the aforementioned bathtub had a built-in seat. I can only assume that this feature is highly sophisticated and aimed, like everything else in this country, at the mythic connoisseur, in this case the überbather who sits up in his tub and will not rudely immerse his/her head and torso in bathwater, i.e., bathe. I mentioned my dissatisfaction to Ali, and my wish was his command. He and a workman procured and installed a new, seatless, perfect tub.)

Even Ali is a glitch. Contrary to what his get-up led me to believe, he is not an Emirati. He is a "bidoon" (Arabic for "without," apparently), i.e., a stateless person, i.e., a person who is everywhere illegally present. I have not inquired into the whys and wherefores of Ali's situation, but, according to *The National*, there are tens of thousands of bidoons in the Gulf States. Most Dubai-based bidoons, I read, are the descendants of foreigners (from Iran, from other parts of Arabia) who settled here before the United Arab Emirates came into being (in 1971, I can declare off the top of my head) and who for whatever reason didn't register as citizens of the new state. Neither *jus sanguinis* nor *jus soli* avails bidoons. They are, as things stand, fucked.

Anyhow, none of this would be my problem if employing a bidoon were not technically cloudy. At Ali's own suggestion, he and I have left things on an informal basis, which I'm comfortable with. Income tax is in any case not payable in Dubai, so no question of tax evasion arises. Because he is not permitted to have a bank account, Ali receives compensation in cash dirhams from my office disbursement account, and quite frankly I treat as a sleeping dog the compliance nuances of this arrangement. *Los dos Batros* have been informed in writing of the payments and their purpose. Sandro has been introduced to Ali and is well aware of what he does. Since it is customary in the emirate to employ bidoons, I can with justification proceed pro tem on the footing that all is hunky-dory or, since the case is not cloudless, that all is not not hunky-dory. That's good enough for me. One can't be Utopian about these things.

I call Ali into my office. I have taken photos of Project X and I bring them up on my desktop and invite Ali to take a look. Over my shoulder, he says, "What is this . . . building?"

"That's what I'd like to know. What do you think?"

This matter has no obvious bearing on my professional responsibilities, but I maintain that without Ali's miscellaneous assistance I wouldn't be able to begin to do my job.

Ali says, "I do not recognize this." He says, "I will check this out." What he means is, he will acquaint himself with the whispers and pass them on to me. I wouldn't actually know anything, but at least I would be in the know.

"No, thank you, Ali," I say. "That's OK. Don't worry about it." Now I feel bad about having involved him. Ali is not, nor likely ever could be, a resident of Privilege Bay. He is never going to be one of the Uncompromising Few. He will always be one of the Compromising Many. My impression is that he lives somewhere in Deira, which is no great shakes but is very far from the end of the world. I will put it this way: I am socially acquainted with people who have lived for a while in Deira. Ali has volunteered very little to me about his personal circumstances and I am not about to stick my nose where it doesn't belong. (This is one of the great perks of living in Dubai: there are few places where one's nose does belong.) Nonetheless, I sometimes need to remind myself that I didn't write the citizenship rules and certainly didn't provide legal counsel to Ali's ancestors. I apprehend that Ali has applied for Emirati citizenship, but I haven't kept tabs on what must be, I don't doubt, a demoralizing process characterized by barely tolerable uncertainty, and I've never asked Ali about how it's going and don't intend to. What it boils down to is, I can't help it that Ali is a bidoon, and I can't help it that being a bidoon is what it is.

I say, "Maybe we'll talk about this another time. Thank you." I am already intently perusing my e-mails, as if there isn't a minute to lose.

I doubt this performance sways Ali. He has seen for himself what my job entails, i.e., a couple of stressful hours of e-paperwork in the morning and an afternoon spent stressfully waiting around in case something should come up. The thought may have offered itself to him that I was crazy to quit what was, on the face of it, a secure and rewarding legal career at a good New York firm. (Ali knows a little about my old job, though he cannot be expected to appreciate what it means that I was of counsel, with a boutique but loyal private-client clientele.) I wasn't crazy, though. The reasonable man, put in my position, might very well have made, or seriously contemplated making, the decision made by me.

White as an egret, Ali exits and shuts the door. He will take a seat at his desk, which is just outside my office, in the reception area, and productively busy himself. (Often he will read a book in English, in a private effort of self-betterment. The luckless fellow is not permitted a higher education, and of course he cannot leave the country to seek his fortune elsewhere.) I swivel away from the desktop, put my feet on my desk, and hope my head is below the parapet.

IT MIGHT SEEM HYPERBOLIC to bring up the proverbial parapet, which calls to mind whistling bullets and, speaking for myself, the Alamo. I don't think it is.

At first sight, my job looks straightforward enough for a man of my qualifications and experience. As the Batros Family Officer, I am expressly charged (pursuant to the provisions of my contract of service, which I drafted) with the supervision of those specialized entities that perform the usual family office functions for the Batroses. These entities are (1) the Dubai branch of the multinational law firm entrusted with the Batroses' personal legal affairs, many of which are governed by the laws of Dubai and the Dubai International Financial Centre (DIFC); (2) an elite wealth management outfit in Luxembourg, which manages over two hundred million USD of Batros assets and devises the family's investment, tax, and succession strategies; (3) the international concierge service, Fabulosity, whose task is nothing less than to make sure that the Batros living experience goes as smoothly as possible and that the family's huge wealth "actually adds some fucking value to our fucking lives," as Sandro has put it; and (4) the Batros Foundation, which is principally operational in Africa but has its head office here, in International Humanitarian City. These supervisees are in a position to commit embezzlement or otherwise gravely fail the family. There is also the risk that a Batros will enrich himself at the expense of another Batros. My job is to make sure these bad things don't happen.

I have two main tools. First, I instruct a Swiss accountancy firm to spot-check and continuously verify the numbers generated by the activities of (1) through (4) above. The Swiss verifications are then verified by me, i.e., I roll a dull and unseeing eye over them. I am not and have never held myself out as professionally competent in the realm of financial scrutiny. I pointed this out to Eddie right at the beginning. He did that thing of waving away an imaginary flying pest and said, "We've got experts to take care of all that. What we don't have is someone we can trust. That's where you come in—as our *homme de confiance*." This brings me to my second tool: I am the General Expenditure Trustee of the so-called General Expenditure Accounts (GEAs). The GEAs are trust accounts held in the name of an Isle of Man trust company, Batros Trust Company Ltd. Monies funnel into the GEAs from all parts of the Batros Group, and the GEAs serve as a reservoir of money for the "personal use" (per the relevant trust power) of Batros "Family Members." ("Family Member" means Eddie or Sandro or their father, Georges. Their wives and children are not "Family Members.") If the trust powers are the dam, I'm the dam keeper: I am not empowered to authorize a GEA payment requested by a Family Member without the agreement of at least one other Family Member. In practice, this means that Georges and Eddie can withdraw as much as they want, because each has informed me that he agrees in advance to all GEA payments requested by the other; whereas Sandro, if and when he wishes to take out money, must go through the process of getting the permission of his father or his younger brother. In view of Sandro's history of profligacy and unsuccessful gambling, this process can be complex.

(Let me say this: I am of course aware of the technical risk of money laundering and/or tax evasion. The Isle of Man trust company is a red flag. Because I have no way to assess the risk, I have sought and received written assurances from each Family Member that to the best of his knowledge all sums credited to the GEAs have been lawfully gained and that all movements of money in and out of the GEAs have a lawful purpose and are free from any taint of illegality.)

There is a very high volume of requests for GEA money transfers, not least because the term "personal use" is very broad and is to be construed, according to Batros custom, as encompassing personal use for a business transaction. The sensitivity and unavoidable complexity of Batros financial doings means that very often the form and/or function of a transfer is opaque or unexplained and involves collateral documents—deeds of trust, contracts, checks, licenses, and other legal instruments— which are themselves opaque, written in foreign languages, etc., and to which I must also put my name. This last obligation is, unfortunately, of my own making. My self-written contract stipulates that I, the Family Officer,

> shall execute such [documents] *as pertain to* an authorized transfer [italics mine]

and I cannot argue in good faith that documents collateral or adjunctive to a GEA transfer don't fall within the ambit of "pertain to." A lot of the time I'm signing off on stuff that, to be perfectly honest, I barely, if at all, understand. I've made Eddie aware of this, too, and here again his response has been to laugh and tell me not to sweat it.

It's kind of Eddie to offer this reassurance, but mine is the inevitable fate of the overwhelmed fiduciary: inextinguishable boredom and fear of liability. To mitigate the latter problem, I am ordering customized stamps of disclaimer to use whenever I sign anything. The document in question will be stamped with a text delimiting the terms on which I lend my signature to it, the document. These stamps are still in the drafting stage. I am the draftsman, and I cannot say that I'm finding it easy: it is not my forte, as my father used to say. ("It would seem that reinsurance is no longer my forte," he stated in 1982, when he was let go by Swiss Re and we left Zurich, where I was born and spent my first twelve years, and moved to Southbury, Connecticut, in the United States, that foreign country of my nationality. (I was so proud of my blue passport. *Mon petit mec américain,* Maman would call me, en route to the school in Zug.) "International business machines are not my forte," my father told me in 1992, when IBM fired him. More than once, after my mother had withdrawn to her bedroom, I heard him say softly, "Boy, the female is really not my forte." Fixing stuff around the house was not his forte, and neither was driving, nor understanding what was going on, nor doing crossword puzzles, nor playing games. A basketball in motion frightened him, as did Monopoly. I cannot forget one particular evening. I had forced him to play with me and some school friends. The board was crowded with red hotels. My father's silver top hat was sent directly to jail, and for a while he was blamelessly and correctly exempt from the buying and selling and bankrupting and bargaining. He wore a huge smile throughout his captivity. If he was ever happier, I don't recall it.

Perhaps my stamp should simply state:

NOT MY FORTE

Trying though these anxieties are, they come with professional territory I have voluntarily entered for reward. It doesn't end there, however. I have to deal, on an uncompensated basis, with extra-territorial bullshit. Every day, I get about two hundred unwarranted work-related messages. From every corner of Batrosia arrive complaints and inquiries and electronic carbon copies invariably written in non-English English or non-French French and/or bearing lengthy and complex attachments and/or referring to matters about which I have no clue. If somewhere a fuckup has occurred or may be about to occur and/or if there is an ass out there that needs cover, you can be sure that the relevant correspondence will be cc'd or forwarded to me. Word has somehow got out that there is a chump in Dubai into whose inbox every kind of trash may safely be dropped. I daily delete about one hundred and fifty of these intruders. That leaves around fifty messages to defend myself against. How dearly I would love to re-forward them! But there's no one to send them on to: I am the final forwardee. Consequently I have become an expert in dead-end messages. For example, today I've written,

> Hi, P——. Please particularize.

And

> This is beyond my ken, J——, but thank you. :)

And

> Many thanks, Q——. The inquiry as stated is premature.

And

> Hi. See previous e-mails, mutatis mutandis. ☺

I'll come right out with it: these incoming e-mails amount to nothing less than an around-the-clock attempt to encroach on my zone of accountability with the intention of transferring to that zone a risk or peril or duty that properly should be borne by the transferor. I've documented my predicament and brought it to the attention of the Batroses. They have not responded and, dare I say it, they don't care. It is not their function to care. On the contrary: they hired me precisely in order that I should be the one who cares.

But what should I care about? That is the question. In order to clarify, circumscribe, and bring order to the scope of my contractual liabilities and responsibilities, I'm drafting (in addition to the rubber stamp disclaimers) what will be, I like to think, the ultimate e-mail disclaimer. One happy day, it will automatically appear in bold print at the foot of my messages and trounce the fuckers once and for all.

There remains another, I fear incurable, problem. My contract provides that the Family Officer

> shall comply with the reasonable instructions of the Family Members in relation to [. . .] other Family Office matters.

Innocuous, mechanically necessary stuff, I must have thought when I wrote this provision. But I had not reckoned on Sandro Batros. Sandro seems to be under the impression that I'm his majordomo. I cannot count the number of out-and-out inappropriate and frivolous demands on my time that he's made.

For example, he wants Bryan Ferry to play a private gig at his fiftieth birthday party. OK, whatever. Sandro gets to do that, and it costs me nothing to tell him, "I'll call Fabulosity."

"No, no, no," Sandro says. "I want *you* to call Bryan Ferry. Not Fabulosity—you. This is very important. It isn't for me, it's for Mireille." Mireille is his wife.

"Sandro, it's not my—" I cut myself off. I want to say that it isn't my job to call Bryan Ferry, but that would be wrong. It is my job, strictly speaking. The organizing of a social event is clearly capable of being described as a *Family Office matter,* and Sandro is a *Family Member* whose instructions in this instance (to personally book Bryan Ferry), though maybe unusual, are *reasonable.* Sandro is of course unconscious of the legal framework, but that does not negate the effect of the service agreement.

"OK," I say. I will underhandedly contact Fabulosity and have them make the arrangements. Once everything is agreed, I will make a pro forma call to Bryan Ferry (i.e., to his agent) and check the box created by my having uttered this "OK" to Sandro.

There are always more boxes to check. It never ends. On paper, I am the hawk in the wind. Off paper, I am the mouse in the hole.

In theory, Eddie should be my ally.

> *Eddie—Is something the matter? I have e-mailed and called you many times these last six months and have not got a response. I know you're very busy, but no one's so busy that they can't even acknowledge e-mail. If you're feeling bad about having dropped me in it, vis-à-vis Sandro, don't. He's not your responsibility. And if it's the case that you can't stop him from making life difficult for me, so be it. But at least respond. Better still, look me up next time you're in Dubai and let me buy you a drink.*

I can't get too mad with Eddie. He and his brother have essentially stopped talking to each other, which from Eddie's viewpoint I totally get, plus Eddie lives far away, in Monte Carlo, plus there are issues, surely consuming and vexing, arising from his relations with his two ex-wives and their five (combined total) children. Plus he effectively runs the Batros Group. I might be hard to get hold of, too, if I were Eddie.

> *Dear Eddie—Sorry about that last, maybe somewhat officious e-mail. All I really meant to say is: Put yourself in my shoes, old friend.*

> *Eddie—Disregard my last e-mail, about the shoes.*

> *E—Never mind.*

The hard truth of the matter is that I don't have to ask Eddie to disregard my e-mails. He's already disregarding them. I have to respect this. You cannot coerce people into having relations they don't want to have. It's my job to give up on the idea that I can ask Eddie to take an interest in how I'm doing and what I'm up to.

I'll catch up with him before long. You cannot keep the world at bay. Exhibit A: Mrs. Ted Wilson.

THE REASON I NAMED HER, right from our first encounter, Mrs. Ted Wilson was not because I find it whimsically gratifying to use a historically oppressive form of address but rather because this designation, while obviously a little old-fashioned, most accurately described the nexus between this person and me: from the outset, I dealt with her as the wife of Ted Wilson. And she set those dealings in motion. That's right—*she* came knocking. I answered the door as it were without prejudice (holding it open only by an inch or two, because visitors are always announced by a call from the doorman and it was the first time I'd heard a knocking on this particular door, and it was 9:00 p.m., and I was in fear, to be honest), and she held herself out as Ted Wilson's wife and *on this basis* sought admission to my apartment.

I had never met Mrs. Ted Wilson or heard much about her. My information was merely that she'd remained in the United States after her husband had come to Dubai. In the Gulf, this is not an abnormal bargain. And if the arrangement had lasted for an unusually long time (it is not disputed that Wilson came to Dubai in 2004), who was I to question it?

Standing barefoot in my doorway in athletic shorts and T-shirt, I said to Mrs. Ted Wilson, "Can I help you?"

"Why—I don't know," she said, looking at me as if I'd said something hurtful. "I'd like to talk about Ted." She told me she'd arrived in Dubai three days previously and that he'd failed to meet her at the airport and she had since found no sign of him, either at home or at work. "He's just disappeared," she said, not hiding her bewilderment.

I said, "Yes, that must be worrying." I said, "I'm afraid I really have no idea where he might be."

While true, this wasn't a comprehensive statement. Reports of people going AWOL were not extraordinary in 2009, which of course saw the beginning of the emirate's sudden depopulation and was the year the famous story went around of hundreds of expensive cars being ditched at the airport by fleeing debtor-foreigners—an understandable occurrence, this being a legal regime in which financial failure, including the failure to make an automatic payment on a car lease, can amount to an imprisonable crime. (There are still such cars to be seen— brown ghosts, as I think of them, on account of the inch of sand in which they're uncannily coated. There's an abandoned Toyota Land Cruiser that's been sitting right here in Privilege Bay for at least a year.)

Again she looked at me with a pained expression. "I thought you were friends. Don't you go scuba diving with him?"

I didn't answer, knowing full well that this was ambiguous. How she resolved the ambiguity was a matter for her. I surely wasn't under a duty to answer her questions or correct any misapprehensions she might have. If Ted Wilson had given his wife to understand that I was his diving partner—a flattering idea, incidentally, my being the buddy of the Man from Atlantis— that was between him and her. I had no wish and no obligation to be dragged into what was, as even a person of modest sensitivity could grasp, a private matter. And exactly what was this caller's status? She was the acquaintance of an acquaintance, which is to say, a member of a remote and almost unlimited class. It might be said: Wait a minute, she was your compatriot in a foreign land. Or, She was your neighbor. To the compatriotist I say, Give me a break. To the second speaker I say, A neighbor? Really? Number one, the Wilson apartment was two floors above mine; number two, Mrs. Ted Wilson's permanent home was in Chicago, not Dubai; and number three, what's so special about neighbors? Since when is residential propinquity a basis for making demands? Let me put it this way: can I ring on the doorbells of those who happen to live in The Situation and expect special treatment? Can I burden random door-answerers with responsibility for my well-being?

She began to cry. This unsettled me, even as I was aware that crying is the oldest, most rotten trick in the book and one to which I have been only too vulnerable. But something else was spooking me. That very day, I'd read on my AOL home page of the death of the little girl who had inspired "Lucy in the Sky with Diamonds." This was news to me—that such an inspirational girl had existed. Her name was Lucy Vodden, née O'Donnell. The obituary reported that back in the sixties, Julian Lennon, John's son, made a drawing of his four-year-old classmate and brought it home to show his father and said, Lucy in the sky with diamonds. The cause of her death, at the age of forty-six, was lupus. This made me very angry. John Lennon being dead was bad enough—but Lucy, too? Little Lucy? No! I Googled "Lucy Vodden" and came face-to-face with a very lovely, smiling woman in her forties with blond shoulder-length hair whom for moment I fell in love with and whom, only hours later, I briefly confused with another woman in her forties with blond shoulder-length hair. I am convinced this hallucination played a part in what happened next: I allowed Mrs. Ted Wilson to enter my apartment.

She sat in one of my armchairs and accepted a Kleenex. She struck me as a vision. How could she not? It was the first time I'd received a female visitor. That's right: in the year and half I'd been there, not even a maid had crossed my threshold.

To be clear, the basis for the exclusion of female domestic help was not sex, and not even my finding it unbearable to have people entering my living quarters in my absence. (In New York, I had no such compunction. Returning home from work on Tuesdays, I looked forward to gleaming wood floors and ironed undershorts and a sparkling countertop, courtesy of Carla the cleaning lady. (What was her surname? Where is she now? How goes it with her no-longer-little daughter?)) The Situation offers its residents a "White Glove Domestic Cleansing Service," but I don't avail myself of it. Why not? Here's why not.

When I first came to Dubai, I stayed for a week at the Westin hotel, which I remember mainly for its tagline—"Between Being and Becoming." From there I moved into a rented suite of rooms near the DIFC, on Sheikh Zayed Road. Beneath my window, six lanes of traffic bowled ceaselessly toward the distant skittles of Sharjah. This was a so-called serviced apartment. "Serviced" meant that I'd come back from the office every evening to find all evidence of my occupation removed, as if I daily perpetrated a crime that daily needed to be covered up. Every one of my few belongings had been put away out of sight; everything, down to the chocolate on the pillow, had been restored to the impeccable state in which I'd found the rooms when I first entered them. This was disconcerting, this non-accumulation of evidence of my existence. But what really rattled me was the mysterious population of cleaning personnel. The mystery lay not only in their alternative geography—theirs was a hidden zone of basements, laundry closets, staff elevators, storage areas—but in the more basic matter expressed in Butch Cassidy's question for the Sundance Kid: Who are those guys? That's not to say I viewed this tiny, timid population of women in maroon outfits as in some way hunting me down, as Butch and the Kid were, poor guys, all the way to Bolivia; but something wasn't right. To go back to Carla: I was aware that she originated in Ecuador, lived in Queens with a husband and a young daughter, got paid around seventeen USD per hour: of

Carla I felt I could do the rough human math. (Carla, I'm so sorry.) The apartment-servicing crew, though, I couldn't work out. I couldn't place those strange brown faces—somewhere in Asia? Oceania?—and I certainly had no data about the bargains that presumably underwrote my room being clean and their hands being dirty. I was confronted with something newly dishonorable about myself: I didn't want to find out about these people. I did not want to distinguish between one brown face and another. I didn't want to know whether these persons were Nepalese, Guyanese, Indians, Bangladeshis, Sri Lankans, Kenyans, Malaysians, Filipinos, or Pakistanis. What good did it do? How did it help anyone for me to know the difference? For their part, these women seemed not to want to be differentiated or even seen, because they always scurried away those few times our paths crossed. Therefore it was a situation governed by mutual avoidance. As the weeks went by, something appalling began to happen. I began to feel a fearful disgust at these scurriers as they intermittently appeared out of the walls and concealed spaces of the building. The feeling was elusively familiar. One morning, as an accidental encounter again dispersed a group of them into hiding, I recognized that my repugnance for these ladies was the repugnance one feels on coming upon vermin.

Out of shock at my monstrousness, I'm sure, I decided (in defiance of the house rules) to tip the service personnel. Easier said than done. My unknown cleaner or cleaners rejected the bills I left under my mattress (and placed them, folded, on my bedside table) and she/they ignored an envelope marked "TIP! PLEASE TAKE! THANK YOU!" Evidently I would have to dispense the cash in person. The problem was, I couldn't make contact with a recipient. My long working hours—this was pre-Ali, when I was trying to single-handedly set up and operate the family office, an experience I never want to revisit— meant that I'd leave my suite too early and return too late to cross paths with the housekeepers, who moreover were trained to observe an extreme lowness of profile, the better to achieve their labor's almost magical effect. One Sunday morning, I finally spotted a distant uniformed figure hastening across the corridor. I practically sprinted after her. When I turned the corner, she was nowhere to be seen; yet, from somewhere behind the walls, a kind of poltergeist chatter could be heard. I opened an unmarked door and found myself in a windowless room with a rough concrete floor and a whining service elevator. For some reason I felt a little frightened. I was on the point of turning back when a cart laden with sheets came in. A small lady was attached to it. There was an exclamation, followed by a statement that was linguistically impenetrable but very clear: my presence alarmed and dismayed her. I gave the lady a reassuring smile. "Baksheesh, for you," I said, and I pulled out a wad of dirhams and made to bestow them on her. She, who appeared to be equally in her thirties and fifties, made a negative hand gesture and, without meeting my eye, drove the cart into the elevator, whereupon she was as it were absorbed still more deeply by the building. I abandoned my quest to privately reward these workers. Apparently that would have been to put them in harm's way.

To avoid another such fiasco, I keep this place clean myself. It's no big deal; I like to mop my marble floor, the cleanliness of which I gauge by the blackening of the soles of my bare feet. When Mrs. Ted Wilson came in, everything was spick-and-span.

She dabbed away her tears and her resemblance to poor Lucy Vodden.

She was intent on staying. Short of manhandling her, I saw no way to get her out. I must admit, I was curious about Ted Wilson; and inevitably I was curious about his wife, especially with her being a damsel, and in distress. But curiosity killed the cat. We all know of those gallant volunteers who rush toward a burning train wreck only to suffer lifelong trauma from the nervous shock caused by the scenes they witness, not to mention the lung disorders contracted from the fumes they inhale or the financial ruin resulting from lawsuits brought against them about what actions they took or failed to take. I resolved to keep as much distance between Mrs. Ted Wilson and myself as was consistent with the basic civility that might reasonably be expected of me, the put-upon stranger.

She got up and wandered to the glass walls, and one might have thought she was going to step right out into the brilliant white tartan of the Marina towers. After a contemplative moment, she gave her attention to the décor: large black leather sofa, two matching leather armchairs, big flat-screen, massive black leather massage chair, mezzanine bedroom, computer desk with computer, framed photograph of Swiss mountains. I'm sure she also took in the air purifier, and the ultrasonic humidifier, and the electronic salt and pepper mills, and the 3-D glasses, and the touchless automatic motion sensor trash can. "This is basically exactly what Ted's place looks like," she said. "Do you guys shop together for furniture, too?"

Now she was inspecting my bookcase. She pulled out a volume of *Decline and Fall of the Roman Empire* and said, "You even have the same books." She said distractedly, "You know Ted's a historian, right?"

I said, "A historian?"

Mrs. Ted Wilson took a seat. She related (unprompted) that when her husband initially went to Dubai it had been in order to teach for a year at the American University in Dubai. No one foresaw that he would almost immediately be offered the job with the advertising agency that was (as he saw it) his big chance to "finally break the 70K barrier" and escape the "humiliation" of an intellectual career that had left him teaching a course called "The American Experience" in a place called Knowledge Village. (I pointed out that Knowledge Vil-

lage was merely the somewhat naïve-sounding (in English) designation given to Dubai's academic hub, but Mrs. Ted Wilson
didn't seem to hear me.) The Wilsons had spent most of the
previous decade "dragging" their two children (a boy and a
girl) from one place to another, and now that both were in high
school they agreed it was "out of the question" to "uproot"
them again. Mrs. Ted Wilson, meanwhile, had "a project that
I wanted to complete." It was agreed that Ted would take the
ad agency job and the family would take things as they came,
on the basis that "life has a funny way of working out." This
plan now struck her as humorous, judging from the little noise
she made.

By now her misconception about the quality of my association with Ted Wilson was beginning to trouble me. I said to her,
"Look, there's something you should know. I'm afraid I don't
know your husband that well. I've just run into him here and
there." I further stated, "I do, or did, scuba dive, but I've never
dived with Ted." As I made this disclosure, I was in the kitchen
fiddling at opening a wine bottle, my back turned to her. This
was my way of giving her space to take in my contradiction of
her husband's story. After a moment, I approached her with a
glass of white wine, which by virtue of having opened the wine
bottle I was now obligated to offer her, God damn it.

I said, "What was his field? As a historian, I mean." I placed
the wineglass within her reach.

Mrs. Ted Wilson seemed dazed. "German history," she said.
Interesting. "Which aspect?"

"Which aspect?" She seemed to be having difficulty. "Sorry,
you're asking me which aspect of German history Ted specialized in? You mean what was his dissertation about?"

"Sure, why not," I said.

"Certain economic features of nineteenth-century Waldeck
und Pyrmont."

There wasn't much I could say to that.

I gave her my card. "In case you need to get in touch," I said. "Thank you," she said. She wrote her contact details on a piece of paper. "Thanks," I said, staying on my feet. As far as I was concerned, we were done.

But I'd forgotten about the glass of wine, and now she reached over and took a large mouthful of it and, for the first time, examined me. "So what brought you here?" she asked.

I said, "Oh, the usual."

"You ran away," she said. "Everybody out here is on the run. You're all runners."

It occurred to me that in all probability she'd had a few drinks earlier in the evening. "I'm not sure that's entirely fair," I said.

"Well, am I wrong?"

I said something about a unique professional opportunity.

"Oh, don't give me that shit."

I was fully aware that this was a person in extremis. That didn't mean I had to give up the customary expectation of politeness. I said, "Do you think you know me well enough to say that?"

"I know you well enough," she said, motioning at my apartment significantly and, I must admit, infuriatingly. "Ted told me about his diving buddy—you're some kind of New York attorney. And you still haven't answered my question."

I understood her mania for enlightenment very well. Her life had become a riddle. I also suspect that she misidentified me as her husband, who was no longer available for questioning. It is fair to say that maybe I took Mrs. Ted Wilson to be none other than Jenn, who was no longer available for answering. For a cracked, treacherous moment, I actually had the notion to tell this woman my story—to have my say at long last.

"I don't have to answer your questions," I said—without hostility, to be clear.

There was that laugh again.

"Is something funny?" I said.

"You should see yourself. You're shaking. What is it? What are you hiding?"

"I'm not hiding anything. I don't have anything to hide."

"I think you do," she said, wagging the index finger of the hand that held the glass containing my wine. "I think you have everything to hide."

I said, "You wag your finger at me? You come here uninvited, you throw yourself on my hospitality, and you wag your finger at me?"

She jumped up. "How dare you. You pretended to be a friend of Ted. You deceived me. You lied. You lied to get me in here. Shame on you."

I looked around for something to throw. To repeat, everything was spick-and-span. The only objects to hand were a copy of *Dwell* magazine and a plastic jar of Umbrian lentils. I picked up the jar, turned away from Mrs. Ted Wilson, and hurled it against the wall. There was an unusual brown explosion as the jar burst.

"Get away from me," she screamed.

"No, you get away from me," I said. I was panting. I could hardly breathe. "This is my apartment. If I want to throw stuff around in my apartment"—here I picked up the *Dwell* and flung it across the room—"I get to throw stuff, understand? You don't like it, you're free to leave."

She left, as was her right.

I swept up. Even so, for weeks afterward I occasionally sensed a lentil underfoot.

It has to be said, my feet were in magnificent shape.

ALL CREDIT FOR THIS GOES TO my old scuba buddy from Oz. One day, on the boat ride back to the shore, he, Ollie, said, "You can't go around like that." He was referring to my long, uneven, gray-and-yellow toenails and, especially, to my horribly fissured heels. Ollie said, "I want you to drop by the spa, mate. We'll take care of you. My treat."

Although a little jumpy at the prospect, I took Ollie up on his offer. Why not, after all? I wasn't to know (and would surely have been scared off if I had known) that he would personally handle the job, which is to say, handle me—wash my feet, trim my toenails, clip my cuticles, patiently carve slivers of skin off my heels with what looked like a miniature cheese slicer, rub a pumice stone over the carved heels until they were pink and new-born. (Afterward, his assistant manipulated my insteps and ankles, and, last but far from least, applied lotions to my feet, shins, and calves.) Ollie was not even slightly queasy about any of this, not even about the flakes of dead skin accumulating like muesli on the towel on his lap. He spoke only in order to utter a kind of podiatric poetry about what action he was performing and which part of the foot was the planum, which the tarsus, and which the dorsum, consistently impressing upon me the enormous importance of feet, those great unsung workhorses whose sensitivity and quasi-magical neural properties had been insufficiently examined and remained wrongly undervalued. What can I say? It was my happiest hour in Dubai.

Things have gone amazingly well for Ollie, I am very pleased to say. In a somewhat unreal turn, he has become an important and fashionable pedicurist who flies around the world to meet high-net-worth individuals who want important and fashionable pedicures: to this day he sends me gleeful, can-you-believe-this-shit texts from St. Petersburg and London and New York. There is a downside, of course: Ollie got so busy he was forced to quit diving; and so I quit diving.

(I tried out another buddy but the guy was full of hot air and even underwater would clown around and bug me with pointless OK signs and make me feel unsafe. He boxed me in, somehow, even in the unpartitioned ocean. When Ollie and I dived, we stayed close; we accepted a severe duty of mutual care; but all the while we enjoyed the feeling of privacy that being underwater offers. This was fundamental to the undertaking, though of course there are those who understand privacy as a business of personal smells and locked bathroom doors.) Ollie and I still have our jaunts, however. Sometimes, to blow off steam, we will James-Bond-drive, as Ollie terms it, on the Gulf side of the Musandam Peninsula. After we cross the Oman border and hit the new and almost empty highway, we notionally race to Khasab. It is no contest. I'm in my Range Rover Autobiography (2007 model, with a Terrain Response™ system designed for rough ground), and Ollie drives the bright red Porsche Cayenne S that is his idea of a concession to family life. He zooms away almost immediately; from time to time, I catch sight of a pepper on a mountainside. Good luck to him. It is a joy merely to motor on this wonderfully engineered road, which curves between bare brown headlands and a blue bareness of open water, and whose rolled asphalt concrete is a kind of lushness. The road follows a dynamited zone of coastal mountain rock, and yet, as it has struck me again and again, my understanding never profiting from the repetition, this destroyed portion seems hardly different from the rest of the mountain, which itself seems to have been subjected to a vast natural blowing up. It is hard not to feel at one with the car advertisements as your vehicle adheres at speed to the surface of the earth, rushing through and over immense geophysical obstacles, then cresting at the pass, and then twisting down to a fjord so blue it seems technological. Who, a century ago, would even have dreamed of such transportation? We are practically in the realm of the incredible. Ollie sometimes urges me to rent something fast for the day—ideally another Porsche Cayenne S, to make a match of it—but I've never done that, chiefly because I don't want to be in an actual race, which would be frightening and dangerous and reckless. So as not to spoil his fun, I maintain that my choice of vehicle is strategic. I tell him, Remember the tortoise and the hare.

More usually, Ollie and I meet up when my feet feel dry. When that happens, I drive over to his salon at the Unique Luxury Resort and Hotel on the off chance that he or one of his helpers will be able to fit me in. It would feel wrong to make an appointment.

The morning after the run-in with Mrs. Ted Wilson, my feet felt very dry.

There's more than one Unique. Ollie is based at the Unique on The Palm, and not the other, older Unique, which is in Jumeira. Driving along The Palm's main thoroughfare, The Trunk, always makes me think of Ceaușescu's Bucharest boulevards: visually coercive concrete apartment buildings that speak of broken Hausmannian dreams. A different gloom descends once I have passed through the tunnel and come to the west crescent, at the tip of which, near Logo Island, the Unique is situated. The west crescent consists mainly of the semi-abandoned construction sites of the Kingdom of Sheba and other failed waterside developments. One or two of the resorts give the appearance of functioning, but there is no getting around it: the drive is a downer. I cannot avoid recalling the automatic plenty of childhood, when a pail and a patch of beach sand are enough to summon us into life's spell.

There is an important drawback to the Unique: I am known there by a false name. The (Assamese? Nepalese?) parking valets have no real interest in who I might be. Not so the pair of jolly, extraordinarily tall, and splendidly robed Nubian greeters whom all visitors must pass on their way into the hotel. (By "Nubian" I am not making an informed reference to the ancient or modern people of the Nile, about whom I am ignorant. I am thinking of the Nubian in *Gladiator,* a very black good giant gladiator who is Russell Crowe's trusted friend in enslavement. Both greeters look like that Nubian.) I have never spoken to either of these gentlemen, and yet every time they see me they very loudly and gladly shout, "Good day, Mr. Pardew!" They have not gone mad. Mr. G. Pardew is how, in a panic, I once identified myself to the front desk when presenting myself as a visitor of one of the female hotel guests.

I pulled into the hotel entranceway at the same time as a Maserati GranTurismo. I recognized the car. Its driver and his beautiful blond female consort were paid to go from hotel to hotel in order to make an impression on tourists. I knew what would happen next: the Nubians would give their full attention to the performance of opening the doors of the Maserati GranTurismo. So it proved. I took the opportunity to sneak by unseen.

"Good day, Mr. Pardew!" the Nubians called out.

I stormed past the front desk with a highly preoccupied air. "Good morning, Mr. Godfrey," a receptionist said. I gave her an austere little bow of the head. This gesture was borrowed from and, I'd like to think, was a homage to the actual Godfrey Pardew, the octogenarian wills and trusts specialist who is my former mentor and remains the most senior partner at my old law firm and is the most correct, respectable, discreet, and altogether old-school person I have ever met. In my assessment, he would rather disembowel himself than show his face at the Unique Luxury Resort and Hotel. I hasten to add that I would never try to pass myself off as Godfrey Pardew, Esq., of New York, New York, or any other actual G. Pardew. That would be wrong. G. Pardew is merely my Unique name.

I once tried to tell Ollie about this, but he raised a hand and said, "I know nothing about Pardew. Nothing." He knew, all right, but of course he didn't know, because what G. Pardew gets up to at the Unique is formally illegal. Of course, everybody knows that the Dubai authorities give sexual contractors a nod and a nose-tap and a say-no-more.

I walked past the Fountain of Ishtar and into the Hanging Gardens. The Unique has a Babylonian theme. What this imports, I do not know. My familiarity with Babylonian matters pretty much begins and ends with the words "Ishtar," "Hanging Gardens," and "Nebuchadnezzar," this last item coming to me thanks to the (indoor swimming) Pool of Nebuchadnezzar, which one passes on the way down to the Unique Spa & Hammam. Here the Mesopotamian fantasia relents somewhat, although it may well be that high-net-worth Babylonians had light-flooded soaking pools and twelve-foot-long towels and whispering attendants dressed in white nursing uniforms. I walked in—and there, in conversation with a technician, was Ollie! Hooray! "Well, well, well," Ollie said. "Need a foot up?" This question is his catchphrase, and I will never tire of hearing it. It invariably prefaces a half hour or more during which I'll sit back and receive ministrations, and Ollie will tell me about his globetrotting adventures and fill me in on local excitements. He is extremely well informed, being the confidant of scores of Dubaian ladies. I am a little sick of tittle-tattle, and almost as sick of only-in-Dubai stories—the lion cub somebody spotted in a neighbor's garden, the guy deported for flipping somebody the finger in traffic, the tipsy girl at the Oil Barons' Golf Tournament who couldn't get a taxi home and drove down Sheikh Zayed Road in a golf cart. But what else are we to talk about? Dubai is where we are.

I don't feel too bad about imposing on Ollie. This is completely to his credit. He always makes me feel that my turning up and putting a large male foot on his lap is the greatest thing that could happen to him. He won't accept a single dirham from me, which makes me uneasy until I remember that a sine qua non of real friendship is a happy freedom from cost-benefit considerations. That said, I don't think I should completely banish from my mind the fact that I played a role in Ollie's success, namely bringing him the corns and chronically ingrowing toenails of Sandro Batros. The introduction had such a triumphant outcome that Sandro would not stop boasting that he had discovered the world's number one foot guy, which led to Ollie being picked up by Fabulosity, which led to Ollie developing a worldwide client roster of luxurious multimillionaires. The rest is chiropodial history.

Sandro—I'm not one to attach importance to small tokens of appreciation, yet even I find it remarkable that you have not once expressed gratitude for, or even acknowledgment of, my role in procuring for you the services of Oliver Christakos. This leads me to wonder if there are any circumstances that would lead you to feel, let alone give voice to, simple human thankfulness.

Hi Sandro—One more thing. You may be tempted to act on one of your many capricious and baseless threats to fire me. So be it. Cookies crumble. But please bear in mind that (1) Oliver holds your happiness in his hands; (2) he is my best friend.

In accordance with our routine, I was first put in the care of one of Ollie's very pretty assistants. She led me to the Human Touch™ massage chair and pressed the buttons that set into motion the marvelous robotic devices, contained within the upholstery, whose actions are designed to approximate the touch of a highly skillful human massage therapist. (I have come to know this particular chair well and like it very much—and I speak as something of an amateur of such chairs and as the owner of a Pasha Royale X400™, perhaps the most "intelligent" chaise de massage in the world. I always feel a tiny, absurd pang of infidelity about giving myself to a massage chair other than my Pasha.) After a fifteen-minute Human Touch™ rubdown, I soaked my feet for five minutes. Then Ollie showed up in the very white, very medical jacket he wears at work.

He gave me a rapid pedicure. "You're in pretty good nick, actually," he remarked, and I wondered if he meant that I was pushing my luck, dropping in on him with healthy feet. But rather than showing me the door, Ollie asked if I would mind if he tried out a new treatment. He produced a small paintbrush and began to coat my skin (from toes to knees) with green enzymic goo. He looked more scientific than ever. He explained to me that an enzyme was a catalyst of chemical reactions, then explained what a catalyst was, then exactly described which enzymes he was using and which particular catalysis they were promoting. This excess of information was so soothing I nearly fell asleep. Little wonder: I'd been lulled into a soporific feeling of all going well in the world, of clever men and women in unseen laboratories toiling and tinkering and steadily solving our most disastrous mysteries, of benign systems gaining in efficiency, of our species progressively attaining a technical dimension of consciousness, of a deep and hitherto undisclosed algorithm of optimal human endeavor coming at last within the grasp of the good-doing intelligences of corporations and universities and governments and NGOs, of mankind's most resilient intellectual/moral/economic foes being routed forever and the blockheads and bashi-bazouks and baboons running for the hills once and for all.

Ollie said, "Oh yeah, listen to this."

To paraphrase him: A friend of a friend, an Iranian, goes to Dubai International Airport. It's his intention to fly home for a funeral. After he passes through security, the Iranian realizes that his return visa is not in order. What to do? He cannot go back through passport control into Dubai, and he cannot fly to Bandar Abbas for fear of not being allowed to return. The Iranian decides to stay where he is, in the huge duty-free area known as Concourse 1, until his travel documentation is put right. (I'm familiar with Concourse 1, even though these days I'm a Terminal 3 man and we have our own, I think better, concourse.) Unfortunately, this takes longer than anticipated. A week passes, then another. Still he is stuck in no-man's-land. His predicament comes to the notice of the mutual friend.

The mutual friend is worried. He asks Ollie to check in on the marooned Iranian next time he flies out, maybe buy the poor guy a drink and a bite to eat. You bet, says Ollie.

Ollie said, "So we meet in the Irish Village. I buy him a Coke and a beef pie, which he just gobbles up. He doesn't say anything. He's just eating and chugging down the Coke. I'm thinking he doesn't really speak English. He's just wolfing everything down. Then he burps—I mean, it's this really loud, kind of contented burp—and starts to tell me about his new life. Mate, you wouldn't believe it."

"Let me guess," I said. "He's happy as a clam."

Ollie looked at me with respect. "Correct. He's a pig in shit. I'm completely wasting my time feeling sorry for him. He's the toast of the town. He knows everybody. They all love him." Ollie put down his green-tipped spatula. "You should have seen him, strolling around and waving to everyone. The cock of the fucking walk. Duty-free? How about just free? Free newspapers, free magazines, free food, free access to a health club, free internet, free everything. OK, the concourse is crowded, it's a shithole—but basically it's a mall. I mean, a mall is exactly where he'd like to be if he wasn't in the airport."

I was laughing hard. Ollie had nailed it. Dubai's undeclared mission is to make itself indistinguishable from its airport. "Where does he sleep?"

"Oh, he's found a nice little spot over by one of the gates. He's got himself a sleeping mat and a sleeping bag and, mate, he couldn't be more comfortable. He looked very well fucking rested when I saw him, I can tell you." Ollie was hunched above my feet, doing the last touch-ups. "Why wouldn't he? He's got nothing to worry about. He doesn't have to worry about work"—the Iranian had some middling finance job— "because they're keeping his job open until the paperwork goes through. And he doesn't have to worry about his family because his salary's still coming in."

"He's totally off the hook," I said.

"Home fucking free," Ollie said. He squinted and frowned at my green limbs as if he'd just finished the *Starry Night*.

I said, "I had an interesting visitor yesterday evening." It wasn't often that I was the one with news.

"Oh yeah?" Ollie said. "Who's that?"

"Mrs. Ted Wilson," I said. "She dropped by. She told me her husband was missing. Vanished."

Ollie grinned—as if the advantage had somehow passed to him. He said, "Which one?"

I told him I was talking about the wife of the Ted Wilson who was the Man from Atlantis.

Still the grinner, Ollie said, "I know that. I'm asking you which Mrs. Wilson you're talking about."

I didn't understand.

"Now this is just what I'm hearing," Ollie said. "I'm not saying anything. I'm just passing on what I'm hearing."

"I don't want to know," I said.

"What I'm told," Ollie unstoppably said, "is there are two Mrs. Wilsons. There's Mrs. Wilson number one, who lives back in the States: your Mrs. Wilson; and there's Mrs. Wilson number two, who lives here."

Yep, I didn't want to hear that.

BUT WHAT WERE MY OPTIONS? Quickly seal Ollie's lips with duct tape? Stuff my ears with wads of cotton wool I kept handy for just such an eventuality?

It might be said I have only myself to blame: I opened my big mouth about Mrs. Ted Wilson: I brought the multiple Mrs. Wilsons on myself. But it is in the nature of a mouth to open, especially among friends. Or am I supposed to avoid Ollie? Why not withdraw completely from society while I'm at it? And why stop there? Why not withdraw from anatomy, too? Who needs a mouth? Who needs ears?

This isn't to say that we're totally helpless and that there's no defending the boundary between the here and the there. That's not my case at all. But there is a limit, if you will, to the fortifications one can build; there is the problem of force majeure. Here's an example. This summer, I have as an office intern Alain Batros, Sandro's fifteen-year-old son. I've never wanted an intern, and, were I to want one, I should certainly not want Alain. However, there's nothing to be done about it. I must accept my instructions. The fortifications fail. Force majeure.

The kid's hours are 11:00 a.m. to 4:00 p.m., Monday–Friday. He sits in a chair at a little desk facing the wall, usually with his head resting in cupped hands, which he thinks conceals his closed eyes. From time to time he makes a groan. This is to be expected. He has the task of perusing unavoidably stale and contextless documents and double-checking the calculations they contain. It is without doubt an ultra-boring assignment, but unfortunately I am not operating a fairground. I have been instructed by the kid's own father that he is not to have access to a computer or electronic devices of any kind and that a spell of drudgery is exactly what he needs. Alain goes to boarding school in England (where things are not going well for him, is my impression) and usually spends his holidays in Beirut, where the Batros family (notwithstanding complicated taxational assertions to the contrary) most actually resides; but, in the words of Sandro, "the time for fun and games is over." The boy has been sentenced to passing the hottest months of the year in Dubai in the Jumeira family compound—Fort Batros, as I call it. "I want him to have work experience," Sandro has explained over the phone. "I want him to learn what work means. Learn that work means work. It doesn't mean play. If it meant play, if it meant fucking around, they wouldn't call it work. See what I'm saying? Work is called work because it's work."

"Yes, I think I follow you."

"That's what you're going to teach him—what work is.

What it is to get your ass into work and work your ass off. Do boring shit and do it all day long. He has to learn. He has to learn willpower. The boy's got no willpower," Sandro says, lightly gasping. "You're going teach him willpower." It doesn't end there.

Eddie—This idea of making Alain's allowance contingent upon his achieving a certain weight loss strikes me as bordering on the unkind. Is there any way you could talk to your brother? Surely there must be a better way to proceed. In any case, I fail to see how my responsibilities extend to this sort of thing. Must I be involved?

Eddie would of course never talk to Sandro about Alain. My phantom inquiry's phantom answer is: Yes, I must be involved.

The awful business is broken down, like the steps of an execution, into small, intrinsically blameless parts. Every Monday and Thursday, Ali accompanies Alain to the corporate bathroom and invites him to step into a stall, undress to his undershorts, and step on the scale. Ali sees the boy's feet step on the scale and sees the indicator jerk well past the 100 kg marker. He records the final measurement and e-mails me the number. I enter the new datum on a spreadsheet that reckons what allowance, if any, Alain will receive that week. The formula is Sandro's (i.e., his accountants'): essentially, Alain's weekly allowance depends on the progress he has made toward his weekly weight-loss target. It falls to me to communicate to the boy the result of this appalling computation, which always produces the same result: zero allowance. I discharge this burden by placing on his desk, during his lunch break, an envelope containing a Calculation Note and a Progress Graph. The Progress Graph charts Alain's progress toward the 90 kg weight target his father has set for him. If and when he achieves this target, he will receive the keys to an Alfa Romeo 1750 Spider Veloce that sits in a garage in the Isle of Man. Why the Isle of Man? Because its residents are permitted to drive at the early age of sixteen—a tantalization that will, it is hoped, induce the fifteen-year-old to achieve his weight target ASAP. (The USA, with its minimum driving age of fourteen to sixteen, was not an option. Alain's portfolio of nationalities—the kid is a citizen of Lebanon, Ireland, France, the United Kingdom, and St. Kitts and Nevis—does not yet include the American one.) Sandro has instructed me to buy an apartment on the Isle of Man with a view to creating (false) residency credentials for his son who, it's safe to say, has no clue where the Isle of Man is. I am happy to take care of the property transaction, but I will not be party to any deception of the Manx authorities. I haven't made an issue of this with Sandro because the issue is moot: the kid has actually been gaining weight, and I would be amazed if he gets down to 90 kilos any time soon. Of course, it's not my job to be either amazed or unamazed. I am not this kid's overseer or Dutch uncle. It isn't for me to counsel him that drinking a giant beaker of Coca-Cola every lunchtime runs counter to his dietary objectives, or to root for him, or to lie awake at night wondering what will become of him and how things could be made better for this large, soft child whose circumstances give one not the slightest basis for hoping against hope that somehow he will acquire the wherewithal to care and be cared for, which is surely the great purpose and the basic meaning of growing up.

Still, it's in everybody's interests that the internship goes smoothly and productively, and to this end I've introduced the little big guy to Sudoku. The puzzles come in paperbacks and therefore do not offend against the no-computer rule; neither do they break the no-fun-and-games rule because they offer a brain workout that's certainly better than meaningless number crunching. To make things even more exciting, I've introduced Alain to the Martial Arts Sudoku series, which has

White Belt puzzles for beginners, and so on, up to Black Belt for real experts. When I call him over to my desk and explain how Sudoku works, he seems uninterested. But not much time passes before he tosses the White Belt book onto my desk and says, "Too easy." "Wow, that's pretty fast," I say. I have the next book ready for him and not without ceremony remove it from a desk drawer and deliver it into his possession. I say, "Check out the *frontispiece*." (I feel it will do the kid good to hear the word "frontispiece," even if I am not exactly sure what "frontispiece" means. I like to slip him the odd ten-dollar word, like "litigious" and "iconoclastic" and "intricate." They might come in useful.) I show him the plate that, in anticipation of this moment, I've pre-glued onto what I think may be the "frontispiece" of this book. The plate reads,

> Alain Batros is hereby admitted to the rank of Sudoku Green Belt.

The kid neither acknowledges the honor nor disdains it. He returns to his seat, assumes his slouch, and sullenly flicks through the pages of new puzzles. For what it's worth, sullenness strikes me as a logical, healthy, and correct stance for Alain. But whether he is sullen or sunny—or in good or bad health, or succeeding or failing—is something I refuse to be dragged into. Once I have satisfied myself that he is for the time being safe and self-sufficient, I am entitled to view him as factically as possible, that is, view him as being on a par with the other occurrences—pencils, microbes, light streams, sounds, galaxies, etc.—out of which arise the accidental phenomena of this room and my consciousness of it. The kid becomes just part of the givens. That he may be overweight or fear the dark or have trouble making friends or enjoy watching basketball is not my concern and cannot be made so by Sandro placing him in the same room as me and counting on this obligatory mutual vicinity to make me act in loco parentis or in loco amicus or otherwise wear some unwarranted caretaking hat. I am obliged to accept the son's presence as my intern and to be a decent and reasonable temporary boss; but I am not obligated to accept and will not accept any responsibility for his greater welfare. Any occasional act of kindness I may choose to do for the kid is of a strictly private nature and between him and me and does not as it were constitute any kind of waiver or abandonment of my right to dwell within the aforementioned limits of obligation.

In order to strengthen and give helpful physical expression to these limits, I have instructed Ali to arrange for a partition to be placed between me and Alain—to, in effect, enclose me in my own room-within-a-room. That way the kid and I won't have to spend the day feeling under the other's surveillance. Although he may be an inept teenager, I would be crazy to lose sight of the fact that he is a Batros and in a position to blab about me. This will not have escaped him. Children are natural snitches and squealers and accusers. This is because adults are natural policers, prosecutors, fact finders, judgers, punishers, torturers, hangers, electrocuters, gravediggers, and defamers of the dead.

The kid is flipping to the back of the puzzle book, where the solutions are set out.

"Hey," I say. "You can't do that."

He slouches some more. Evidently he is stuck.

"Let me see that," I say, and there is a loud squawk of chair legs as he gets up. I take a look at the puzzle. "Mm," I say. "Not easy." I'm not lying. It isn't an easy problem; and the fact is, I'm only a Brown Belt, and just barely. A lot of Brown Belt puzzles stump me, and too often I am faced with the choice of making a guess or abandoning the puzzle. Guessing is out of the question, of course, since that would defeat the point. The trouble is, not finishing the puzzle also defeats the point.

(I am in awe of Sudoku Martial Arts Black Belts. I would love to meet one of these logical warriors and find out how he or she does it—how, in particular, s/he masters the challenge of bifurcation. Bifurcation is called for when the path to the solution fatefully forks and it is no longer possible to induce whether numerical path A or B is the correct one. (Maybe it would be clearer to think of it as a "symbolic" path, since the nine Sudoku numbers are not mathematical objects and function only as representations of nine unique things.) At my skill level, the player/martial artist has no option but randomly to choose one of the two paths and provisionally follow it in the hope that the guess will turn out to be correct. This process of tentative exploration is the hard part, because (assuming you don't cheat by lightly penciling numbers into the puzzle with an eraser-tipped pencil) it is far from easy to keep aloft in one's mind the multiplying number-scenarios produced by your progress. If the provisional path proves to be a dead end, the player must backtrack all the way to the fork in the road (bifurcation is sometimes called Ariadne's thread) and take the alternative path—which could itself bifurcate, down the road. I have never met a Black Belt and find it hard to believe that actual Black Belts are out there, in the real world.)

Before I disclose the solution to his problem, I say to Alain, "This here is the wall in the puzzle. You've hit the wall. And beyond this wall, there's probably going to be another wall. That's why you play Sudoku in the first place—to *scale* the walls." ("Scale": a sneakily high-value verb for the kid.) "I'm going to give you a little bit of help this time, but next time you're going to do it yourself." Throughout this little pep talk he looks into space with an expression of vacancy I completely respect. He thinks I am very, very lame, and he is right. Still, we must go on. I show him a way to figure out his next move. He catches on and rapidly fills out a few more boxes. "OK," I say, "now we're cooking with gas." As he makes to leave, I say, "Hold on there, mister." I get scissors. I cut out the solutions pages and toss them into the trash. "We won't be needing these. Our *prowess* renders them *superfluous.*"

And he drags himself back to his seat ten feet away from mine and I begin again to boil with rage that I have had taken from me a work space that by rights should be mine alone and in which I should be entitled to put up my feet and pick my nose if I want to and live my life on my own fucking terms.

> *Eddie—I want to go back to the last responsive thing you said to me. You'll recall this was back in November: I asked for your help with the Luxembourg thing, which as you know put me in an untenable position. The gist of your response was: "If you don't like it, you're always free to leave." Out of shock, I said nothing at the time; and also, to be honest, out of some idea that you were right. But let me now say: "Always free to leave?" You know as well as I do, it's not that simple. And suppose I were "free" (I take it you mean "at liberty") to leave—well, you were likewise "free" to help me out, and your freedom (liberty) preceded mine, and the cost to you of exercising your freedom would have been much smaller than the cost to me of exercising mine. So let's not kid ourselves. You were the chooser, not I, and you chose to strong-arm me to the maximum degree permitted by your bargaining position. Eddie, that's not amicable.*

Writing mental mail eats up time and energy. An hour passes before I have worded the foregoing to my (relative) contentment and I'm able to think about attending to my real work and my number one priority, which is drafting my personal disclaimers. I lack attentiveness, though. I am too worn out and bothered. Normally I would take forty winks but God damn it I cannot on account of the stoolie in the corner.

———

THE DAY AFTER MY PEDICURE, Ollie called to say that "the diving community" was putting together a "search and rescue party" for Ted Wilson. Ollie said, "I guess they're asking us to go out and look for him. Leave no man behind and all that."

Of course the correct response to this ridiculous idea would have been to ridicule it. But no—I was flattered to have been identified as a significant member of the "diving community" and to have been handpicked for this special operation, I who had not pulled on a set of fins in over a year. I solemnly agreed to "report" at "0430" the next morning at the Spinneys in Jumeira and from there head out to Oman in what was subsequently referred to, surely erroneously, as a "rolling thunder" convoy.

I arrived at Spinneys in my silver-gray Autobiography just as Paolo Weiss was arriving in his silver-gray Autobiography. I recognized a few other faces/cars. Dionisi Ottomanelli was there in his Jaguar XJ220, as was the Ferrari F430 of Jesper and Ingrid Poulsen. Keith Botha's Bentley Arnage T was unmistakable, even in the dark. We stood around in the parking lot with the restlessness of men and women on a mission. If anyone was a close friend of Ted Wilson, they didn't say so. Jesper Poulsen disclosed that he had once asked Wilson what drove him to dive. "He said, 'Because nobody can phone me underwater.'" This drew a laugh of assent. Trevor Winters, the diving school owner and the chief instigator, planner, and leader of our venture, conducted the briefing. He reminded us that Ted Wilson's "diving transport" was his Mazda MX-5 Miata Sport automatic, and that the first sign of his whereabouts could well take the form of this vehicle. There was no need for Trevor to mention that the peninsular waters are practically unlimited and that the likelihood of any one of us finding the Man from Atlantis, or what remained of him, in the ocean, was very slight. For this reason, perhaps, nobody made mention of it, although Keith Botha did ask whether, in view of the troubling passage of time since Ted Wilson had last been seen—it had been a week—our outing should be "downgraded" from an "S&R" operation to a "search" operation. Trevor said, "Keith, I'd like us to go out there today with a little hope in our hearts. But you're right. We have to be ready for the worst."

It was a somber and burdened and exhilarated group of coffee-drinking, scuba-qualified automobilists that set forth from Spinneys at 0500 on the dot, and we must have offered an inexplicable spectacle as we moved in the morning-night through Dubai and Sharjah in a slow-moving, tailgating, fifteen-strong procession of, inter alia, C- and CLC-Class Mercedes-Benzes, Porsches Cayman and Cayenne and Carrera, a 1 series BMW, two Audi A3 Sportbacks, and a Nissan GT-R. The undertaking was governed by a mighty mood of adventure. Certainly, and speaking for myself, it was that very rare occasion when one's fictitiousness feels euphorically correct. I was no less animated and purposeful than if I'd been setting out to look for Red Rackham's treasure; and, as I traveled through the nocturnal cities, it was as if an existential transfer or translation had taken effect and it was the case without counterfactuality that I was an aquanaut and the cabin of the Autobiography, dark except for the dashboard's fire of needles and numerals, was that of a submersible passing between batholiths and brilliant upright reefs; and it was the equally real case, as the convoy turned east onto the E88 and quickened through the desert, that the moon gave the slip to a constabulary of moon-brightened clouds. Usually I find dawns disgusting: up in the Hajar Mountains, the appearance at the ocean's edge of yellow and apricot hues provoked a happy sense of daybreak I had not felt since, it may be, I was a just-qualified attorney and in the first purr of Midtown Tunnel traffic I walked to work through empty, wintry Murray Hill, and the overnight snow, cleanly banked on every sidewalk, loomed for me as the cliffs of Dover once loomed for English seafarers. What a home the world was! What a drama! It didn't matter that my part was that of the lemon hurrying to its juicer. I still had the verve, after twelve-hour days, for an office romance with The Beautiful Jennifer Horschel.

(That was the name applied to her by certain wistful male co-workers. In secret fact, Jenn's legal name was simply Jenn. This monosyllable, whose dwarfism I found only endearing, was one of the things Jenn held against her parents even as she accepted that in this instance they had not sought to injure or handicap or shortchange her but merely to give her a nice name. To make Jenn feel better, I let her in on my most embarrassing secret: my first given name. This unutterable word had been written on my birth certificate in honor of a Swiss great uncle. From high school onward, I disclosed its existence only under bureaucratic duress, when filling out forms. Jenn said, "You have a secret name? What is it?" Very vulnerably, I told her— which is to say, wrote it down on a piece of paper. She stifled a shriek. "Oh my God," she said. "You poor, poor thing." (Not long after, a busybody in the law firm's HR department saw fit to exhume this forename "as a matter of good order." Ridiculously, my professional name thereafter began with the initial "X." "It'll make you stand out," the busybody said. "It'll give you an X factor." How right he proved to be.) My revelation did make Jenn feel better, but her hatred of her own name was not lessened. I believe that having a stunted or halved name must in her mind have symbolized the improvidence of her chaotic upbringing in and around the Lehigh Valley, Pennsylvania, which left her unsuffixed in some broader sense and certainly did not equip her with the familial support enjoyed by so many of her peers at Dartmouth (to which she transferred from Penn State) and at law school in Georgetown, evidently few of whom had to combine their studies with crappy jobs or needed to make room in their lodgings for a half-sister fleeing a violent boyfriend or, for several weeks, another half-sister released on parole from Lehigh County Prison. When I met Jenn, she was holed up in a doorman building on Second Avenue, up by the Queensboro Bridge. She was twenty-six—one year younger than me but (as a result of three wavering semesters I spent at grad school) one year my senior at the firm. Her seniority wasn't just chronological. Jenn seemed unnaturally more experienced than me, able somehow to see things more quickly, as if an all-seeing tipster whispered in her ear. I guess she saw a lot, growing up—more than I saw in Zurich or Connecticut. We were both in Corporate—I in insolvency and restructuring, she in securities. She was regarded as a young superstar. We got to know each other in the cafeteria, late at night. At first we talked about the partners, those improbable fascinators; but as we continued to meet, Jenn offered a monologue, amusing and ethnological in tone, about the dark difficulty that was her youth. Combining the mentalities of the caseworker, the confidant, and the one who has a crush, I listened to her in a state of moral and romantic excitement; I even thought of taking notes, so importantly communicative seemed her disclosures of the Horschel clan's fuckups and tribulations, the likes of which I had never come across except on TV and which left me, in relation to Jenn, with an edgeless feeling of duty. I somehow came to believe that this very lovely and intelligent and in all respects admirable person was gravely in need of help and, by fantastic good luck, this added up to a need for me. When Jenn and her Conran sofa moved into my rent-stabilized one-bedroom (in August 1998), it gave me great pleasure to write letters to her parents and siblings to the effect that she was now under my protection, that her days of housing and bailing out and bankrolling Horschels were over, that any communication with her would have to come through me, and that anyone who tried to interfere in her affairs would have to deal with yours truly. I described myself as Jenn's "partner." There was no question of our getting married because Jenn's parents had gone through six marriages between them and as a consequence their daughter feared the blessed estate. I, too, feared the blessed estate, even though my parents married only once. Work sanctified our union. We were always working. When I try to think of times Jenn and I were actually in the same room and happy to be there, I think of those early days when she would bring home work and I would spend hours at her side, helping to draft client letters and notes of advice. My contribution was chiefly linguistic; Jenn, the much better attorney, contributed the analysis. She made partner at thirty; I never did, and in due course moved sideways, into private client work. At our tête-à-tête dinner to celebrate her elevation, Jenn said that she would have a baby when she was thirty-four. That should give me enough time to establish myself, she said. Very good, I said, interiorly running to keep up. What about buying an apartment? she asked. I told her that I liked the rent-stabilized one-bedroom and that the financial logic of surrendering the rent-stabilized lease in favor of property ownership was unclear. OK, Jenn said, contentedly galloping on. But we'll get a bigger place after the baby, OK? OK, I said.

(Wrongfully, I withheld from her my developing interest in room theory. For example, how many more rooms did two persons in occupation of a one-bedroom need in circumstances where (i) the two persons were almost never simultaneously in the one-bedroom; (ii) on the rare occasion that the two persons were simultaneously in the one-bedroom, almost always one or both of them was asleep and therefore unconscious; (iii) on the still rarer occasion that the two persons were simultaneously in the one-bedroom and simultaneously conscious, almost always one person was in the bedroom and the other was in the bathroom or the living room? (A footnote: when we quarreled, which wasn't often, we would be in the same room. After a while, I'd tire of the quarrel, and I'd exit the room and go to the other room, in order to be by myself there. Jenn would follow me in, in order to continue saying things, and eventually I would leave that room and go back to the first room, and again she would follow me, and finally I'd have to go to the bathroom and lock the door, and still she would come after me, standing by the door and following me into the bathroom vocally, as it were. That happened consistently, which is interesting, because when we were not disputatious an opposite dynamic was typically in effect, namely, that if I entered the same room as Jenn, she would quite soon leave that room, as if the point of an apartment was to ensure that its occupants lived apart from one another. (This partly explains my resistance to moving to a larger place and thereby enabling our mutual dodging, whereas it was my hope that one day we would enjoy being in the same room together. It wasn't right to keep this motive secret. The right thing would have been to mention to Jenn that I resented all the dodging, and let her know where I stood, emotionally, even if my previous attempts at this kind of communication had not been productive, very possibly because of my own inadequacies as an emotions-communicator. (As it happens, my wrongdoing in this specific instance—i.e., resisting a move to a larger place for reasons kept secret—turned out to be consequentially good, because we were spared a conflict about how to dispose of a jointly owned property. To that extent, all's well that ends well.))))

So there it was: we had agreed on a plan. When Jenn turned thirty-three, we made the premeditated reproductive effort; sexual intercourse became focused and timeous. After six months, Jenn elected to receive fertility treatment. This necessitated that she self-administer certain drugs. The drugs made her depressed and anxious and paranoid for a week of each month—an especially disconcerting turn for her, because she naturally tended toward emotional efficiency. These painful symptoms bothered her for three consecutive months. During the third, something bad happened at work the details of which Jenn would not reveal but which involved, I gathered, strange behavior attributable to her artificial biochemical state. Soon afterward, she said that she didn't want to take any more fertility drugs. I said, OK, we'll do without them, and Jenn said, No. I can't do it anymore. She was very upset, as far as I could tell, or perhaps very relieved, or both. There can be little doubt that her family background complicated for her the issue of children, among others. I said, OK, let's think about it again in a little while, OK, love? and she said, OK. We said no more about it. Then Jenn turned thirty-five and said she wanted to try again. It was now or never, she said. She said that there were no two ways about it, we had to find a bigger apartment, with more rooms. It was financially ridiculous not to, apart from anything else. I said, OK, even though by this point I had lost my cameral idealism and room-wise was on the same page as Jenn, i.e., my interest in our being in the same room together had waned. To quote an old, possibly wise, legal colleague: There comes a point when there comes a point.)

At Dibba were dhows and inflatable speedboats loaded with diving equipment. Our group disbanded in teams of two. Some headed for Lima Rock, some to Octopus Rock, some to the Khor Mala Caves, some to Ras Qaisah, others elsewhere. Ollie and I were assigned the Ras Lima headland. The decision had been made to cover the well-known dive spots, even though Ted Wilson had become a legend precisely for his avoidance of these sites, which furthermore attracted so much scuba and snorkeling traffic that it was hard to believe that a findable diver in distress would not already have turned up. It wasn't until our boat was in the water that I began to feel preposterous. Ollie and I looked like Dumb and Dumber in our yellow flippers and matching short-sleeved O'Neill neoprene shirts.

I said, "So what's the plan, exactly?"

He made a grimace. "Let's get on with it."

We toppled ass backward into the Gulf of Oman.

Everything beyond ten meters was lemonade murk. I was tense; I had forgotten about the unlimited expectancy that is a feeling of being in the sea.

Ollie went along a shallow trough. I followed. We had dived this site before, and soon I recognized a grove of lavender coral. On we went, through enigmatic marine vales. The blue-and-white striped fish were out and about, as were the small black triangular dawdlers, as were, in a disorderly shoal, the innumerable now-glossy, now-dull colorless guys that are the pen pushers of the reefs. My Fish Identification Course did not cover these little fellows, and in fact the whole enterprise of human discernment, of passing what is sensed through the sieve of what is known, is more or less annulled underwater. Perhaps for this reason, I've never been able to dive without loneliness—and never could have gone into the water like Ted Wilson, without human corroboration. Always I would need to sense, close by, friendly foot fins idling in the deep. And yet while looking for Ted Wilson's body, if that's what we were doing, I hardly felt companioned by my intermittently effervescent old buddy. We were present as searchers, not sightseers, and I felt a terrific pressure of intentionality. The sunbeams in vertical schools, the alien phyla, one's unnatural litheness—I was used to submitting without thought to these marvels and their incalculable *Welt.* Very few human ideas survive in this implacably sovereign element; one finds oneself in a realm devoid not only of air but of symbols, which are of course a kind of air. There are moments when even the sunniest diver has forced on him or her certain dark items of knowledge, among them, if I may extrapolate from my own diver's experience of being simultaneously a vessel and a passenger, that one is a biological room in which one is the detainee. None other than Cousteau, as I learned from watching his *Odyssey,* understood that a corollary of his oceanographic adventures was the contemplation, inevitably gloomy, of the processes of decomposition and disappearance that finally govern organic life and, for that matter, the lives of civilizations, ancient traces of which are apparently to be found everywhere in the depths of the Mediterranean Sea in the form of coins and urns and ruins. None of this is to propose a special category of submerged truth; but there is no point in denying that diving changes things.

We came to a drop-off and went down.

Right away we saw a leopard shark, at rest on the white sand. On another day, I would have been overjoyed. Convulsively, I kicked away from this animal, from the abominable sound of my breathing, from the inertness of everything. I have to think this was provoked by the fraudulence of my situation; but in any case, panic displaced all notions except that of surfacing. I signaled to Ollie. We went up without delay.

"I can't do it," I said, gasping. "I'm not breathing right."

Ollie said, "OK. Let's get on the boat."

I haven't fully recovered from this freak-out, which one might more precisely describe as a traumatic episode of extra- or supramural apprehension. A few months ago, I had reason to spend a discounted but still very expensive night in the Neptune Suite of the Atlantis Palm. The special feature of the Neptune Suite (aside from the two complimentary Dolphin Encounters, with dolphins supposedly flown in from the Solomon Islands) is the huge blue water-window that gives on to the Atlantis's famous Lost Chambers aquarium and promises the experience of "exploring the mysterious ruins of Atlantis." My companion asked if the curtains might be left open overnight. Sure, I said. I got into bed and switched off the lights. The incandescence of the aquarium flooded the room, which now was subsumed by the thalassic realm and, so it felt to me, teemed with silent pelagic beings. "This so cool," my companion said. I smiled at her and hid my face under the bedclothes. Eventually I peeked out and, in the hope of overcoming my terror, forced myself to watch the approach of eels, sharks, and other fishes. A small ray scooted up the window with its white underside against the glass—charming little spook, from one point of view, monster of otherness from another. I was in the latter camp. For hours I lay in an insomniacal agony of submersion that ended only when a pair of frogmen, each in a cloud of fish, swam toward us and began to wipe the glass.

The speedboat operator gave us tea. "I say we head back," Ollie said. "This isn't working out."

Dibba was hot, hot, hot. It was July, easily over forty degrees Celsius. Waiting around for the other divers was not an option. Later we heard that Trevor Winters, who was far from being a bad guy and not long afterward was himself the subject of one of those Dubai evaporations, thanked everyone for their efforts and distributed commemorative T-shirts bearing the words TED WILSON POSSE.

By the time I got back to The Situation, I was wiped out. I took a cold (i.e., lukewarm) shower, dressed to my under-clothes, and watched a jet skier fooling around in the lagoon. Then I climbed into my Pasha Royale X400™ massage chair and programmed a twenty-minute Full Body Integrated Shiatsu Massage, Intense mode. I selected Ambient Classics (the Pasha has built-in speakers) and pressed Start Bodywork. The chair and I began to tremble.

THE PASHA REMAINS MY GO-TO COMFORTER. I'm not sure how I would cope without it. Arguably this reveals something inadequate about me, but what is a private dwelling if not a redoubt against the tyranny of adequacy? And what's wrong with having a favorite chair? What difference does it make if its components include motors and rollers and air bags? Are these to be distinguished, analytically, from casters and springs and cushions? So what if one's chair produces physically pleasant vibrations and frictions? Or is an uncomfortable chair better than a comfortable one? Bottom line: the Pasha hurts nobody. It's not as if it's stuffed with minuscule underlings coerced into massaging me.

About nine minutes and fifteen seconds into a twenty-minute Full Body Shiatsu, the Pasha's heavy-duty twin rollers—Cagney and Lacey, I call them—get serious and rumble up the S-track and start the Deep Tissue Knead action on the muscles that surround my upper spine. Here, I invariably open my eyes and look out the windows. It is soothing to look out the windows in combination with a Pasha massage, especially if there's an active construction site in view. I have become an aficionado of this species of vista. Admittedly, this has a compulsory aspect: I have yet to live in a Dubai apartment that does not give on to a scene of buildings being built. There has never been a time, in fact, when the stupendous and beautiful Burj Dubai/Khalifa itself has not been in sight from one window or another. The slow theater of its years-long rising, its growing little by little taller and more slender until finally it achieved its last sheen and height, so that a person in almost any populated part of the emirate now has the option of looking up and contemplating nothing less than a wonder of the world—this excitement has been and continues to be a must-see part of the Dubai experience, a great theme of which has been the turning inside out of the optical fictions for which the desert sands have been notorious from the earliest ages. I still think about the afternoon when, at a spot not far from the wilds allocated to now moribund Dubailand, I stopped the Autobiography and got out into the heat and wind to take in, without the mediation of the windshield, Dubai's little row of towers, visible as if adrift, miles away across the level desert. The city could not have more resembled a fata morgana—and that was the whole idea. If I might psychologize, the reliance on the mirage/wonder equation, which of course has an etymological basis, is not just a marketing ploy: it is a secret revenge on the mirage itself, and only one facet of the Dubaian counterattack on the natural. The crimes of nature against man, in this part of the world, are not restricted to the immemorial mockery of the visual sense. The slightest effort of reflection must yield an awareness of the suffering and lowliness that these barren and desolate sands have without cease inflicted on their human inhabitants;

and it cannot be a surprise, now that the shoe is on the other foot, that the transformation of this place is characterized by attempts at domination directed not only against the heat and dust but, as is evident from the natives' somewhat irrational hostility to solar energy and their unusual dedication to the artificial settlement of marine areas, against the very sun and the very sea. This is what happens when you fuck with people for a long time. They fuck with you back.

There are some who would raise an eyebrow at my favorable aesthetic assessment of the Burj. I'd invite them to come here and see the unprecedented perpendicular for themselves, but first of all to put away ideas formed in advance about this country, the brand of which, it's fair to say, places unusual reliance on the *Guinness Book of World Records* and in particular the sections of that book for children that are concerned with the breaking of records having to do with immensities. Unless I'm mistaken, in addition to the world's tallest artificial structure, our many Officially Amazing feats/features include the longest driverless metro, the tallest hotel, the largest gold ring, the most floors in a building, the building with the largest floor space, the biggest mall, and, I read somewhere, the most nationalities washing their hands at once. Even this last exploit (undertaken to mark Global Handwashing Day, and not, as the pre-judger might think, a mindless stunt) suggests to me that there remains intact in this small country a joyful, properly childlike sense of the lofty. Excelsior!

The construction process is interesting and sometimes gorgeous. I can't pretend to understand what I'm looking at, but nor can I deny the spectacular pleasure I get from tall rebars standing in thickets in concrete, or from the short-lived orange plastic mesh that is like orange peel, or from the patterns made by construction lanterns shining in exposed concrete interiors. Most compelling of all are the tower cranes. The Dubai skyline is unimaginable to me without their masts and jibs and guy lines. Each of these marvels would impress Eiffel himself and stirs one as much as any spire or minaret. If I had my way, they would remain permanently in place, in great numbers. A Dubai that is not under continuing construction would make less sense. I'm pretty sure that nobody is looking forward to the day when everything has been built and all that remains is the business of being in the buildings.

Let me add: I'm not blind to the job-site laborers, South Asian men who are most conspicuous in the earlier stages of site work and in whom, from the high-up and distant vantage point from which I inevitably observe them, one might take an almost entomological interest as they crisscross and here and there swarm, seemingly one and the same in their color-coded corporate uniforms. I emphasize the qualifiers "almost" and "seemingly." I'm aware that I'm looking at individual persons. I have taken steps to inform myself about the oppressive and predicamental working conditions, not to say near-enslavement, to which many of them are subject from day one. (Or even before day one: many are instructed, so I've heard, to don the abovementioned corporate attire in their country of origin so that they travel to and arrive in Dubai already color-coded.) I also know enough to not give weight to the emotion of solidarity by which I experience, from inside my chilled apartment, a one-sided connection to these men, who are in the blazing hot outdoors. I'll simply say this: I have run the numbers, and I'm satisfied that I have given the situation of the foreign labor corps, and my relation to it, an appropriate measure of consideration and action.

(I don't want to dwell on this or pat myself on the back (if back patting is what's called for, which I'm not saying it is). I will only, quickly, say:

1. The subjection of persons to unjust, harsh, and otherwise wrongful treatment constitutes mistreatment of persons.

2. Laborers in Dubai are mistreated.

3.   The problem of mistreatment is widespread.

3.1   Mistreatment is not confined to laborers in Dubai.

4.   The concept of personhood is a valid basis for an ethics.

5.   The personhood of all persons is equal.

5.1   Locality of a person is an invalid basis for preferring the personhood of one person to that of another.

5.2   A corollary of personhood is the freedom from mistreatment.

5.3   A corollary of an ethics of personhood is a practicable duty to promote all freedoms that are corollaries of personhood.

5.3.1   A practicable duty is a duty to take action that is reasonably practicable.

5.3.1.1   What is reasonably practicable depends on the facts of the case.

5.4   I ought to take practicable action to prevent, stop, or reduce the mistreatment of persons.

5.4.1   In doing as I ought pursuant to 5.4, I ought not to act for the benefit of laborers in Dubai in preference to acting for the benefit of persons located elsewhere on the basis of my and the laborers' coincidental locality in Dubai.

5.4.1.1   I cannot establish a basis alternative to the basis referred to at 5.4.1 for acting preferentially as aforesaid for the benefit of laborers in Dubai.

6.   There exist organizations that take action to prevent, halt, or reduce the mistreatment of persons ("organizations").

6.1   An organization may be effective.

6.2   It is practicable for me to identify effective organizations.

6.3   The effectiveness of an organization relates to the continuing receipt by the organization of donations from the public.

7.   It is impracticable for me to directly prevent, stop, or reduce the mistreatment of persons.

8.   It is practicable for me to donate to effective organizations.

9.   A donation by me to effective organizations will have the effect of supporting the freedom of persons from mistreatment.

10.   A donation by me to effective organizations is a doing of my duty as described at 5.4 if the donation is commensurate with what it is practicable for me to donate.

(Or something to that effect. I'm sure this reasoning is full of holes. If I were to show it to professionals, they would fall around laughing. Let them. I'm not trying to move the world-historical philosophical needle here. I'm trying to figure out how to do the right thing, and last I heard that wasn't something you needed a Ph.D. to do.)

Human Rights First (HRF) and Human Rights Watch (HRW) are nonprofit, nonpartisan, independent, and reputable international advocacy and action organizations with global reaches. They are effective organizations. In my first year in Dubai, after I had had the chance to consider matters, I set up and activated automatic bank transfers of 18.5 percent of my gross monthly salary to HRF and 18.5 percent to HRW. (These are U.S.-tax-deductible charitable contributions, of course, but that's between me and the IRS, and by the by. (I arrive at the 37 percent number by calculating the maximum donation that's consistent with my making reasonable and prudent provision for my long-term comfort and solvency. A monthly cash-in-hand of six thousand USD, net of taxes and mortgage payments, strikes me as reasonable and prudent for these purposes. (Note: the Autobiography is a corporate car, owned and paid for by Batros Family Office (Dubai) Ltd.))) I cheated a little by asking HRW to allocate my donations to the struggle for migrant workers' rights in the Gulf States, but only if in HRW's judgment this would be appropriate. HRW confirmed this was appropriate, thanked me, and did as I asked. I admit that I'm uneasy about maybe not doing the right or valid thing with this allocation, the self-serving purpose of which is to make it easier for me to walk around Dubai without feeling too guilty. I can live with that uneasiness, which is not as bad as the alternative uneasiness. While far from saying that one can purchase rectitude or that I've now got some kind of get-out-of-jail card, I do feel I'm acquitting myself well enough so as not to have to lower my eyes to the ground when I meet someone.

(One last point: because I accept as a given that Dubai laborers are very badly treated, I don't owe it to the laborers to take steps to find out about exactly what kind of mistreatment they suffer from. Knowing those details would make no actionable difference to me. By contrast, HRW and HRF must go into the details, since that is their job, and what they find out is knowledge that can be imputed to me, that is, whatever they know, I know, even if I don't actually know what they know. It sounds counterintuitive, until one bears in mind the concept of outsourcing.))

On the afternoon of the Ted Wilson mission, I drew little relief from looking out the window. From the Pasha, I could see the Astrominium site (as it then was). All work on that mighty tower-to-be had just stopped. The sight of the huge abandoned pit was demoralizing. When the Full Body Shiatsu came to an end, I did not move. I lay limp in the Zero Gravity position, dreading the empty and shameful hours and days and weeks and years ahead. Normally I'm tolerant of my lot, but sometimes I am gloomy and cannot bear it and I question the rationality and desirability of personally sticking around for a further (all things being equal) three or four decades, and I find it calming that I have no dependents of any kind and am always at liberty to hang myself. The gloom passes, and gives way to the more searching notion that one's conduct is, by definition, a leading of the way, and we are all conductors, and not even the man without dependents is an island, and one's body is not one's own. It follows that to put oneself to death would offer a dispiriting example and one ought to not do it; one ought to biologically persist. Even though it thankfully remains the case that almost no one in Dubai—or elsewhere, at this point, I believe—really gives a shit what I do, I am still bound to try to do as little damage as I reasonably can. This mainly involves lying low. From the moment I arrived in this country, I have deliberately tried to be by myself inside my apartment as often and for as long as is consistent with not turning into an oddball.

I'll say one more thing about no man being an island: it isn't the whole story. I'm of course referring to one's inner Robinson and the inward island on which he must be marooned.

My face skin felt dry. I got out of the Pasha and found my moisturizing sunscreen. I used (and still use) a brand named "hope." Maybe this is because tubes of "hope" display the following statement:

> philosophy: what was
> is not what will be. let
> hope light your path in
> life's journey, and it will
> set you free.

My phone shuddered. Mila! The text of her text:

How are you?

What timing!

MILA I MET BACK IN MY EARLY Dubai days, on a night I got drunk at the Hyatt Regency Premiere club bar. I had never cal-

culatingly spoken to a hooker before, so the encounter was
nerve-racking as well as pleasant; as I say, I was drunk, and
Mila was and is very good at being kind and delighted, and
very much presents on the *fille de joie* end of the sex pro spec-
trum. We talked about Minsk, her hometown. We established
that the Danube fails to flow through Minsk, fails indeed to
flow through Belarus. With a pen and a paper napkin, Mila
plotted for my benefit the whereabouts of her cryptic coast-
less country. Belarus is surrounded by Latvia, Russia, Ukraine,
Poland, and Lithuania.

An unpredicted result of befriending Mila and Mila's friends
is that I've become really quite curious and knowledgeable
about the layout of Russia and the post-Soviet states. I not only
know the difference between Kazakhstan and Uzbekistan but
have on my map Omsk and Bishkek and Yerevan and Perm
and Poltava and Ternopil. This isn't to say that I'm interested in
these ladies' circumstances. Absolutely the last thing I want to
get into with them is their backstory. But I've always been interested in geography; and often, after she has left, I will Google
the place a given girl says she's from and I will learn a little
about the world. My investigations are mainly photographic. I
have contemplated the smokestacks of Magnitogorsk and the
poplars of Gharm. A gas station in burned grassland; a munici-
pality approached through a wood of silver birches; a window
among thousands in a sovietic housing complex—these are the
icons of personal desolation with which I have come to associate the women I pay to have sex with, and sometimes it requires
an effort of reasoning on my part to resist emotions connecting
them to Rapunzel and Andromeda and the Little Mermaid and
to remind myself, first, that the women Mila introduces me to
are members of a special class, namely tourists who choose to
fund their vacation or other financial objectives by engaging
in a night or two of remunerated sexual-social activity, and
are not sex slaves trafficked by criminal gangs; and second,
that it would be ridiculously grandiose and/or patronizing of

me to think that it falls to me to "save" these women from their choices and/or from those circumstances that may, to one degree or another, have left them with imperfect options, for it must be recognized that prostitution of any kind is a far from ideal line of work and that, put in possession of a magic wand, like anyone of ordinary sensitivity I would see no reason not to wave out of existence those things that lead a person to become a sexual servant or reluctant equal-footing erotic contractor. Unfortunately, I am not a wizard. I am a john, and cannot escape the john paradigm. This does not mean I cannot do good. I can: a john can do good. He can meet the (regrettable but pre-existing and by him uncorrectable) on-the-spot needs of the woman whose company he pays for. This entails making as generous a bargain as he is reasonably able to make; keeping his side of the bargain (by which he is bound not only by terms of payment but by terms of courtesy and respect); and abiding by the etiquette that serves all parties well. This last requirement means making no personal promises or demands; refraining from embarrassing the other or snooping around into her undisclosed motives; and offering nothing less than full face-value acceptance of her self-presentation as a good-time girl lightheartedly making an extra buck.

Of that first night with Mila, strangely it is not the night itself I remember most happily (and I do remember it happily) but the morning after. I woke up with a woman who seemed pleased to be in a room with me. True, Mila headed out at the first drone of the imams (she was disguised in an abaya, which was logical but astounding); but she was also all smiles, and gave me her phone number, and uttered emphatic words of satisfaction. Apparently the night had been a great success for her, too. Apparently Mila's interests and mine not only were not in conflict, they were in identity. Apparently she and I had injured no third entity, animal or mineral, and our dealings had produced neither an increase nor a decrease in the total sum of human hope. Apparently it was a win-win-draw-draw.

(In my book, the win-win-win ideal, valuable advance though it is on the mere win-win, does not go far enough. It seems unsatisfactory to restrict the stakeholders in a given transaction to the two transactors plus the inescapable third party, to wit, the planetary/global lot. There is a fourth, admittedly subjective and conceptually vague interest at stake, namely the effect of the transaction in terms of the human race's susceptibility to downfall or glory. And I suspect, uselessly and a little awfully, that by definition there must be a further, fifth plane of moral reality, beyond our animal comprehension, involving interests that transcend even the destinies of our planet and of the human soul. I do not mean the divine or the universal as such. Nor am I mystically hinting at some cosmic good news. If only I were!)

In my victoriousness, I actually laughed out loud. The funny part wasn't just that the me-and-Jenn deal, when it was extant, had always felt like a draw-lose-draw-lose. It was that during all those years of trying to do the right thing with and by and for Jenn, I never felt in the right. Always I sensed, close by, the doghouse. Not that I blamed her for this. Even as I understood the doghouse as an outbuilding of the phony coupledom for which surely both of us were responsible, it was clearly a doghouse built by me, with my name on it. Chronic self-misrepresentation and inner absenteeism are inconsistent with the performance of the duties of a loving partner. They make a wrongdoer of one, and it must be the exceptional wrongdoer who does not of his or her own volition inhabit a place of fault and penalty. But when I look back on that doghouse, I see that my sense of it has grown foggier. For example, it occurs to me that a doghouse implies a dog, and a dog implies a master. The identity of the dog is clear enough—I was the dog. But who was the master? Not Jenn, surely. The role would have been too burdensome: a dog must be taken for walks, etc. So who, then?

It was during those doghouse days, as it happens, that I went through a phase of being in a sort of love with Matilda, the gray, breathless, arthritic pit bull mutt who lived immediately downstairs from Jenn and me and could sometimes be heard howling. When Matilda's owners were out of town it was my job to feed her and take her to the dog run at Madison Square Park and sometimes even spend the night with her, at her place. I was not a zombie with Matilda, who for her part was purely Matilda. When the neighbors moved away, I missed her; it was painful to walk doglessly past the dog run. I suggested to Jenn that we might want to have a four-legged friend of our own. "I'm being serious," I said.

Jenn was sitting up in bed, laptop open, leafing through work pages: A4 lever arch binders surrounded her. She put down the binder. We had never discussed the question of pets before. There was a look of interest on her face. It was exciting—to connect to her like this.

"I don't want to live with a dog," she said. She picked up her binder.

Jenn was not being unkind. Far from it. She was honestly ascertaining her wants and communicating them economically and clearly. It was her form of considerateness, and I received it as such, and I still view it as such. Another way to state the matter would be: she was being Jenn. This was enormously consequential. Since I had made a binding commitment to Jenn the implied condition of which was to be with *Jenn,* i.e., the person characterized above all by Jenn-ness, it followed that, (i) if Jenn was being Jenn, then (ii) I had no good grounds for complaint about those actions of hers which, though they might provide grounds for complaint if they were the actions of another, were essentially instances of her being herself. Jenn understood this. When I said, "Why not?" in response to her saying she did not want a dog, she, evidently anguished by my persistence, said, "I'm not interested in dogs. I'm not a dog person. You know that. What do you want from me?" There was no good answer to this question, which of course had not been asked in order to solicit an answer but to make point (ii) above. But for some reason I decided to hear her literally, and I blurted, kind of jokily and experimentally, "How about a little bit of attention?" She, Jenn, looked at me. "You want my attention? I'll give you my attention." It was a menace, obviously, and it scared me—rightly so, as subsequent events showed. So I said nothing more about it, and not only out of fear. Her threat had silently expressed a valid accusation: I was a zombie fraud and not speaking in good faith and deep down did not want Jenn's attention and had no good reason to ask for it. Therefore, even though she'd menaced me with the intention of cowing me, there was legitimacy in her stance; and, on the question of the dog, she also had right on her side, because I was in effect asking her to be other than who she was, which was a non–dog lover. I let it drop—slunk off to my doghouse, which of course also operated as a shelter. Though sometimes I did fantasize about Jenn coming home from the office to discover that I had punched two holes in my torso and impaled myself on the rings of a man-sized binder.

I continue to think it would be lovely to have a dog. I sometimes imagine this faithful, pleasantly malodorous hound— saved by me from the municipal killer—snoozing happily at my feet, or leaping to greet me on my return to The Situation. As a basis for action, the fantasy is problematic. I could handle the emirate's pet-owning regulations, pursuant to which dogs must without fail be microchipped and be annually re-registered and wear collar disks issued by the authorities. So be it. But The Situation (I discovered too late) is a no-dog building. Even if I sold up—not possible, unless I'm prepared to take a 40 or 50 or, God forbid, 60 percent hit—and found somewhere dog-friendly, I would still be confronted with the rules that prohibit the walking of dogs in all public parks and on all beaches; and of course there is no question of a dog setting foot in a mall or even on Marina Walk (where often I take an evening amble and—though I am the opposite of a sailor and in fact loathe boats and regard boating, with its never-ending mopping and knotting and bucketing, as a dangerous, disagreeable form of cleaning house—I enjoy reveries in which I commandeer one of the more modest Marina vessels and weigh anchor in the dead of night and make a life as a lone salt who knows every cay and current and for whom happiness is a matter of cigarettes, stars, and something to drink). Where the public presence of dogs is permitted, it is on condition that they are kept on a leash. There are stories of dogs running free on a beach near Jebel Ali, and I've heard about sandy waste areas on the outskirts of the city where unleashed dogs are unofficially tolerated. The fact remains that man's best friend, in this country, is practically an outlaw. I find it all somewhat disheartening.

I'm aware that a cat is a viable option. I draw the line at cats.

Mila very rarely personally fucks me these days. Only when one of her associates no-shows does she sometimes step in, whereupon she kindly encourages me to imagine that we are old flames stuck in a romance that will not die, try as we might to extinguish it. Our much more usual arrangement is that Mila books a room at the Unique (where she has her contacts) in the name of the person who that night will entertain G. Pardew; I pay her an up-front fee of five hundred USD (out of which sum she compensates her friend/associate) plus the cost of the room; and, after the event, I pay her in cash for room service and any overnight guest fee. Unless something has gone awry, I add a tip, also paid to Mila on trust, since my strong preference is not to have to think about money when I'm with my companion. (Something goes awry, in this context, if my companion is not nice. I'm not told in advance who Mila has set me up with— "Surprise better," as Mila says—and I am very flexible about the physical type of the lady in question and have never turned my nose up at anyone on arbitrary and demeaning grounds such as not liking this or that about her natural appearance, about which she can do little, although I might afterward express some private opinion to Mila. But niceness is a must. I cannot not have niceness.) It comes to about a thousand USD a pop, about twice a month. It's both a luxury and a benign circulation or trickle-down of my wealth. I'd happily increase the frequency, but Mila's network operates by word of mouth, and it cannot astonish that her supply of dependable holidaymaking part-time hot women of the night is erratic.

I took a nap and woke up in the early evening. Then I re-showered and shaved so as to be Pardew-like and presentable. I was all set for an enjoyable evening: after the morning's search and rescue debacle, I felt I deserved it. I stepped into the elevator and ran into Mrs. Ted Wilson.

I could have not been more shocked if it had been Dracula. I think I let out a small yelp of fright. The doors shut quickly. There was no getting out. It was me and her and the decorative mock hieroglyphs. I must believe that she found it as terrifying as I did, for she turned toward the corner of the car and stood with her face almost touching the stainless steel. Not a word was spoken. When the elevator reached the lobby, she ran away as if from a danger.

My companion that night was a merry Kyrgyz. She had a sweet Chinese face and was very talkative, even though she spoke no English. I saw that she'd already finished most of a bottle of room service Veuve Clicquot, which, in the live-and-let-live, do-unto-others, let's-not-sweat-the-small-stuff spirit of these occasions, was absolutely fine by me. It was certainly no fault of hers that I was not able to relax. I was too shaken up by the encounter in the elevator. I found it intolerable that I could no longer go about in my own building without fear or favor, that I had to watch my step, duck and dive, keep myself to myself, accept a fate as a Quasimodo. I had to take action. *Dear Mrs. Wilson,* I conceptually wrote while the Kyrgyz sucked my cock,

Allow me to communicate my regret about the unfortunate outcome of your recent visit to my apartment. Please understand that it was an exceptional and most uncharacteristic occurrence. I am most assuredly a non-violent person. I cannot offer you an explanation of my conduct without burdening you with the long story of my personal history and the idiosyncratic sensitivities that are mine to bear. I would merely ask you to accept that I am aware that things got the better of me, and that you suffered as a consequence. Also, with great tentativeness and with a view only to your edification, I would humbly suggest that you inquire into your own possible contribution to what happened. It is not my place to say anything about this, and in any case I have nothing to say. Yours etc.

Not for the first time, I felt the lack, in English, of letter closings available to the French. How fitting it would have been to end with

Je reste à votre disposition pour toute précision complémentaire et je vous prie d'agréer toute l'expression de ma très haute considération.

I pulled away from the Kyrgyz. "Please excuse me for a moment," I said. I got out my phone and e-mailed Mrs. Ted Wilson,

Nice running into you today. May I buy you a coffee? I have information regarding Ted that may be of interest to you.

MRS. TED WILSON DID NOT get back to me. I sent her a follow-up e-mail (which also got no reply) letting her know that in any case I would be at Al Nassma café, on Level One of the Mall of the Emirates, at 11:00 a.m. on Friday. Dubai Mall, which is newer, has more buzz and glitz than the Mall of the Emirates, but I have a soft spot for the latter's staid, almost déclassé vibe, which is most pronounced in the textiles and home furnishings section, where Al Nassma is to be found. Al Nassma specializes in chocolate made with camel's milk. Camel-milk chocolate not only tastes good but works as an icebreaker and talking point. I arrived early, carrying a copy of *Philanthropy*, the magazine for philanthropists. I am not strictly a philanthropist, but I am an officer of the Batros Foundation and try to keep up with what's going on in the giving industry. It must be confessed, I was hoping the publication would make me look good, or at least philanthropic, in the eyes of Mrs. Ted Wilson.

I don't think it's very wrong of me to dwell with a little pride on my part in the founding of the Batros Foundation.

Very early into my new job, I noticed that my e-mail inbox was the terminus of chaotic requests for alms, handouts, loans, donations, etc., received by the family. Sandro was the chief forwarder of these requests. He might add,

> pls do something for this man his mother was my mother's friend

or

> $3,000????

or

> tell him to screw himself.

I had (and have) no authority to make ad hoc payouts from the Batros Family Office (Dubai) Ltd. account. When I formally requested, on Sandro's behalf, the consent of Eddie and Georges to the withdrawal of small charitable sums from the

GEAs, I got no reply. No doubt they figured Sandro could easily make the payments from his own funds. Yet it seemed to me that there had to be a way lawfully and conveniently to give effect to the Batroses' benevolent intentions. I advised that the family consider setting up a private foundation, with clearly defined purposes and powers and criteria, as an effective and potentially tax-efficient vehicle for their giving. There was no answer. Some weeks later, I got a call from *le père* Batros. This was a surprise and a big deal. It was Georges Batros who'd transformed the family business, a venerable if smallish shipping agency with offices in Beirut, Tripoli, and Latakia, into the vast international concern known and trading as Entreprises Batros. The story of his commercial adventures was told in his self-published ghostwritten memoir, *La vie est belle,* in which he described as a series of very lucky breaks his successful forays into one market after another (marine insurance agenting; automobile insurance for developing countries; exportation and distribution of generic pharmaceutical products to French-speaking Africa). Perhaps his biggest coup was Banque Batros S.A.L., a specialist in custodian services for Middle Eastern and West African clients founded in 1984: in 1996, he sold the bank (Batros interest: 32 percent) hook, line, and sinker to an American consortium for 440 million USD. The memoir did not mention it, but the family's real estate portfolio has grown in value (if my back-of-an-envelope calculations are correct) by at least 160 million USD since the mid-eighties; and now Eddie is making new fortunes, notably by betting big on agricultural holding companies in Argentina and Brazil. I have no reliable way to estimate the total value of Batros assets, but I would guess that it's not less than half a billion USD. (If the financial crisis had a negative effect on the family's wealth, I have not heard about it.) I cannot be any more specific. I'm not really sure where all the money comes from and what it all comes to.

Georges, a little fellow who looks like Charles Aznavour,

gave me a signed copy of *La vie est belle* at our very brief first meeting. This took place on his fuck-off yacht, the *Giselle*. Named for his deceased mother, it was moored in Beirut harbor most of the year and, according to Eddie, was where Georges now spent most of his time, playing cards and shooting the shit with his crew and old pals. My dedication read, *Bonne chance, fiston*.

"*Fiston, écoute bien,*" he said when he called me in Dubai. I did as instructed. The next morning I packed a bag, got into the Batros Gulfstream 100 (*"l'autobus,"* in the family slang), and flew to Antalya, Turkey. From there I took a two-hour taxi ride to Finike, a small coastal town. The *Giselle*, too big for the marina, was anchored well offshore. A crew member collected me in a rubber dinghy, incidentally trying to break the world water-speed record. Waiting at the top of the boarding ladder was Georges Batros. He wore a naval peaked cap, shorts, and no shirt. "OK, *yallah,*" he said to the captain. To me he said, "Welcome aboard," and he kissed me on both cheeks.

Somebody took my bag, somebody took me to the dining deck, somebody made me a gin and tonic. I didn't want a gin and tonic, but what the hell. It was good to have got out of the desert, and I'd never been on a private cruise or visited this part of the ancient world. The yacht, or ship, slipped past aquamarine inlets and between small islands where wild olive trees grew out of gray and white rocks. The littoral mountains, precipitous and forested, were beautiful. A cool breeze blew. I inhabited the World of Rolex.

And yet I was jumpy. Why? Because I am not a total dope. I wasn't going to fall into the trap of equating beautiful surroundings with a beautiful state of affairs. When, in Beirut, Eddie introduced me to his father, he said, "You're going to like him. He's mellowed a lot since the old days." People who are said to have "mellowed" always make me nervous. Meanwhile I had already figured out that to even begin to understand the

Batros family you had to understand the money. The Batros sons are highly remunerated (salaries, bonuses, stock options, employment benefits), but many of their largest capital assets— houses, boats, lump sums from the GEAs, interest-free loans, etc.—have essentially remained in the gift of their father, who is the majority shareholder of Batros Holdings Ltd. (incorporated in the DIFC), which in turn wholly owns the Batros subsidiaries, of which there are more than fifty, which in turn own who knows how many sub-subsidiaries. Georges still controls most of the money, is what it comes down to.

He joined me. He had undressed and wore only a white towel, around his waist. He unknotted the towel and draped it over the seat of his chair. Now he was naked. A pharmacologistical young woman (*"Une lesbienne,"* Georges later whispered) began to shampoo his hair. Most of the ultra-HNW individuals I've met are idiosyncratically demanding, and everyone is familiar with the larger-than-life, I-make-my-own-rules display of power, and I understand from Ollie that gratuitous domestic nudity is prevalent among the rich and famous as a kind of very authoritative informality. But even though I had willingly entered into the company of Georges Batros and maybe "on some level" had sought him out, I began to feel that my situation was objectionable as well as precarious. I had no idea how long I was expected to stay on this boat or why I'd been summoned. The *Giselle,* I knew, was making its annual odyssey from Beirut to Saint-Jean-Cap-Ferrat, where Mme. Batros (née Alice Rourke, in Mullingar, Ireland) was already summering in the Villa Batros, a magnificent cliff-top mansion with a private jetty. Where was I supposed to get off? Piraeus? Portofino? Surely there is more than a trace of false imprisonment about hospitality from which there is no escape.

Georges got to his feet and took a shower. The female crew-member trained a high-powered hose on him as though he were on fire. He thoroughly lathered himself, dick and balls especially, and rinsed his hair and hopped around in the water jet. He kept chatting to me, even as the crew-member toweled him down. There was something faintly villainous about his showiness. He reminded me of those clever murderers who for a while run rings around Lieutenant Columbo.

"And how is your old friend Mr. Trompe?" Georges, taking his seat, said. He was still in the buff, though now he wore his commodore's cap.

"Fine—I guess," I said. "I don't really know him."

"Come, you're being modest," Georges said. "Weren't you invited to his wedding? At Palm Beach?"

This was correct—up to a point. Godfrey Pardew was the invitee, on account of the good work he had done for Donald Trump and especially Donald's father, Fred, in the realm of wills, trusts, divorces, prenuptial agreements, and other sensitive matters. But Godfrey had declared himself "regrettably unable" to fly down to Florida, and at the last minute he notified the Trump people that I (plus one, Jenn) would be attending on behalf of the firm in the stead of Mr. and Mrs. Pardew. The wedding was a lot of fun, as it happens, and I shared certain amusing details with Eddie on the night of our reunion at Asia de Cuba. That was a highly consequential anecdote, as things turned out, because it was my connection to Donald Trump that prompted Sandro to approve my appointment.

I'm not sure what Eddie told him, but out of the blue Sandro flew to New York, bought me dinner at the Rainbow Room, and (making zero mention of the London fiasco) questioned me for over an hour about that magical night at Mar-a-Lago. I was able to tell him what it was like to stand next to Shaquille O'Neal, and to listen to Billy Joel playing the piano six feet away, and to take a leak with the great Trump in the adjoining urinal. Sandro was deeply moved. He confided that it was his dream to take part in *The Apprentice*, the Trump TV show in which job-seeking contestants compete for the approval of the magnate and are each "fired" by him, save one—the apprentice. Sandro was in his late forties and presumably more qualified for the role of master than apprentice, so I was a little surprised. I began to understand his ambition to earn Trump's blessing only after it became clear that Georges neither trusted nor esteemed Sandro and restricted his role to that of running the Dubai holding company—a titular job—and chiefly expected of him, his older son, that he spend enough time in Dubai so as to serve as a human data point for technical legal purposes. When Sandro asked me about getting on Trump's TV show, I told him I would see what I could do. This I duly did. I could do nothing.

"I went as a representative of my law firm," I said to Georges. "I'm not close to the Trump family."

"Ah, this was not my impression," Georges said. Then he was telling me all about the crewing arrangements—two Norwegians (captain, chief engineer), a Greek chef, and five others from ethnically prestigious parts of Western Europe. Their uniform consisted of white Lacoste shirts, white sailing shorts with the *Giselle* monogram, and classic blue-and-white boat shoes. They all wore the same sunglasses. Uniformity aside, they might have been gung-ho young bankers on holiday. Georges said, "These people are the best in the world."

I said something like "Yeah, they look like they're really stoked."

He called out to one of deckhands. "Giancarlo!" The fellow came bounding over. Georges said something to him in Italian. Presently the boat dropped anchor. I heard splashes: Giancarlo and two others had plunged into the sea. They swam to the shore, climbed over the tricky rocks, and made their way up the hill to where a herd of goats was feeding on bushes. There was no sign of a goatherd. Giancarlo turned toward us and waved. He gestured at a black goat, and Georges gave him a double thumbs-up. The three men jumped on the black goat and wrestled it to the ground and instantly roped its legs. I might have been watching a rodeo. Giancarlo slit the animal's throat. They held it down while it kicked and bled out. This lasted for some time. Giancarlo towed the carcass back, trailing a messy red stream. The three men stood on the deck wet and bloody. They held up the dead goat. "Bravo, bravo," Georges Batros said, applauding. Everyone applauded, me included.

"You see?" he said to me. "This is the quality of these men."

"Unbelievable. Wow," I said. There seemed no point in raising the issue of compensation for the owner of the goat.

A short while later, the chef arrived with a serving dish. "The liver," Georges said. "Fresh, fresh." He cut a piece off the red mass, squeezed lemon juice over it, and began to eat. "Fantastic," he said. "Take some. There is nothing healthier." I accepted a piece, against my will. I did not want to put a part of the goat inside me.

Georges said, "This idea you have, to have a foundation, this is a good idea."

It took a second or two to figure out what he was talking about.

"Tell me," Georges said. He was very fastidious with his white napkin and was taking a long time to clean his mouth and wipe his hands. His huge helping of raw liver was suddenly gone, as if by prestidigitation. "Who do you think we should help?"

"Whoever you want to help," I said. "It's your money." I added, for some stupid reason, "You have the honor of deciding."

"Honor?" He laughed. "This is not my area of expertise. I would like you to decide."

"Uh, I'm no expert, either," I said. "It was just a suggestion. I just thought it might be a good idea. From the Batros standpoint. I mean, it's my impression that you get a lot of requests for help."

"This is very true," Georges said. "A lot of people ask us for money." He pointed at my chest. "Tigers. Maybe we should help the tigers. They are very noble. I remember seeing them in Las Vegas. Poor Mr. Roy, that was the tragedy of tragedies. Or was it Mr. Siegfried? My question is, do you think we can save the tigers? How would we do it? How much money would it take? The problem is the Chinese," he said. "They eat tigers. I believe they will eat anything. Dogs, of course. They love the meat of the dog. It is not just the Chinese. The Indonesians, too. Let me tell you a story. I was in Indonesia once, in Sumatra. A savage place. I had to go up into the hills to speak to a big man. On the way up there, my driver is looking, looking, like this." Georges gripped an invisible steering wheel and peered from side to side. "Then"—he turned the wheel—"*boum*. We hit something. The driver gets out. He goes into the street. He picks up the dead dog by the legs and throws it in the back of the truck, like this. He says to me, We will give the dog to the big man. And this is what happened. The big man cooked the dog, and we ate it. Eating dogs isn't so stupid, in my opinion. In Switzerland they eat dog sausages, and I cannot say the Swiss are stupid. Cold, yes. Avaricious, yes. Stupid, no. But eating tigers for medicine? Very stupid. Maybe this should be our focus, the fight against stupidity. It's a very serious problem. There is a lot of stupidity in the world. It does much harm. You must understand this very well, coming from the United States."

"I—yes," I said. I was more taken aback by his comment on the Swiss, which on one view amounted to a comment on my mother.

"The people of China work very hard, but still they are stupid," Georges Batros said. "Our problem is, they are"—he searched for the English word—"*nombreux*."

"Numerous." I was wondering why he'd decided to have the conversation in English. In Beirut, we'd spoken in French.

"Exactly. They are numerous. There are more than one billion Chinese, *si je ne me trompe pas*. Also one billion Indians, and many of them are stupid, and again the tiger suffers. I am not sure where to begin. What do you suggest?"

"I don't know," I said. "Perhaps you could—"

"What are your arrangements?" Georges said.

I didn't know what he meant.

Georges said, "What arrangements have you made to help others? That would be very good to know. I could follow your example."

"I'm not sure that would be instructive," I said. I smiled humbly. "Our situations are not comparable," I said. "Unfortunately, I'm not in a position—"

"Yes, yes, yes—I understand. But you make good money. Eddie has taken care of you. You are in a position to help others, even if only a little. It would be a guide, an inspiration, to hear about your personal efforts."

He was trying to push me around. I declined the top-up an attendant was offering me. To Georges, I said, "My arrangements are my business, with respect." (I had no arrangements at that time. I had only recently arrived in Dubai. I had not yet put in place my automatic transfers to HRF and HRW.)

"But what I give to charity, what I do with my money—that's your business?"

"I think there's been a misunderstanding, Mr. Batros. I don't have an opinion about this. I was just trying to be useful as the family officer."

"I like you," Georges stated. "You're Eddie's old friend. And Sandro trusts you. This is a point in your favor, because my sons can't agree about anything. So let me explain something to you. You have one function. You know what this function is? It is to make sure nobody steals. This is your function."

Various ripostes came to mind ex post facto, but at that moment I said, "Absolutely. Understood." If Georges wanted to flex his biceps, put me in my place, show me who was boss, ream me out—whatever, sticks and stones. Fundamentally, spiritually, he had no standing. All I was interested in was keeping my job and getting the fuck off the yacht.

So it came about. Somebody took away my glass, somebody gave me my bag, somebody ushered me to the dinghy. Georges was at the top of the boarding ladder, waving. "Please give my regards to Mr. Trompe," he called out. I was quickly transported to the nearest coastal village. I made a deal with a villager and was driven to Antalya. The *autobus* was long gone. I flew back commercial, via Istanbul. A week later, I was informed that the Batros Foundation had been incorporated in Dubai and that the board of directors had appointed me to the (pro bono and essentially honorary) office of Treasurer.

The Batros family endowed the Foundation with forty million USD. I signed the GEA authorization myself—an unforgettable, vertiginous moment. Almost four years later, the Foundation (through sub-charities and in cooperation with partner donors) supports medical clinics in Abidjan, Libreville, Tunis, and Kinshasa. These projects are going very well, judging from the brochures and the websites, which feature photographs of very happy-looking Africans. I have no involvement in the operational side, which is carried on by a mainly Lebanese team based in International Humanitarian City, over by Business Bay. The team reports directly to Georges but copies me in on about fifteen e-mails a day, few of which I am in position to make much sense of. I do, as Treasurer, have power to authorize payments from the Foundation accounts, which in theory I oversee. This power enables me to ensure that the Foundation makes miscellaneous donations authorized by the Batros directors. To date I've received authorizations from Alice Batros, in support of CARI (working for Irish victims of childhood sexual abuse), and from Sandro, in support of Operation Smile (surgical repair of facial deformities in children) and the Heritage Foundation (development and dissemination of right-wing ideas). I have given the relevant instructions to the Batros Foundation employees and followed up personally. The donors can be sure that their benefaction has been effective.

It has never been explained to me by what process Georges Batros decided to green-light the Foundation. I believe I played an instigative role, even if this has never been recognized by any Batros. When I question the worth of my life, it comforts me to think that, but for my instrumentality in this matter, a significant number of humans would likely be living less healthy, less happy, less worthwhile lives. One might say that this unforeseen good contains nothing less than the hidden meaning of my move to Dubai.

My dealings with the Batros family are confidential, and I'm not one to toot my own horn, so there was no question of sharing any of this with Mrs. Ted Wilson at Al Nassma—if, that is, she showed up. I drank a cappuccino; I drank a second. As I watched one person after another who wasn't Mrs. Wilson walk into the café, I passed into an awareness of another person—the one waiting for the arrival of Mrs. Ted Wilson. What was he doing? Who did he think he was? Was it really his plan to inform Mrs. Ted Wilson of an unverified rumor that there was a second Mrs. Ted Wilson? As if she hadn't heard it already? As if he had some kind of standing in the matter? As if he was an Extraordinary Gentleman? As if she was really going to meet up for a coffee with an unstable lentil thrower who didn't even know her husband? And then what—take a romantic stroll in the mall? Fall, for no reason, for a supererogatory weirdo? LOL.

I rolled up my *Philanthropy* and went to the office.

SPEAKING OF WHICH, who should drop by today but Sandro. He enters unannounced and catches me and his son working on a Green Belt Sudoku problem.

"What's this?" he says, picking up the puzzle book. Before anyone can reply, he lets go of the book and advances to my side of the new partition and with a great sigh takes a seat in my chair. Sandro must have the mistaken idea that the partition creates an acoustic barrier, because he says loudly, "We need to talk."

I pause him with a raised hand, which I suspect irritates him. I go to the kid. "Why don't you sit at Ali's desk for a while." The kid picks up his chair and follows me out. Ali gets up and offers the kid his own chair, behind the desk. I veto that. Ali must sit in his chair and the kid must sit in his chair.

Sandro is fiddling with my mouse and looking aggrieved. He tells me, "I'm not happy with my doctors."

"Which ones?" I say. Sandro's healthcare profile is complex. There's an orthopedist in Lausanne for his bad knees, a pulmonologist in London for his bad breathing, and a cardiologist in New York for his bad heart. In Dubai, he retains physicians who provide 24/7/365 concierge medical services to a very small clientele. (The Batros family has its own in-house emergency room in both the Dubai and Beirut compounds. Each has an X-ray machine, CT scanner, blood-analysis facilities, ultrasound equipment, etc. The *Giselle* has an ER cabin, albeit a relatively rudimentary one. (Sandro's yacht, the *Mireille,* has no special cabin, but does have a defibrillator. (Eddie has no yacht.)))

"Lieberman," Sandro says. Lieberman is the Park Avenue cardiologist. "He's got me wearing this for the next couple of weeks." To my dismay Sandro lifts his Notre Dame T-shirt (Notre Dame is his alma mater, though he never graduated). Even as I avert my eyes, I see that wiring has been taped to his breast tissue. "It's a monitor. This way they can follow my heartbeat second to second."

"OK, that makes sense," I say. Sandro suffers from cardiac dysrhythmia.

"Yeah, but get this," he says. "The results show up in India. There's a computer in India watched by Indian guys. They see something, they call New York. I mean, what the WTF? Indian guys? I'm putting my life in the hands of Indian guys in India?"

"I'm sure they're highly qualified."

"Yeah? I'm sure they're highly fucking minimum wage."

I make a big show of getting out a piece of paper and taking a note.

Sandro sighs and heavily swivels. "So . . . ?" He bobs his head toward the door, in the direction of his son. "How's it going?"

"OK, I guess," I say. I decide to try my luck, carefully. "I have to tell you, Sandro, I'm not sure this is the most productive setup. And this thing with weighing him . . ."

Sandro says, "Tell me this: you got kids?" Another swivel, a big roomy one that surely puts my chair under huge strain. "I didn't think so. However . . . Point taken. We've got to make this work. I think the answer is, you should take him under your wing."

I am very, very silent. I am William the Silent and Harpo Marx and Justice Thomas.

He is saying, "You're telling me it's not super-productive. OK—so make it productive. You're a smart guy—teach him something. He's got a bunch of summer homework he needs to do. Help him with that. His mother isn't exactly the professor of brain surgery type."

I'm not going to get sidetracked into a consideration of Mireille Batros, an exceedingly complicated person. "Sandro—"

"You're going to teach him some values," Sandro says. "What's right and what's wrong. This is going to be your top priority."

"Sandro, there's no way I—"

He begins to weep. "I can't do this by myself anymore."

Here we go again. *Krokodilstränen*. *Les larmes de crocodile*. The human tear, once a great currency, is now worthless everywhere.

He says, "You know our ATM machine?"

I do know. At Fort Batros, the family has an HSBC ATM for its exclusive use.

Sandro tells me that Alain underhandedly borrowed his ATM card, somehow figured out the PIN, and attempted to withdraw money. They caught him red-handed, the numbskull, because he couldn't quickly work out which way to insert the card.

"Oh dear," I say. "That's unfortunate."

Sandro relates that he and Mireille cross-examined their son for an hour, made various threats, inflicted various penalties, and still he refused to say how he'd got hold of the card or the PIN, or how much he was planning to withdraw and for what purpose. Mireille's participation in this questioning is ironic, because Mireille's own debit and credit cards have been taken away from her on account of her alleged inability to control her spending.

"We got nothing out of him," Sandro says. "Not a word."

I'm impressed with the kid. He didn't crack.

"I want you to find out what's going on," Sandro says.

"How am I supposed to do that?"

Sandro points a thumb at himself. "Bad cop." He points an index finger at me. "Good cop. Make friends with him. Make him feel like it's safe to talk to you."

The demand is so absurd and unenforceable that it doesn't occur to me to object.

"You'll make it work," Sandro says. He somehow raises himself out of my chair. "We all set with Bryan Adams?"

"You mean Bryan Ferry," I say. "Yes, we—"

"I mean Bryan Adams. What am I going to do with Bryan Ferry? Mireille loves Bryan Adams."

"You asked me to book Bryan Ferry. You didn't ask me to book Bryan Adams."

"Bryan Adams. I told you to book fucking Bryan Adams. You booked Bryan Ferry?"

"I booked who you asked me to book."

Sandro points at me again. He's always pointing. "Now you're fucking with my sex life." He goes to the door, where, in a cheesy move, he turns to face me darkly. "Do not fuck with me on this. You got nine days to get Bryan Adams."

Exeunt Sandro and all of his bullshit. Re-enter the kid and all of his.

I'm so angry, I can't even mental-mail.

"I'm stepping out," I announce to Ali and Alain and, for all I know, Allah.

There is still a problem, however: where to go once I have stepped out. It is an old problem: the problem of the exit. If it is a difficult thing to leave a room, it is still more difficult to find the room's alternative.

My office is in the DIFC, which I consider to be a beautiful place to do business and to be human in Dubai. The semi-autonomous Dubai International Financial Centre, with its regulatory structures that remove it from the emirate's archaic justice system, is not just a financial free zone. It is also an architecturally free-floating environment. In contrast to almost any other place in Dubai, substantial amenities are offered to the person who wishes to be an outdoor pedestrian. Here are broad gray plazas and pools with charcoal or dove gray water. There are green lawns, and blue-gray-brown footbridges, and cafés with silver chairs, and cool gray-brown breezeways and charcoal gray sculptures. The beautiful office buildings are gray and gray-blue and silver-gray. Gray-brown doves go about near the dove gray pools and beautiful women go coolly across the plazas in dark jackets over white or blue shirts, and the men on the plazas have charcoal or silver hair and blue shirts and dark suits or beautiful white robes. These harmonies and con-

sistencies of tone and demeanor are nothing other than indi-
cia of an agreement in feeling between all of us who partake
in and of this polity, namely that, in essence and in potential,
ours is a zone of win-win-win flows of money and ideas and
humans, and that somewhere in our processes and practices, as
we sense in our bones and sometimes almost sniff in the air, are
the omens of that future community of cooperative productiv-
ity, that financial nationhood, of which all of us here more or
less unconsciously dream.

My difficulty, at this moment, is that I cannot feel at one
with the people who coolly go across the plazas, who after
all have the intention of going into the interiors of the gray
buildings, i.e., into rooms, whereas I am going out of my building with no intention of going into another building. I would
even say that the harmoniousness of these people and their surroundings depends on the viability of the indoors as a place for
those outdoors to go to, because after all there isn't much that
can be accomplished by walking between buildings. In other
words, I feel anomalous as I go across the plaza, and very hot;
also, it is unsustainable to keep going across plazas. I must go
back indoors, into a room. And here is a room: The Empty
Quarter, one of our DIFC art galleries. I go in.

The exhibition is titled:

The Worst Journey in the World
Captain Scott's Antarctic Expedition 1910–1913
The Photographs of Herbert Ponting

I'm not a big art fan. Even so, I would have to be a very
strange person to be uninterested in these photographs.

Because I'm broadly familiar with the story of Captain Scott
and know that gloom and doom lies ahead, I start with *An
Emperor Penguin*. Upright haughty bird! Good chap! The
resemblance to the Ruler is startling. (If another expat were
present, I might share this impression with him/her, sotto voce,

and we'd have a nice little laugh. However, I have The Empty Quarter to myself.)

The Terra Nova *held up in the Pack, Dec. 13ᵗʰ, 1910*

The good ship runs afoul of the ice. Yes, I can see how that would happen. To judge from Mr. Ponting's astounding black-and-white images, this sphere of land-ice and sea-ice and air-ice, so-called Antarctica, is barely a place at all but, rather, an enormous and enormously weird natural activity, so that the spectacle of this doughty, three-masted silhouette trying to get somewhere seems multiply fallacious, as if an attempt were being made to sail a shadow into a hubbub, audible only in the form of coldness, emanating from sources that are not a whereabouts.

Ah, here are the huskies.

Each has its own portrait. Husky Tresor, Husky Wolk, Husky Vida. They have pensive, trusting faces. This makes one sad, inevitably.

And here are the humans.

C. S. Wright on return from the barrier, Jan. 1912

Portrait of B. Day on return from the barrier, Dec. 21ˢᵗ, 1911

These men are clearly in shock. What happened to them? What is the "barrier"?

There's a book of writing for sale, *The Worst Journey in the World,* by Apsley Cherry-Garrard. This is a fine name for an explorer. However, the book is enclosed in cling wrap and I cannot leaf through it. I must go back to the photographs on the walls.

Capt. Scott, Apr. 13ᵗʰ, 1911

The great/flawed man himself, with one foot on a sled. The face is emotionally ajar, and discloses a slippery modern soul— self-absorbed, ambivalent, newly metaphysically brave. It's a face you see a lot. Walk into any DIFC office and you'll spot a Bob Scott.

> *Portrait of C. H. Meares on his return from the barrier, Jan. 1912*

Again the barrier? They had to keep making the men go there?

> *Portrait of Dimitri on return from the barrier, Jan. 29th, 1912*

It is much too much for me. Out I go.

IT MUST HAVE BEEN A DAY or two after my non-meeting with Mrs. Ted Wilson that I ran into Brett Hutchinson in a DIFC parking lot and accepted his invitation to Friday brunch. I felt like I had to. A few months before, I'd loaned Brett twenty thousand AED. As soon as he'd been fired, his bank accounts were automatically frozen in accordance with the local law, and the guy was up to his neck in liabilities and tied to the U.A.E. for personal reasons and unable to make a run for it. Talk about being in a tough spot. Now that he was bravely back on his feet and relatively liquid (he'd repaid me fifteen thousand AED and promised the balance in short order), he wanted to signal his gratitude and reclaim some lost acre of honor. It must be said, I didn't know Brett that well. I loaned him the money because he approached me as one American to another. I had misgivings about whether shared nationality was a valid reason for assisting co-national A rather than alter-national B, particularly where B's needs might be as great as, indeed greater than, those of A; yet I said yes to Brett without hesitation. It was striking how, when the shit hit the fan and people suddenly if temporarily found themselves in the same tight corner, loyalties of country were re-discovered in the matter of asking for help and giving it. Which isn't to say that there was an abrupt territorial re-organization of moral feelings; there were many who were kind without reference to kindredness, and in this sense may be said to have admirably rescued the language of goodness from its primal dirt. I might add that I feel more cleanly American than ever. Leaving the U.S.A. has resulted in a purification of nationality. By this I mean that my relationship to the U.S. Constitution is no longer subject to distortion by residence and I am more appreciative than ever of the great ideals that make the United States special. I pay my federal taxes to the last dime, and, without in any way devaluing citizenship to a business of cash registers, I can assert that I am well in the black with my country.

Anyhow, Brett was a proud man from Little Rock. If he needed to buy me brunch to look himself in the eye, I wasn't going to stand in his way, even if the thought of another all-you-can-eat-and-drink Friday afternoon shindig was basically worrying. It didn't help that the event had as its stated theme "F*** the F****** Financial Crisis."

The venue for the brunch was the subject of debate between a dozen or so of the brunchers. Some were in favor of the One & Only, others Al Qasr, others the Park Hyatt, others the Fairmont, others The Address (in Downtown Dubai, not The Address Dubai Marina). I would guess that two hundred messages went into circulation. The initial volley straightforwardly considered the hotels' relative merits (in the matters of value for money, lobsters, cigar availability, ambience, house champagne brands, etc.); but this give-and-take quickly frayed into off-topic threads, the most popular of which, this being Dubai, inevitably concerned the question of service. To be fair, I suppose it's theoretically possible that the affluent expat population largely consists of people who arrived with bees already in their bonnets about the performance of waiters, lackeys, and help. But most of us here would shamefacedly agree that something about the local gradient eventually means that pretty much everyone who's white and/or well-to-do slides into bossiness and haughtiness in relation to pretty much everyone who's not white and not well-to-do. According to some commentators, our domineering cadre is essentially drawn from the same stock of provincial, socially second- or third-tier Europeans who, in the days of empire, populated the lesser despotic positions—policemen, clerks, overseers—and it's far from surprising, therefore, that members of what was once the taskmaster or slave-driver class should be given to pushing people around and looking down their lower-middle- or middle-middle-class noses at their supposed social and/or racial inferiors. Maybe this holds some truth; there's no denying I've seen repellently *de haut en bas* behavior here from men and women about whom it might in all neutrality be said that in their own homeland they might not be widely perceived as having the socioeconomic status to as it were plausibly claim for themselves a relative superiority. I have to wonder, though, if the negative critique of these individuals is a function of the critics' care for the well-being of the dominated persons or if it is, rather, self-serving viciousness and snobbery about persons who the critics feel have no entitlement of their own to viciousness and snobbery, a feeling that's detestable on the intellectual level among others, since, unless I have been thoroughly misinformed, the so-called top or upper or upper-middle societal tiers cannot be said to have brought glory on themselves, whether historically or contemporarily, in the matter of the kindly or just treatment of less powerful others, e.g., serfs, peasants, defenseless foreign populations. It's ugly, however you look at it. It's not uplifting or entertaining to read, as I did on the aforementioned thread about the imbecilities of the servant classes,

> I got one. Our cleaning lady whose from Indonesia and a very nice young lady, put away some books with the spines facing INSIDE.

> Think I can beat that. I was at Starbucks yesterday and the Indian gentleman waiter tried to "tidy away" the newspaper I was reading. He had no idea that the whole point of sitting down was to read the newspaper. He didn't know what reading a newspaper was!

> Try explaining that L socks go with R socks! Never works. They always think L goes with L because it looks the same. Drives me potty.

Normally, I would never think of intervening. On this occasion, I don't know why, I was prompted to write, it must be said hesitantly,

> I think that here in Dubai, there's a widespread confusion of the notions of service and servility. Restaurant/ hotel service focuses on fawning and obsequiousness rather than efficiency. The question is whether this is due to the customer expectations (i.e., we demand servility), or inexperienced management, or both. We know that it cannot only be due to the imported culture of the staff, because Indian waiters who work in New York, London, etc., are highly competent and resourceful. Ditto cabdrivers. Btw, has anyone noticed how disenchanted the taxi drivers here are, compared with those in New York, say? What is our role in this, I wonder.

Nobody responded to my wonderment, either online or at Yalumba, the restaurant at Le Méridien where the brunch was, in due course, held.

I turned up on the late side, at 2:00 p.m. Brett and his two English co-hosts had booked a huge banqueting table for thirty, and surrounding our table were other tables at which other champagne brunches were taking place, and there was a very happy, very loud, restaurant-wide brouhaha to which my table was contributing its fair share of laughing and yelling. A majority of heads wore pointy bright party hats. Not wanting to be a Buzz Killington, I put on a gleaming red fez.

Brett aside, I recognized only a few faces at my table, and only faintly. Brett seemed a little confused, or distracted, when I greeted him, and it took some rearranging of chairs to make room for me. I wandered Yalumba's famous buffets. They were wasted on me: I don't see anything great about crab displays or giant vats of macaroni and cheese, etc. Still, when in Dubai; and boiled potatoes, garlic mussels, and a T-bone steak found their way onto my plate. At the table, I accepted red wine, and champagne from a salmanazar of Laurent-Perrier that happy aproned waiters wheeled around on a mobile ice bed, courtesy of someone somewhere in the restaurant. Who was my benefactor? It seemed wrong to accept the drink without some sign of thanks (even though I was entirely satisfied by my red wine and had no selfish wish to drink champagne). In the end, I decided to raise my glass of bubbly to a table of generous-looking French dudes wearing berets, and they raised their glasses back, though it remained unclear if this was to acknowledge my gratitude or simply to return my friendly gesture.

The chief excitement in my section of the table was provided by the presence of a Scotsman named Jimmy. Jimmy was that very rare bird—the new arrival in Dubai. Here was a chink of economic light! Here might be the recovery's first swallow! Our joy was lessened by his revelation that his was not an open-market hiring but, in point of fact, a U.A.E. government job—a six-month contract to work on supplementary procurement issues connected to the Metro construction. Never mind, he was a fresh face, and he gave older Dubai hands the chance to once more indulge in what may be our most indestructible conversational trope, that is, tutoring the newcomer to the Emirates about the outlandish legal hazards he or she faces in the areas of buying and consuming alcohol, gambling, having sex, driving, drunk driving, using recreational drugs, incurring debt, and so on and so forth, with illustrative cautionary tales whose invariable moral is that, contrary to its accommodating and modern appearance, for the non-national the emirate is a vast booby trap of medieval judicial perils, and Johnny Foreigner must especially take great care when interacting with local citizens (who constitute only 10 percent or so of the population) because de facto there is one law for Abdul Emirati and another for Johnny Foreigner, so that, for example, if Johnny is involved in an automobile collision with Abdul, responsibility for damage caused will in practice not be determined in accordance with familiar qualitative assessments of the acts and omissions of the parties involved but in accordance with considerations of identity, the local concept (supposedly alien to the person accustomed to Romano-Judeo-Christian jurisprudence) being that the applicability of the duty of care (known to some as the neighbor principle) is subject to modification by the nationalitative interrelation of the involved parties. I.e., it's not what you *do,* it's who you *are* vis-à-vis the person who does unto you or unto whom you do.

Jimmy was asked about his first impressions. "I love the huge posters of the Sheikh you see everywhere," he said. "I wouldn't mind getting hold of one. I could make a fortune on eBay."

A fork was waved in Jimmy's direction. "That sort of hipster irony doesn't go down very well here."

"Yeah," someone said. Making quotation fingers, this person added, "He's not 'The Ruler,' he's the fucking Ruler."

The fork waver warned Jimmy, "You want to watch it. They don't have a sense of humor about that sort of thing. Just so you know."

"They like to be ruled. It settles them down. I'm not against it, to be honest. Not in England, of course, but here."

"He's a good bloke, Sheikh Mo. He's done a lot of good for his people."

Jimmy: "Is it true he's got a private jet just for his falcons?"

"Yes. So they say."

"And he's got cheetahs, too."

"No, he doesn't. That's total rubbish."

The cheetah guy threw his party hat at the rubbisher, who in turn threw his napkin at the cheetah guy. There was a brief storm of things being thrown. Bread rolls flew from one end of the table to the other, to shouts of approval.

When things calmed down, somebody said, "They say he's after getting married again."

"That's what I heard, too. Sheikha number four."

"Could be number five, for all we know."

Jimmy: "Why's it so hush-hush?"

Somebody began to air a theory (which I paraphrase and, to be honest, save from disjointedness) to the effect that the Ruler's overt power depended on an inner zone of secrecy for secrecy's sake, and this centrum of inexplicability (which deprived outsiders of data relating even to royal matrimonial and domestic arrangements) tacitly communicated the existence of broader political arrangements by which entitlement to significant information was made the subject of concentric separations, with the Ruler at the center and the populace distributed more or less at the perimeter, etc., etc., with the inevitable reference to the Wizard of Oz.

To my left was a kind-looking blonde in her thirties. She must have been as restless as I was, because she said, "Hello, I'm Samantha. What's your name?" She was drinking a cocktail involving champagne and Rémy Martin. The neighboring table gave a hilarious roar as I answered her, and we both smiled, because it was good to have so many relaxed and happy souls assembled in one room, and at that moment, in fact, the music came on and a kicking conga line instantly formed and people from every corner of Yalumba joined in, laying hands on shoulders and waists and shuffling along singing the olé song and tooting on party blowers. Samantha said, "Come on," and I added myself to the shambling human concatenation, and I had fun, obviously because I was well on my way to getting loaded. It was a full five minutes before the music stopped and we all returned to our tables in the best of spirits.

Samantha told me she was heading home to England, to get a divorce and "start all over again."

"That must be very painful," I said.

She suggested in a sensitive tone of voice that I might have gone through something similar, and I said, "Perhaps I have."

"Well, either you have or you haven't," she said.

I laughed. Samantha seemed to be upset by this, which was the last thing I wanted, because I was really rooting for her, this spirited and good person, and I said, "Sorry. I was just remembering something. My ex objected to me using that word—'perhaps.'"

Samantha said, "What do you mean, she objected?"

"She just didn't like it. It got on her nerves."

"I suppose it depends on the context," Samantha said with great pensiveness.

"Yes," I agreed.

The Perhapsburg Empire—that used to be my unspoken nickname for the Jenn-me realm.

I said, "And 'henceforth.' 'Henceforth' really, really irritated her."

Samantha giggled.

My theory, kept from Samantha, was that Jenn objected to this fancy (in her mind) vocabulary because it was (as she saw it) the tip of an iceberg of European haughtiness. I suspect she equated my Swiss ancestry with being looked down on from an alp. It sounds crazy, but I don't think she could quite accept, or understand, that an American could through no fault of his own know French (a language spoken by normal people all over the world), and that the whole thing wasn't just some kind of trick of one-upmanship designed to knock her back down into the Lehigh Valley.

The salmanazar! Three men hoisted the inexhaustible Brobdingnagian bottle and, not without anxiety, filled our glasses. Samantha was looking very appealing now, and I recognized that I was imagining myself alone with her and prospectively knowing the bliss of being with her, and it took a real effort to avail myself of the technique I've developed to protect myself and the woman in question at such moments, which is to fast-forward through the joyful scenes of carnality and closeness, valid imaginings though these may be, and slowly play in my cerebral cinema the moment when it's pain-pain and lose-lose-lose-lose and she's heartbroken and I'm boarding a boat to Tristan da Cunha.

Samantha declared, "Henceforth I'm going to start saying 'henceforth.' Perhaps." She laughed very hard, and her elbow dropped into a jumbo shrimp combo, and several of the jumbo shrimps sprang from the salad onto the table. A cheer went up.

"Bloody elbow," Samantha said, wiping her arm with the tablecloth. "Story of my life." She laughed courageously.

I decided to not give voice to my deep, untrustworthy compassion.

Samantha told me that her husband, Gavin, had been unfaithful to her with a twenty-four-year-old he'd met while "seal bashing" at Barasti. "That's when he took up 'scuba diving.'" It was her turn to make air quotes. "He'd tell me he was 'scuba diving' with this friend from work, Ted, and then he'd be gone for the day. Very easy, really."

Unthinkingly, I said, "Ted? Not Ted Wilson?"

"You know him?" she said.

"Only very slightly," I said, as if I were under accusation. "He seems to have gone missing."

"*Cherchez la femme,*" a bruncher interposed.

"*Cherchez la voiture,*" another said. "I hear from a little bird that a very naughty little blue Mazda has been seen in some unlikely places."

"Really? Where?" The topic had everyone's attention.

Our informant paused deliciously. "Sharjah," she said.

"Of course."

"Of course what?"

"It's the perfect place to keep his floozy. Then the wife comes over from the States, and old Teddy says no thanks and does a runner. I bet you he's lying doggo there right now. He'll be back as soon as the missus flies home."

I said, "That doesn't make much—"

Samantha said, "I wonder if he was in on it with Gavin."

"Wouldn't surprise me. Scum collects."

The fork waver pointed at me. "Hold on—weren't you in that search party?"

Everybody turned to examine me.

I said, "I—yes. I was asked to take part, so I did."

Samantha said disgustedly, "You're a scuba diver, too?"

"Not really," I said. "Not anymore. I mean, I used to dive, sure. Yes. But never with Ted."

"You must be a bit pissed off, mate, going to all that trouble while our Ted dips his wick in Sharjah."

"Did he even really go diving? It was probably a cover, wasn't it?"

"He went diving all right." There was laughter.

"Sounds to me like he's a psychopath," someone said. "I'm not saying he's going to murder anyone. I'm talking, you know, psychiatrically."

More ha-ha-ha-ha.

"No, no, think about it," the psychiatrist said. "The fake diver thing, the shag pad in Sharjah, all the lying and cheating. The whole double-life thing. No conscience. No empathy for anyone else."

"OK, here we go." This bruncher was consulting his iPhone. "'Psychopathy Checklist.'" When he started to read out the alleged characteristics of psychopaths, I removed my fez and left. I should have gone earlier, as soon as it became clear that the dignity, and in particular the privacy, of the Wilsons was going to be violated. Privacy is in many respects an indistinct ideal, but surely we can agree that there is such a thing as misappropriating another's biographical belongings.

I'd texted Ali an hour earlier. The stout fellow was waiting for me in the Méridien lobby. He drove me and the Autobiography home. Then he took a taxi back to his place or wherever it was he wished to go, Friday theoretically being his day of rest and liberty. I gave him taxi money, of course, and slipped him a hundred dirhams for good measure.

Of that group of brunchers, I would guess that less than half are still in Dubai. Evanescent conga!

Brett Hutchinson is one of those who went away, whether by choice or not I can't say. He has not stayed in touch, even though he still owes me five thousand AED. The day after the Yalumba event, he e-mailed me this:

> Hey bud. Great seeing you. I may be wrong, but I think you left without paying? Give me a buzz when you get a minute or just send me a check. Cheers.
> PS: Dh 700 a head inc. giant bottle of bubbly!

I LIKE TO THINK I TRY to be curious about others in the way I'd want those same others to be curious about me, namely in a way that is not alienated from the root meaning of curiosity: to care. I try to not be a busybody. I reject the idea that one can enter another life at no cost. I guard against the lowness of the detective. (When I first came out here, I would daily Google Jenn, then my old firm, then me. It was as fruitless as it was compulsive. I was like the dog with the empty bladder that nonetheless goes from tree to tree, stopping at each one to cock his leg in vain. Later, I went through a phase of Googling the Batroses, and, regardless of the search results, the outcome was the same: my degradation: my falling farther down the slope of Parnassus.) On the other hand, a measure of inquisitiveness is sometimes called for. If the petition "Help!" reaches us, obviously we should want to look into it. I'm not arguing that the Wilsons cried out to me. But I did come away from Brett's brunch with the feeling that Ted Wilson, and Mrs. Ted Wilson by association, had been run over in absentia. I don't know why such a little thing should have got to me. Every day, the immaterial ear of conscience—surely the organ that must distinguish a human being from the remainder of animals—receives other, louder calls.

Anyhow, I decided to Google Ted Wilson.

Predictably, Wilson had a LinkedIn page. I used to be LinkedIn, because my old law firm required it. Membership of LinkedIn or any self-revealing network is, however, incompatible with the sensitive and confidential nature of the family office job. It would be wrong if my "profile" were visible to John and Jane Q. Public as a source of connectivity to, potentially, the Batroses. It's a relief that Googling my professional name these days produces next to nothing. This is because, virtually, I am legion. Anyone searching for me could easily get the impression that in the preceding twenty-four hours I have pitched victoriously in a high school baseball game in Long Island; worked as a fire marshal in Idaho; jumped bail in Corsicana, Texas; and passed away in Maryland and Ireland and Australia. For all practical purposes, I am completely camouflaged by my name's commonness. If you look deeply into the image results and scroll past the pictures of scores of my namesakes, most of them on Mugshot.com, you can dig up a photograph of me from a long bygone corporate softball event in Central Park; but even there, the legend confuses me with a certain Graham Herold as we stand next to each other in a lineup of seven squinting softball players. As to why I find my online absence pleasing, I will only say that I also find pleasing my absence from the African wilds.

Ted Wilson, another almost unsearchably ordinary name, became distinctive when qualified by the word "Dubai." In this way, I was able to find the LinkedIn page of "Dr. Ted Wilson." It was informative. Wilson attended Reed College and obtained a Ph.D. in German economic history at the University of North Carolina at Chapel Hill. He held "adjunct and visiting professorships, fellowships, and other faculty positions" at (chronologically) Duke, Emory, University of Hawaii at Manoa, Coventry University (United Kingdom), Lund University (Sweden), University of Illinois at Chicago, and finally the American University in Dubai, where he taught in the International Studies program. In 2004, he joined his current employer, RCF (Reality Creativity Futurity), an Emirati-owned advertising, PR, and branding (or, their website put it, "Presence Management") agency. The "Overview" stated:

> Dr. Wilson has taken his deep scholarly knowledge of the processes that give rise to the historic perception of nations, and applied it to the contemporary arena of country branding, public diplomacy, and reputational risk management. At RCF he has been instrumental in the successful development of Brand Dubai and other country brands. Dr. Wilson's expertise at measuring, building, and managing Arabian Gulf national and commercial assets has been internationally acclaimed, with his team at RCF winning *Brandweek's* Best Emerging Market Story 2006 (for the "Do You Really Know Dubai?" campaign), and also winning UAE Tourism's Most Valuable PR Campaign 2007 ("Hospitality of the Desert").

I visited RCF's site. Under the "Our Team" tab, Ted Wilson was designated "Team Leader, Country Branding Visions and Operations." The photograph showed a smiling Wilson. Resting neatly on his forehead was a pair of round red spectacles. The caption asserted,

> Ted is so ridiculously bright that at RCF we call him Two-Brains. User-friendly to the max, he is unsurpassed in his commitment to making Total Branding concepts a reality for our clients. When he's not burning the midnight oil, Ted enjoys scuba diving. "I'm very lucky to have the best diving water in the world right on my doorstep," he says.

I went further with my investigations, if that is the right word. It turned out that in addition to LinkedIn, Wilson had Friendster and Facebook and MySpace and Vimeo and Twitter accounts to his name and in each case had opted to make public the content of his pages, so that even I (who was then, and am now, a non-member of any such site) could freely and immediately access their content and, by implication, Wilson himself. I well understood that in Wilson's work circles, a certain trendy visibility was advantageous. Still, I was taken aback by the man's forwardness, which struck me as unbecoming as well as surprising. The surprise was of my own making: extrapolating from my sense of him as a furtive aquanaut and standoffish elevator rider, I had had in mind the conception of a lone wolf or lone ranger—by which I of course mean a man who keeps himself to himself, not a masked searcher for truth and justice. As for my judgment of unbecomingness, I quashed it right away, and not without guilt. I was the unbecoming one. I had no right to pass judgment on Wilson on the basis of some unexamined taste preference or, come to think of it, on any basis, especially as I knew very little about social networking services and their norms and could easily have been misdirecting at Wilson a more general horror founded on little more than my unfamiliarity with these virtual communities, whose character struck me as falling bafflingly between the stools of *Gesellschaft* and *Gemeinschaft*. If Wilson was innocuously and/or self-servingly into this sort of socializing, that was entirely up to him. *Laissez faire.* To each his own. Mind your own business. Judge not, that ye be not judged. *Honi soit qui mal y pense.* Take a look in the mirror. Turn the other cheek.

With hindsight—with retrospective knowledge of Wilson's complicated arrangements—it appears that I missed an important function of his Web presence. There is no reason to believe that Wilson's incessant posting (he offered across his various platforms a not unusual mix of family and leisure photographs, day-to-day bulletins, whimsical observations, links to enthusiasms and amusements) wasn't genuine. I'm sure he got real satisfaction from his social networking, including the entirely understandable satisfaction of being (and being seen) at his most optimistic, interesting, and well behaved. But I think it becomes reasonable to theorize a further objective: Wilson was making a hiding place out of conspicuousness. The concealed space was created negatively, from his advertisement of a comprehensive or filled life, a life apparently without room for much else: where would such a man find the time to have a second life?

Facebook was Wilson's most important forum, and his use of other sites was relatively light. He had 264 Facebook friends, which back then seemed like a lot. These friends were located all over the world. His "Wall" (which served not the enclosing and defensive function suggested by the noun but the contrary function of disclosure and welcome) saw much activity, with Wilson posting up to ten times daily and eliciting many Likes and messages. I must confess that I was quite moved. The gatherers at this Wall were clearly touched by the better angels of their nature. They were cheerful, funny, and supportive. They deeply loved their children and their spouses, they cooked experimentally and generously, they read revisionist histories and challenging novels, they loved music and art and even dance. They were civil. They had grit.

They cut each other slack, gladly granting one another the footing that, man or woman, black or white, Christian or Muslim, whether in Oslo or Dhaka or Windhoek, she/he was doing a good job, in trying conditions, of whatever it was he/she was trying to do. They shared educated and thoughtful insights into world politics and trustworthy links to pictures of cute dogs and new monkey species. They made common their feelings. They grew. They rooted for and bore sympathetic and useful witness to the others as, one by one, each made her or his way along life's rocky path, facing en route the loneliness, discouragement, and pain that are the inevitable and persistent highwaymen of our ways. Ted Wilson, I was given to see, was a talented underwater photographer and a typeface buff. He loved listening to Gomez, Wilco, Nick Lowe, Squeeze, Fountains of Wayne, and Brandi Carlile. He had watched *The Life Aquatic with Steve Zissou* "at least fifty times," tearing up every time Bill Murray beheld the jaguar shark.

From the beginning, I'd been wary of Facebook and similar venues of connection, precisely out of a fear of the pyre of memories that awaits a match and, once lit, will set a blaze—of old friendships, old places, old desires—that would serve only to grieve me. But if *this* was how it worked—as a second chance, with new friends; as a rewriting of the record; as a festival of mutual absolution—I wanted some of it. I wanted to divulge my playlists and movie favorites, my moments of wit and hope and wry gloom. I wanted to become a sharer and a good egg and booster of morale, too. I wanted to friend Ted Wilson and his friends.

I couldn't friend him, though. He had disappeared. His Facebook account had been inactive for weeks. To be exact, there

were no signs of activity by Ted Wilson. His friends continued
to leave concerned and bewildered messages on his Wall. One
of these, from someone who went by UnderservedDeserving,
caught my eye:

> Teddy honey, please get in touch. Don't worry about
> anything. Whatever it is, we'll fix it. Just come back.

UnderservedDeserving, whose sex was evident, had been
consistently leaving messages for Ted Wilson for at least two
years. Many of these struck me as intimate and very nice.
About an upcoming dive, UnderservedDeserving wrote,

> Be careful out there. x

About a photo of Ted posing poolside,

> Wow—hot! Must take a cold shower while watching a
> Dick Cheney video.

I wondered what Mrs. Ted Wilson made of all this.

"UnderservedDeserving" had an institutional ring. I
Googled it.

I'd guessed right—it was a small nonprofit with the mission
of "connecting national charities to economically and social
neglected communities in Chicago." The home page carried a
photograph of its founder and managing director—Mrs. Ted
Wilson. Oh, right, I thought. Now I get it.

There's no such thing as "to get" something. The inevitable
consequence of resolving knotty unknown A is the creation of
knotty unknown B, in this instance: what was the deal with this
Facebook thing between Ted Wilson and his American wife
(whom I cannot bring myself to call Mrs. Ted Wilson I)? What
was the deal with their marriage?

These questions are unanswerable. Even if I'd been a confidant of both Wilsons and a professor of psychology to boot, there remains the problem of matrimonial mist. Who can say what goes on between couples beyond closed doors? Not even the couple behind the doors, if my experience is anything to go by. But without claiming a right to peep through a keyhole or to appoint myself adjudicator, and invoking only the human need to interpret, a need without which thought of any worth would not be possible, I will say that I was intrigued by the Wilsons' practice of communicating, not without intimacy, on publicly visible message boards. Always aware that I was taking the shaky and finally indefensible position of the conjecturer, always conscious of the importance of granting only a provisional and faltering status to whatever conclusions might offer themselves to me, I gave the matter some thought.

I surmised that the Wilsons Skyped from time to time; occasionally if rarely met in the flesh in Chicago; and supplemented their contacts on these message boards. I found this impressive. It suggested that, in spite of the distances of time and space by which they had divided and tested their pairing, they used whatever resources were available to generate the closeness and solicitude and playfulness that give substance to a marriage and make possible a distinction between a loving staying together on the one hand and, on the other hand, a pact whose principal aim, guided by considerations of perceived utility, is the sustenance of the marriage qua conjugal belonging, as if it were a piece of property or going concern in which the partners held a joint interest whose socio-economic and instrumental value was deemed by them to exceed a human being's potential for that brand of intimate feeling that draws together two persons for whom the good of the other is indivisible from their own good, which feeling transports us, I would suggest, as an incidence of itself and of the good-faith actions taken pursuant to it, away at long last from the natural violence and nothingism of the earliest dealings of *Homo sapiens*—a transportation that remains, I want to believe, the underexplored source of hope of any lasting sort. Ted and Mrs. Wilson's commitment to Facebooking revealed adaptability and goodwill and mindfulness. How easy it would have been for them to give in to the difficulties of intercontinental human bonding and instead tend to the formalities of their situation, all the while, perhaps out of unconscious anger or a malign search for consolation by vengeance, increasingly associating themselves with the external forces insistent on the punishment and lowering in dignity of those who fail to sacrifice themselves to the perceived interest of the collective in controlling the doings of its members by imposing on the members stringent and potentially precipitous rules of conduct in the form of marital laws. It illuminated the foregoing to recall the night of our breakup, when Jenn said, "You've murdered my marriage!" I was taken aback by every part of this statement—my characterization as the sole actor; the accusation of intentional killing; the "my." In the turbulence of the moment, I was able to voice only one point of incomprehension. "What marriage?" I said. "This marriage," Jenn cried, making a waving gesture with both arms. "But we're not married," I said. "Of course we're married, you clown," Jenn said. "What do you think this is? A nine-year date?" She was right: there was no equitable difference between the coupledom we had and the one we would have had if, at some point, we'd spent half an hour at City Hall. To my surprise, Jenn didn't pursue this line of argument. This was logical, in hindsight, because she wasn't calling upon the analytical framework of marriage with the intention of gaining a better understanding of the nature of our rapport; rather, during this final, frightful argument, she was digging and putting down the conceptual foundation for subsequent extreme action by her the legitimacy of which in the eyes of the officious bystander, that spirit who cannot be placated yet must be, depended, first, on the transformation of the history of our private feelings and dealings into a thing (in the legal sense) from which Jenn might derive (quasi-) proprietorial/contractual rights; and, second, on the license customarily granted to persons claiming to enforce (quasi-) proprietorial/contractual rights and/or claiming to redress a violation of those rights as a justification for actions that would, in the absence of the license, be viewed by the bystander as unruly and deplorable. It should be noted that the officious bystander/licensor invariably takes pleasure in watching such licensed hostilities, which offer the spectacle of the falling of two persons.

Going back to the Wilsons and the virtual meeting room they'd made for themselves, I was at first uneasy about the public nature of their chosen venue, as if they could only meet as part of a larger gathering and were one of those couples who are lifeless unless they're at a cocktail party. But when I paid attention to their actual comments, it was obvious they were basically just having fun and that if Ted Wilson's Wall was a kind of cocktail party, it would have been silly for them not to join in. There are many twosomes who seek out and enjoy the company of society, and being out and about from time to time is healthy for the one-on-one, and why should society, for these purposes, be limited to the physical? It occurred to me that I might be witnessing at first hand a historic psychic enlargement or exploration, that the quickening and tantalization felt by today's pioneering virtual communitarians was something like that of the early phenomenologists as they reconnoitered their dawning new dimension. These written interactions of Ted Wilson and Mrs. Ted Wilson fortified my non-acceptance of the whispers about Ted Wilson's secret Dubai romance. This was incorrect of me: one should not entertain rumors about others, not even for the purpose of dismissing them, because to do otherwise is silently to accept the premise of the rumors, which is that people have a right to call balls and strikes about how other people lead their private lives. They don't. One should recognize and mistrust this judgmental propensity, belonging as it does to an animal whose so-called ethical sense comes not from above but from a primeval epoch of natural selection in which cooperative grouping resulted in better outcomes for individuals coping with a savage natural world. Five minutes of driving alone in the Dubai desert will bring home a forgotten zoological fact: solo survival is not and has never been humanly feasible. It has occurred to me that I should take young Alain Batros out to the Empty Quarter (the wilderness, not the art gallery) to dramatize for his benefit the lowly pragmatic origins of morality and to impress on him two things. *Uno,* it's a somewhat disagreeable reality that conscience, at root, is no more than a productive biological sensitivity to the reciprocity that is essential to our specific survival. The sense of fairness familiar to all societies has come to us from and because of the apish age of literal back-scratching. *Due,* that a life in which an honest attempt is made to transcend the original quid pro quo is a life that has a shot at glory. The kid may not get it right away, but you never know.

What am I going to do about this boy?

"BRYAN ADAMS SUCKS," HE TELLS ME.

"He does?" I say. I'm startled by this declaration out of the blue, which may be the first entirely voluntary utterance he's made to me in the weeks he's been my intern. Nor is there a previous instance of his leaving his desk and standing at the entranceway of my part of the room. I beckon him in. "How come?"

"His songs are so bad."

That doesn't accord with my assessment of Bryan Adams, but hey. And I'm biased. Bryan Adams took on the Batros gig on a week's notice and at a considerable discount on his advertised minimum fee of one million USD. (Bryan Ferry's people were unhappy, understandably, but that was mediated by Fabulosity to everyone's relative satisfaction.) I wasn't at the Adams concert (not invited), but Sandro and Mireille are very pleased about how it went, I've heard (not from them).

Hi Sandro—You're welcome. De rien. *No trouble.* Nichts zu danken. *Any time.*

"What's so bad about them?" In an ideal world, Alain would have more complex critical skills.

"I don't know. Everything."

(His "don't know" comes out as "døn't knøw." For all his devotion to mumbling and drawling, the kid has this fancy English-Norwegian accent that must be, I guess, a payoff of his expensive schooling in England. (I like it just fine. (That said, I have a real soft spot for the habitual accent of Arab speakers of good English, in whose mouths the language, imbued with grave trills, can seem weighted with the sagacity of the East. (See Alec Guinness in *Lawrence of Arabia*.))))

I tilt my head respectfully. "So who's good? Who should I be listening to?"

He shrugs. "Slayer. Or maybe Dying Humanity."

I decide against saying something that I would find funny but Alain wouldn't. "Maybe I'll check them out," I say. The kid's still hanging around, and I feel the touch of opportunity and duty. This outburst of musical opinion is the first sign of any knowledge on the boy's part. I know he's only just turned fifteen, but in the course of my minimal involvement in his summer assignments (as per Sandro's instructions), I've been astonished and re-astonished by just what a know-nothing he is. He can't point to Rome on the map. Somehow he has never heard of St. Paul. He thinks "the present tense" may have something to do with "feeling worried." I am giddily reminded that the

human race refreshes itself in absolute ignorance and that without an enormous, never-ending labor of pedagogy, everything
would go to hell.

I ask the kid to tell me more about Dying Humanity. He tells
me they're from Germany.

"Where in Germany?" I say. He doesn't know. "Let's look it
up," I say. "Pull up a chair." I figure this is without the ambit of
the prohibition against the kid using a computer in the office.

Unfortunately, only German Wikipedia offers details of the
band. Fortunately, I still have my childhood German. "See this?
It says they're from Annaberg-Buchholz." He doesn't seem to
care very much. "Let's see where that is," I say. Interesting:
Annaberg-Buchholz is in the Erzgebirge—in English, the Ore
Mountains, in the southeast of the country, by the Czech border. "Wow, no wonder their music is so tough. These guys are
from a tough area."

"Tough how?"

"One thing at a time," I say. I get him to look up "ore"; then
"heavy industry," then the Deutsche Demokratische Republik,
which is as remote to him as the civilization of the Incas was to
me; and this is how we continue for a full hour and a quarter,
chancily hopping from one link to another until we end up,
anticlimax, on the topic of Dallas, Texas. "I've been to Dallas," I tell Alain. "Don't go there. Not unless they're paying
you well." "Why?" "Why?" I'm closing the files we opened.
"Because life's too short. Avoid D-Town like the plague."

As Alain takes his leave—he looks worn out, poor guy, and
I have to say I'm pretty worn out myself—it occurs to me to
say, "Hold on there, Al." I say, "You know about the plague?
About the Black Death?" He shakes his head. "That's your
homework. Find out about the Black Death and write down
ten interesting things about it. No, let's make that five things.
We'll take a look at it tomorrow. You OK with that?"

He seems to be. He goes back to his desk. He knows as well

as I do that it's noon, and at noon he must be weighed. To avoid the weighing is one reason I pop out, back to The Situation, for a couple of hours. Another reason is that I like to take a shit around midday, and I've made the executive decision that the round trip is well worth it. (It's definitely not the case that I'm snubbing the facilities available to all in my office building, which are first-rate.) I may be wrong, but I seem to do more shitting than ever. Certainly I often find myself thinking, when I take a seat: Again? Still, I'm not complaining. In there, in the bathroom, everything is out of your hands. Time out. Pax. And am I the only one to appreciate the sweet egality of it all? For a little while, you're no better or worse than anyone else. You're shooting par.

Or are you? Among the more embarrassing criticisms of the emirate is that it cannot deal, on a municipal level, with the huge and booming volume of digestive waste produced by its population. Much of the sewage is collected in septic tanks, whose contents are moved to the treatment plant in fleets of trucks. Apparently the lines of trucks waiting to enter the plant are so long, and the waiting is so unendurable and/or cost-ineffective, that some truckers have resorted to illegally dumping their loads behind sand dunes and in the city's storm drains, the latter practice resulting in unfortunate incidents of fecal stuff turning up in Dubai's otherwise tip-top swimming waters. I believe the situation is now under control, though incorrigible naysayers continue to attach a negative symbolic meaning to the issue. There's nothing I can do about it, in any case. The call of nature must be answered.

Today, as ever, it's a relief to withdraw to the privy and lock the door, even though the front door is locked and there's no one else around.

Or is there? By a startling olfactory or digestive coincidence, the smell I make is exactly the smell made by my father.

Done. But the midday intermission is not complete without a look-see at Project X.

Still nothing. The structure of mystery is unchanged. Is that pile of dirt fresh? How come nobody ever uses the portable toilet? Curiouser and curiouser.

It is reassuring to look over to my left, where, just beyond Privilege Bay, a construction project is indubitably in progress. Today, I see, prettily green truck-mounted cranes are on site and, taken together with the abundance of yellow hard hats and primrose blue overalls, grant the scene a vernal air. Incredible, how they manage to work in that heat. Almost thirty floors have gone up of what will clearly be a nondescript residential proposition. Although situated across the water channel and so belonging to a discrete niche of the market, this tower will be our visual neighbor and, I fear, put at risk the distinctive silhouette of Privilege Bay. This is another reason, as if we needed one, why it is vital that Project X develops quickly into a top-dog building. As matters stand, we are in danger of suffering the fate of downtown Manhattan, whose skyline, as I recall, seems these days to be situated in Jersey City.

Which reminds me: the other day I received a nasty report. Apparently people have started to refer to The Situation and The Statement and The Aspiration as "Tampax Towers," on account of the allegedly high number of female flight attendants who are said to live among us in shared accommodation, an arrangement seen by some as running counter to the Pioneers of Luxury and Dreamers of New Dreams and Uncompromising Few narratives. I don't share this perception. I have nothing but respect for the flight crews of Emirates, who can be rightly proud of their indispensable role in the great success of their corporation and specifically of the Emirates Experience for which the airline is uniquely and rightly world-famous. Any residential community would and should proudly welcome them. *Willkommen,* I therefore say. *Soyez les bienvenues.* Добро пожаловать!

(How clearly I remember my first exposure to this superior polyglot race, which is how these ethnically elusive women with smiling creaseless faces first struck me. They seemed indigenous to the skies. Uncannily Eurasian- or Afro-Asian- or Latin-Asian- or Eurafrican-looking specimens in red pillbox hats and white head scarves, they made me think of the calm interstellar travelers familiar to us from the Star Trek entertainment franchise. When it was announced that the "team" of flight attendants between them spoke English, Arabic, French, Latvian, Russian, Malay, German, and Tagalog, I fell into a state of admiration that has, if anything, only been deepened by the passage of time, which has of course seen a decline in the fortunes of almost all economic things Emirati and, unless I'm mistaken, has led to an adjustment in the profile of Emirates passengers, who these days would appear to be drawn largely from the same market the Dubaian migrant working class is drawn from, a development, dare one say it, that puts into question the image of the airline as the transporter of choice of the voyaging elite: yet our indomitable multilingual female highfliers still go about their work as brightly as ever. One evening not that long ago, in circumstances that are beside the point, I found myself on the roof of The Situation's parking lot, which is located about fifty yards behind the residential proposition itself. I had an accidental view into the lower floors of The Situation, and I could not help seeing the young women in their illuminated apartments as they pedaled on exercise bikes and watched television and cooked dinner. How courageous they were! How young and adventurous! I must have been fascinated, because a good few minutes went by before I became conscious of myself as a voyeur cloaked in the dark of night; whereupon I left. I have since felt, and fought off, the urge to return to that roof and take another look. What is this urge? What would I be looking for? What could I possibly be hoping to see?)

All that said, no residential proposition should be dominated by any single class or demographic, and "Tampax Towers" is not a value-adding moniker. For the good of all, the situation must be monitored with care.

It's as I'm turning my gaze away from Project X that out of the corner of my eye I see, or half-see, or imagine, a small dark dropping motion to my left. My guess is, a gull or other large bird. Bird life in the emirate is booming, by all accounts. Migrant birds pass through in great numbers. Tweeting and cooing may be heard every morning, in every neighborhood. I've heard tell that, some decades ago, the Dubai authorities netted a large quantity of our feathered friends from around the Gulf region and released them in the city. This sounds apocryphal, but you never know. The abduction of an entire avian population is by no means beyond our Rulers.

My bowel movement is normally followed by an internet-fueled episode of self-pleasuring. This coy verb comes to mind ironically, I'm sad to say. Although I'm not going to deny the element of sensational gratification, I register with dismay the growing difficulty I'm having in sticking to my goal of jerking off at least four or five times a week, without which I would be in danger of not extinguishing, or not keeping in check, the natural desire to copulate and then mate. Including my time with Jenn, I've spent over a decade going from one dirty website to another, and, at this point, I'm running out of juice. I must acknowledge that, as an ultramarathoner of masturbation, my devotion to amateur or homemade pornography, which kept me going during the Jenn years, has in Dubai been swept away by the never-ending search for novel and effective stimulation. There isn't a porno twist, tweak, or twang I haven't exhaustively gone into. Asian babes, MILFs, BBWs, celebrities, extremists, Africans, naturists, insertion specialists, acrobats, horny bosses, straponistas, Italians, mature lesbians, vintage sluts, cuties, horny boot wearers, randy yachtswomen, exhibitionists, busty teens, hairy cougars, anal queens, cum gobblers, wife swappers, nerds, bottle fuckers, beauties, strangers, bored natural housewives, brunettes—I've been through all of these and many more. I don't like the way this is trending. Some months ago I went through a phase of jerking off to scenes of (grown-up and, I honestly believe, consenting and professional) women being penetrated by enormous dildos attached to what were called fucking machines. That was a gray area.

A week ago, I had an unambiguously very bad experience. What can I say? I was watching a woman and four men doing various things. It was all proceeding as one might expect, until one of the men punched the woman in the face, and then another pulled on her ponytail so that she could be punched again in the face, which she was, by the other men, and the female performer was crying and bleeding at the mouth and trying to not be punched, and in the blink of an eye the fake orgy had turned into a gang sexual assault—and yet I couldn't stop the movie, my hands were full, I was about to ejaculate, there was no stopping that, and even though I did turn my eyes away from the screen, I kept jerking off until I was done. Only then did I shut the laptop and quit the scene of the crime. Too late. I had already acted in concert with the sexual assaulters. It will be objected that the crime victim, as I believe her to be, was an actor, as were the other actors in the filmed events: they, too, were actors; I'd seen the *performance* of a crime. My retort: Actors are in the first place persons. It cannot be forgotten that the phase of public pretending is preceded by an initial private phase of pretense in which the person assumes the part of actor. When I re-visualize the video in question, I see that the female actor ceased to pretend to be an actor. She reverted to naturality with the first or second punch; and it seems clear that after that reversion she did not consent to being punched repeatedly in the face and to having sexual interaction, vaginal and oral and anal, with the men punching her. It follows that the female actor was not an actor pretending to be raped. She was a person being raped. This isn't automatically to incriminate the men as rapists; their relevant mental states are open to argument; one would need to hear from them. Me, I have heard from myself. I know what I did. I saw the rape happen and used my seeing of it for my own sexual benefit.

What am I supposed to do now? Turn myself in? To whom? Where are the authorities when you need them?

And I cannot jerk off anymore because I'm afraid that, if I do, I will see the female person being punched and I will want to see that.

What do I do? I go back to work. I turn myself in to Alain and Ali.

Where is Ali, though? Not in the office. Only Alain is here, and he is in my chair, and on my computer. What the fuck.

"Excuse me?" I say.

The kid smoothly closes his windows and, if I'm not mistaken, clears his history. He says, "I was finding out about Black Death," and goes back to his desk and opens his Green Belt Sudoku book as if nothing has happened and it's all been my bad dream and not his bad.

I take the responsibility. I forgot to shut down the computer, and boys will be boys. Still, the kid and I need to talk.

"That's my computer, Alain. You need my permission to use it. You don't have my permission unless I say so."

I get nothing back from him. He stares at the wall. Fair enough. I've said what needed to be said. Regarding exactly what he was doing on my computer, I'm not going to get into with him, even though his explanation was brazenly false. He would deny falsity, and there would be a factual dispute and a battle of wills, and that's too much to ask of me. I'm not his parent. His parents are his parents.

Meanwhile, Ali has returned. I step out to talk to him and shut the door of the office so that he and I can talk beyond the earshot of the kid, who is inside my office.

"Everything OK?"

"Everything OK, boss," Ali says.

"Listen, Ali, you can't leave the boy here by himself. You have to wait until I come back."

"I went to the dry-cleaning," Ali says.

The evidence, as if it were needed, is next to his desk: a dozen hanging shirts.

I say, "Yes, that's good. Thank you. But next time, do me a favor, wait until I get back. We have to look after Alain. If there's a problem, you can always call me." I can't understand why he has slipped up like this. It's not like him at all. The man is straight as an arrow.

"No problem, boss," he says. "What do you want me to do for this afternoon?"

"Let me see," I say. "Has the Range Rover been serviced?" He tells me he's already taken care of it. "Very good," I say. I'm racking my brains. The office is shipshape and I can't think of anything I might need from him in the way of errands or tasks. The truth is, I have the family office and my domestic arrangements in very good order; at this point, things pretty much run themselves. I can't think of anything for Ali to do. This is a problem, because Ali's raison d'être (in the work context; his other contexts are not visible to me) is the doing of things. I have toyed with the notion of a gentler, happier, less perplexing, and more comic world in which Ali is not so much a factotum or office boy as a companionable sidekick, a world in which the infrastructure of injustice that supports the terms "valet" and "manservant" is marvelously absent or made harmless, and Ali unproblematically is a Jeeves or Passepartout to my Wooster or Fogg, and the two of us have adventures in which we extricate each other from amusing and diverting entanglements and difficulties, our solidarity sturdy and unstated, our needs always mild, and the evil of the day forever sufficient unto it. This ridiculous daydream is founded on Ali's extraordinary real-life consistency of deportment. He is never out of character, and his character is that of the rock. In over three years, he has never been noticeably joyful or miserable, irritated or pleased, obtuse or over-clever, obsequious or big for his boots. He is free of nuance: no cloud passes across the sun when Ali is around. If he has a *Binnenleben,* I am not privy to it. Ali's dignified two-dimensionality coheres in his garb, the shadowless white dishdash and white head scarf which I've never seen him out of, even in winter, when other Emirati men turn to blue and brown fabrics in order to mix things up a little. There's a story, who knows if it's true, that at some point, maybe in the seventies, the then Ruler essentially took control of the national wardrobe and instituted the dress code we see today, a sartorial initiative that, if it indeed occurred, had the effect of transforming a dusty, scruffy, jumbled-looking male populace into the bespoke toothpaste-white strollers we see today, and whom we cannot help perceiving as emblematic substitutes for their homeland's hygienic new orderliness and coolness. It's a look that's working out for them, you'd have to say. I would love to wear a dishdash and head scarf myself, albeit for reasons of crypsis.

I've thought of something Ali can do. I toss him the keys to the Autobiography and tell him to go down to Project X and see if, by any chance, he can find out what's happening.

I'M STILL IN A SOMEWHAT agitated state, however, and when I notice that there's a good-sized FedEx box on my desk, I rip open the box as if tearing a foe limb from limb. The box contains more boxes; a moment goes by before I understand: my stamps have arrived! My stamps!

(When was the last time I felt such joy? Easy: Christmas 1980, when Santa Claus, descending the chimney for me for the last time, brought with him a sky-blue Tigra seven-speed racer. (In the spring, Dad and I bicycled together on the shore of the Zürichsee. With the aid of an illustrated map we picked out, in a multitude of white-hatted Alps, Chammliberg and

Schärhorn and the Tödi. (*Et pauvre Maman nous a attendu à
la maison et à notre retour m'a fait une petite bise alcoolisée.*)))
Everything I ordered is present and correct. I'll admit it, I
splurged. I've got myself:

- A metal high-quality date stamp (self-inking in
black ink) with the custom text BATROS FAMILY
OFFICE (DUBAI) LTD.
- A chrome desktop embosser with a circular plate
for embossing a mark of the Entreprises Batros
logo (in which curlicued E and B are entangled as
if in a bathrobe monogram) and the circumscrip-
tion BATROS FAMILY OFFICE (DUBAI) LTD.
- A "gold" desktop embosser with a rectangular
plate. The EB logo comes with the custom text
GENERAL EXPENDITURE TRUSTEE BATROS TRUST
CO. LTD.
- A small circular wood-and-rubber stamp (text:
FAMILY OFFICER, BATROS FAMILY OFFICE
(DUBAI) LTD.) with a stamp pad and a bottle of
blue ink.
- A small triangular wood-and-rubber stamp (GEN-
ERAL EXPENDITURE TRUSTEE BATROS TRUST CO.
LTD.) with a stamp pad and a bottle of green ink.
- A large square wood-and-rubber stamp with
a stamp pad and a red ink bottle and the text
SIGNED SUBJECT AND WITHOUT PREJUDICE
TO TERMS AND CONDITIONS SET OUT AT
WWW.BATROSFAMILYOFFICER.COM.
- A large rectangular wood/rubber stamp with a
stamp pad with orange ink. Text: SIGNED SUB-
JECT AND WITHOUT PREJUDICE TO TERMS AND
CONDITIONS SET OUT AT WWW.BATROSGEA
TRUST.COM.

- A "rocker" ink blotter.
- A green leather desk pad (38" × 24").

I remove the leather desk pad from its wrapping. I put it on my desk in front of me. I place the embossers to my west, the stamp pads to the north, and the stamps to the east. I keep the ink bottles at hand: slowly, carefully, and not without alchemy, I imbue each stamp pad with its color. Done.

I put away the ink bottles in my filing cabinet, which is always locked and which only I have the key to. The stamps and embossers will in due course also "live" in the filing cabinet, in which the embossers will be kept in a further lockbox (again, only I have the key) and will be doubly under lock and key and doubly secure. Now I'm ready to start stamping and embossing. One thing at a time, however. Let's first of all give these guys a workout.

Before I shut the partition door, I want to make sure the kid is at his desk, doing Sudoku or something. He is.

I place a sheet of white typing paper on the leather pad. I get out the date stamp. I adjust the band by turning the oversize wheel: now it's set to today's date: 01 Aug 2011. OK, here we go. *Ke-thunk.* That sounded good and that felt good and that looks good: the black tattoo is very professional and very sharp. I am repelled by, and untrusting of, smudged or blurred documents. They are indistinct enough as it is, as it were.

I successively tint and then bang on paper the blue, the green, the red, and the orange stamps. *Dumb. Dumb. Dumb. Dumb.* Very good.

The (superfluous, because the imprints are superb) handheld seesaw blotter? It is as fun as I suspected a handheld seesaw would be.

Last, and most, the big guys—the embossers. I have to stand up to grip the lever steadily. *Cramp,* the chrome one says. *Cramp,* repeats the gold one. Wow. OMG. O. M. G.

To be clear: centrally, my happiness isn't aesthetic or recreational. To be perhaps less clear: these two modes of pleasure are but the flowering branches of practicality's tree. What I'm saying is, my new office items are not bureaucratic toys. The point of the embossing is not to make a pretty design on paper but to make life harder for any scoundrels who might want to forge my signature. They will not be thrilled that there has been added, on top of my John Hancock, a further stratum of identification and authentication personal to me, i.e., my boss. The two smaller stamps add a third baffling stratum, and will be useful in various administrative situations. Most important of all, though, are the big bright stamps, which are not big and bright by accident. The red/orange texts they impress on a document serve to vividly qualify, I'd like to say helpfully elucidate, the scope and effect of the act constituted in the putting by me of my name to the document. The mechanism of qualification and elucidation is one that's now common in the world of legal dealings in writing: the reader is referred to a website that functions as an addendum or rider to the document in question, alternatively as a collateral contract between the referrer and the referee or, in the further alternative, in some way that I haven't yet figured out, as something that otherwise gives to the reference the legal effect I want, i.e., an effect protective of me. A nit-picking technical analysis isn't my priority. This is real-world stuff. I'm not going to get hung up on niceties.

With Ali's help, I've created two websites. They respectively set out the standard terms and conditions on which I sign stuff qua Family Officer or GEA Trustee. I have to say that writing those provisions was trickier than I'd anticipated. For example, it turns out that creating a website creates issues particular to the creation of a website. I had no option except to begin with a disclaimer about the website itself:

> No warranty or representation of any kind, implied, expressed, or statutory, including but not limited to

warranties of non-infringement of third party rights, title, or freedom from computer virus or any other harmful or destructive electronic or Internetian agent, is given or made by the Trustee [or Family Officer] with respect to the contents of this website. The Trustee [etc.] does not accept any responsibility or liability for the accuracy, content, completeness, legality, or reliability of the information contained on this website or for any loss or damage of whatever nature (direct, indirect, consequential, or other) whether arising in contract, tort, or otherwise, which may result or follow from your use of (or inability to use) this website, or from your use of (or failure to use) the information on this site. No legal or other kind of advice is given on this website. The legal and other kinds of information on this website are "as is." You must not rely on the information on this website as an alternative to seeking and receiving legal advice from your attorney or other professional legal services provider.

That was the easy part—the preliminaries. I cannot exaggerate how testing I found it to draft the main matter, i.e., to state efficaciously that which I wanted to say. The problems I encountered—conceptual, verbal, juristic—were horribly comparable, in their stubborn, enigmatic vitality, to those poison-resistant super-rats that, we are told, threaten to defeat every hostility of modern science precisely because they, the super-rats, have been strengthened by scientific hostilities. I'm suggesting that every attempt I made to eliminate a textual vagueness or errancy or inadequacy of sense resulted only in the making of more, less eliminable problems of sense. It was as if the very project of making sense was being mocked; as if the words I typed on the word processor's white page, words of black letters, were not the symbols for which I'd mistaken them; as if, that is, each word, with its little lucifer of denotation, was in fact consubstantial with the darkness of uncommunication against which it supposedly was a counteractor; that is, the significance of a word lay not in its letter-by-letter symbolism but in its literal presence on the page, a presence that, though obvious, was a secret; that is, a word was exactly and covertly what it appeared to be, a letters-shaped blackness, which is to say, a kind of verbatim detail of the immovable, possibly entropic, and in any case finally annihilating, residual super-reality of blackness; so that every mark I made by pressing a key of my keyboard had a consequence opposite to the one I'd intended, namely, a decrease in the totality of light brought into the world and an increase in the totality of gloom. Or so it began to seem to me, after several months of futile refinements and do-overs, and a million miscarried meanings. I became so confused—so lost in a fantastic vigilance of ambiguity, obscurity, and import—that one morning I sprang out of bed with a madman's idea of a breakthrough: I had been trying to kill, or cage, the rats of complexity. Wrong! Let the revolting fuckers multiply! Let them run wild! Let them turn on whoever dared to approach! And who were these approachers, anyway? The transactions I signed off on, to which my disclaimers applied, were between professional bargainers doing everything to maximize their own advantage. There were no vulnerable parties here—no minors, no uninformed consumers, no persons acting under duress or undue influence, no judicially recognized or protected weaklings. Nobody here was being forced or duped into doing anything he/she didn't or wouldn't want to do. Nobody was going into this thing with her/his eyes not open. In a weekend-long lingual-legal rage, I composed a heartless, fearless, terrifying work of negation that burdened every person save myself with every conceivable responsibility and loss and risk, that in every instance unfairly and unlimitedly and gratuitously and disproportionately favored me at the expense of the world and, most repellently of all, that withheld the basic hospitality of writing: my disclaimer, as completed, was a graphic monstrosity, a cruelly rambling, almost agrammatical near-balderdash of baffling dependent clauses and ultra-boring, ultra-technical phraseology that enveloped the reader in a dingy, alien, almost unbreathable word-atmosphere offering barely a vent of punctuation, indentation, or line breakage. Put that in your pipe and smoke it! At the same time, I was mental-mailing. *Eddie— Remember when you told me (I paraphrase) that, by accepting the position of Family Officer, I was accepting the termination of a camaraderie that went back to our time on Lansdowne Road? You said something about hardball. So be it, my sometime amigo. Think of this as a brushback pitch.* At three in the morning, I went to bed. I was still brainstorming, however. It struck me with great power that romantic human dealings also might profit from the availability of standard terms and conditions—from articles of association, one might less forbiddingly say—spelling out the footing of A's entry into B's intimate company and the precepts A would wish to apply to the conduct of such intimacy. Why not? Were we not always being told that good communication is the be-all and end-all of successful emotional transactions? Ideally, B would have articles of association of her/his own: A and B could openly discuss, from the outset, the question of how to proceed jointly, and come to an agreement—or disagreement—that would save them a bunch of he said-she saids and who knows how much else of the havoc caused and powered by human misunderstanding or claims thereto. To those who would ask, Gee, do we really need to have a heavy-duty convention before we get to date someone? I would answer, (a) Take it from me, it beats the alternative; and (b) It could be made fun, in a screwball comedy kind of way. To repeat: why not? Users of dating sites freely expressed requirements about a prospective partner's intentions, not to mention stipulations about hobbies, height, ethnicity, smoking, looks, sexuality, etc. My idea was to go farther—go beyond the superficial pre-sorting of matchmaking, go beyond, especially, the (unspoken) mutual oaths on which (quasi-) marriages were founded and the apparatus of coercion by which the oaths were guaranteed. What this "beyond" might involve, specifically, was for another day. I was tired as a workman. I went to bed.

Just as I was about to drop off, I had one last moonstricken rush of insight—that human articles of association, in their nobility like the great constitutional documents of the Age of Enlightenment, should promulgate a mission of human attachment surpassing of reciprocity. I could not understand this, my own thought, except in this respect: as I fell asleep, it seemed to me that I'd spied, like stout Cortez, a beautiful and unexplored ocean.

I woke up in daylight a few hours later. I looked again at my draft disclaimer. Filled with incredulous disgust, I deleted it. As for the "articles of association": where had that folly come from? What was the matter with me?

Still, it was a constructive episode. In my post-delusional clarity, I found myself able to quickly produce the text that now appears on my websites. The text makes plain in straightforward terms that I'm signing papers as a mechanical agent; that my signature should for all substantive (as opposed to formal) purposes be treated as that of my principal (i.e., the relevant Batros(es)); that although I might be aware in very broad terms of the nature of the documents, I have no personal knowledge of their contents or any authority or expertise applicable to the contents; that I have accepted my mechanical agency on the basis of appropriate assurances received from my principal as to the lawfulness, efficacy, and adequacy of the papers I sign and the actions or outcomes connected to them; and that my principal, not I, bears all and any relevant responsibility and liability.

Is that too much to ask for? Is it so wrong? I might equally have ordered this stamp:

PLEASE DON'T HURT ME BECAUSE I'M SIGNING THIS

I notified the Family Members in writing of the websites and of my intention to refer to them by stamps and bosses. There was no reply, which was logical. I was merely proposing to make explicit an unstated but well-understood state of affairs.

I've spent over an hour quite joyfully stamping and bossing—an activity that isn't without its physical demands—when Ali returns from his outing to Project X.

He gives me to understand that a few men were gathered at Project X but that on approaching he learned they were not connected to the inexplicable structure. They were gathered on the bank of Privilege Bay to rubberneck the construction site across the water.

"A man fell down from the building into the water," Ali explains.

"What?" I say. "Fell down? When?"

"Before I arrived. Maybe half an hour before. They were getting him out of the water."

"What do you mean, getting him out? He died?"

"I believe he was dead," Ali reports. He says, "He jumped. It happens a lot. Every week it happens. Every week, always one or two of the men jump from the buildings."

I saw the jumper from my apartment. The dropping thing I saw out of the corner of my eye at lunchtime—that was the jumper. Or was not. I did not really catch sight of that which was dropping. I glimpsed, I should say I think I glimpsed, a shadow-like movement, and whatever it was was gone as soon as I turned to look. It could have been anything. It could have been a bird; it could have been something inanimate. That cannot be ruled out. Nor can it be ruled out that it was nothing. Nothing can be ruled out.

Ali offers to go back to Privilege Bay tomorrow to pursue his investigation. I tell him there's no need. "It's nearly three o'clock," I say. "Why don't you take Alain home now."

To my amazement, Ali doesn't jump to it. He stays right where he is, motionless—except for his bearded mouth, which he is twisting into significant shapes. I'm about to give voice to my bemusement when the penny drops: he is signaling something in connection with the kid, who is sitting on the other side of the partition and no doubt overhearing our every word. "There is a problem with the car," Ali announces volubly. "I need to show you."

"Very well," I say. "Let's go take a look." I lock my computer. I say to the kid, "Al, sit tight for five minutes."

Down in the entrance lobby, Ali and I find a quiet spot where two black leather chairs have been specially set aside for conversationalists. A certain kind of showy private confabulation is big in Dubai. Wherever you go, there always seems to be a pair of brazen conspirators in the corner.

Ali looks rattled, which is a first. Here is a glimpse of his third dimension. Here is a cloud. Uh-oh.

He says, "Boss, Mr. Alain is a big, big problem for me."

He tells me that the kid has been shaking him down. On three occasions during the last ten days, Alain has asked Ali to give him five hundred dirhams. Ali gave him a hundred a couple of days ago, hoping that would put an end to it, but today, during my lunchtime absence, the boy repeated his demand. There's no need for Ali to spell out what lies behind the demand: he is a bidoon, and the kid is the son of the big boss. No doubt the kid is ticked off with Ali for weighing him, as if Ali were somehow at fault. They're a family of messenger shooters and cat kickers, the Batroses.

I can see that Ali is very nervous about having spoken about this at all. He is still afraid of the kid, and rightly so, because the kid is a kid and, because he is a kid, has no real clue that anybody other than him is a human being. I would guess that he barely knows that he, the kid, is a human being. Still, I'm shocked. I did not see this coming. I tell Ali not to worry. I take a bill for one hundred dirhams from my wallet and direct Ali to accept it as a reimbursement of the money screwed out of him. "Thank you for telling me about this," I say. Then I direct him to clock out.

Of course, I am anything but thankful. It would have been much better if Ali had ponied up for a couple of weeks or found some other way to not involve me until the kid was off my hands. Now, however, I am seized with knowledge of the facts. That's not good. A fact is where it all starts to go wrong. A fact is a knock on the door.

I chauffeur the young extortionist home. He has taken a seat in the back. I say nothing. He says nothing.

We pull up across the street from Fort Batros. A high white wall surrounds the property's several acres. Behind the wall one can see a sizable cluster of palm trees and, aloft amid the palms, a gaping three-meter satellite dish that would interest me very much if I were a pterodactyl looking for a nest.

"OK, see you tomorrow," I say. In accordance with protocol, he doesn't move until two security guards have hastened over from the guardhouse and opened the passenger door. They escort him to the enormous metal double gates and lead him through the doorway that's built into one of the gates. One of the guards indicates with a wave that the kid is safely home. I don't doubt it. Fort Batros has a round-the-clock security presence and alarms and floodlights and various other defensive measures in part attributable, as I understand it, to the requirements of the kidnapping insurer. I have never been inside the property, which is managed by an Italian gentleman hired away from the Four Seasons Hotel Milano, but I have gone online and aerially surveyed it. In addition to the family villa, the grounds contain a tennis court and two swimming pools and outhouses and cabins: the expectable inferno.

THIS ISN'T TO SAY THAT high walls and swimming pools and luxury cabanas are intrinsically bad; and I absolutely don't have anything against the ideal of the family home. As a matter of fact, sometimes I long for the experience of being made welcome by a family in its domain. I'm no Norman Rockwell, but I do believe in the existence of families that are not units of suffering and power. My own nuclear family was not one of these success stories, sadly for all concerned, and I'm forced to conclude that neither was the group comprising Jenn and me and, spectrally, our not-to-be child; but one can hardly fall from these particular disappointments into a general theoretical gloom about familial love or the special domestic comfort that a successful household can offer a visitor. The specialness, here, does not consist in giving a guy/girl the best chair and pouring him a glass of wine and lending him a sympathetic ear and generally bending toward her, indispensable though these things are; it consists, fundamentally, in exercising for the guest's benefit the power of shelter and exoneration that is the prerogative of the family in its residence, which constitutes (the family home, that is) a private enclave within larger, all-too-hostile dominions. At home—*chez soi*—one is a potentate; one may grant an outsider relief from the outside; and this must be what I yearn for.

It's possible that this old question—of the stranger and his reception—detains me because it detained none other than Ted Wilson. This was made apparent by his short advertising film for the Dubai Tourist Board, the award-winning *Hospitality of the Desert*. In the film, which I Googled without difficulty, a man in tattered Middle Eastern robes walks alone in the desert. It's a timeless scene, shot in black and white. He is in difficulty, this wanderer. The sun is in that mood we recognize as "pitiless," and the sand formations have the undulating immenseness we associate with the phrase "sea of sand." The wanderer covers his face with his scarf and trudges on, up a dune. There is a second man in the desert: an unambiguous Arab in blazing white. He sees someone approaching. The Arab carefully watches this figure: there is something menacing about the slowly advancing silhouette. With a concise gesture, the Arab issues a wordless command to his servants, who have materialized along with goats and camels and a modest encampment of tents. Cut to a tent's shade: the sheikh—for that is who/ what the Arab is—proffers the traveler a cup of water and, on a silver dish, dates and white cheese. That is the drama: the humility of the aristocratic host before the vagrant: the reversal of station. In a burst of color and pop music, everything skips to present-day Dubai, where a family of ecstatic Western tourists checks into a hotel with the help of an Emirati guide/ friend/host; whereupon we see the foreigners enjoying a series of stock touristic pleasures, the scenes punctuated by close-ups of the sagacious black-bearded face of the Emirati host/helper. Next, the tourists are waving goodbye to the Emirati at the airport; and then we're back in the timeless desert, where the traveler, in fresh clothes, heads out into the desert on a horse supplied to him. The sheikh wears a wise smile. The legend appears:

WELCOME TO DUBAI

I'm no expert, but I detect a difference between this ad and the others. I'm thinking of the little films brought to us by the "Reaffirm Your Uniqueness" and "The Prestige of Excellence" and "Dubai: The Exception" campaigns. These obviously laughable and tawdry productions push without irony the idea that Dubai is where an elite of beautiful cosmopolitan tastemakers convenes in order to lead lives of extraordinary *luxe* and cachet and to buy and use and disport themselves in and with famous handbags, clothes, bathroom fittings, etc. We see men tossing car keys to smiling parking valets, and women emerging long-leggedly from sports cars, and childless couples in their late thirties getting together to drink champagne on yachts. The cheesier, the better, I say. There is a transparency of falsity in this absurd idea of a good-looking socio-economic

Weltklasse that almost confers a kind of blamelessness on the falsifiers, whose misrepresentations are (no offense) not far removed from those offered by very young children caught red-handed, and may be regarded, even enjoyed, as good old-fashioned hogwash. Wilson's effort, by comparison, was sly. I'm not one to pick on a man or knock down the efforts of someone who's just doing his/her job, and in any case whatever I might think about any of this is subject to the universal rule that dooms to futility a private effort of vigilance and so won't make a difference to anything. Still, I'll allow myself a small say.

"Hospitality of the Desert" proposed to do battle with the (of course calamitous and disgusting) prejudices directed against Arab/Muslim peoples (the terrorist-towelhead travesty) by offering an alternative mischaracterization, namely the whole wisdom of the desert–slash–ancient custodian of hospitality–slash-ethics thing. The latter is hardly on the same scale of wrongdoing as the cartoons it opposes, but it trawls the same swamp of plausibility; it calls forth fresh species of toads and snakes and slime. There is no high ground here, admittedly. There never is. Maybe the best that can be done, in terms of not making a bad situation worse, is to stick with the vivid fantasia of opulence, or, even better, to go back to the straight-forward before-and-after photographic montage that was once very popular here but now seems to be falling out of fashion, i.e., the juxtaposition of a "before" photograph of the acreage of sand that Dubai until very recently was, and an "after" pho-tograph of the extraordinary city we now see. This captures something honorable and true, if you ask me.

No one will ask me, I can safely say; the question is deeply moot. So, too, is the more personal question of my own recep-tion by others, since it hasn't happened since I got here. That's right—for reasons that have, I hope, more to do with local custom than with what I'm (perceived to be) like, I have barely crossed the threshold of a private residence in Dubai. I haven't even been to Ollie's house, in Arabian Ranches. For that matter I have only once met Ollie's (English) wife, Lynn, and that was the time I ran into the whole family in Dubai Mall. The term "family" in this instance includes the live-in Filipina nanny (Winda? Wanda? Wilda?), who, on the occasion I'm thinking of, took complete care of the little boy, Charlie, so that Ollie and Lynn were at liberty to stroll around in a carefree manner and permit themselves a measure of public parental insouciance that would be unavailable to them back home in Australia/England or, if available, would not be totally free of stigma, there being in those places people who frown on the conspicuous assignment to an employee of responsibilities deemed to be proper to a mother and/or father, and there being for the time being in those countries a degree of social uneasiness about noticeable master-servant relations. Here in Dubai, there's nothing particularly unseemly or unusual about one's children and one's child-minders trailing behind one at the mall, especially since Emirati women amble at some distance behind their menfolk, often with the little ones. Nor is it suspect or *de mauvais goût* to have a residential domestic workforce: on the contrary, integral to the appeal of the expat experience is that the labor of mopping and dusting and washing and cooking that typically forms part of the *in patria* experience may, *ex patria,* be transferred at a low cost to others—the so-called help. What about their experience—the labor transferees? This question, inherently valid, arises especially in the minds of the self-appointed inspectorate located overseas and to our northwest, where news agencies periodically run stories of women who have escaped from domestic service as if from slavery and reportedly are found desperately wandering the malls of Dubai without a penny to, I was going to say, their names, except that these escapees evidently are usually deprived by their employers of their passports and suffer from an official namelessness, not to mention denationalization. I completely accept the factual soundness of these stories. The imbalance of power that inevitably characterizes the employment by the relatively rich of persons radically relocated from poor parts of the world must perforce give rise to cases of mistreatment of the powerless. However, no consideration of this problem would be satisfactory without the paying of some attention to the trope by which it is publicized, namely the trope of the scandal. I am not such a theology ignoramus as to be unaware of the time-honored sense of this word: a stumbling block on the true path of religious virtue or, in a different context, Christian faith. This is hardly applicable to the present case: the mistreatment of help in Dubai is hardly a shocking reverse in the sacred project of human goodness to which the scandalized bystander is committed. I say this not out of cynicism but out of a recognition that real-life scandalization is a delight, conferring as it does a wonderfully unpaid-for feeling of righteousness. So let's get it straight: most of the tut-tutting we hear is the sound of nothing other than opportunistic moral hedonism. And let's acknowledge that it would be wrongheaded to disregard the fact that a large number of low-net-worth workers in Dubai enjoy relatively satisfactory outcomes, the pertinent point of comparison being the outcomes they would have enjoyed but for their employment in Dubai. Ollie and Lynn retain an Ethiopian live-in housemaid whom I've never met or seen but who is most unlikely, knowing her employers as I do, to be a detainee. I think it may fairly be assumed that she's better off cleaning the nice house of nice people in Arabian Ranches than doing whatever she'd be doing in Addis Ababa, fine city though it may be.

Anyhow, we all walked over to Morelli's Gelato for ice cream. Lynn Christakos is very pretty, in the sporty, clean-cut way of a star golfer's girlfriend, and I found her good-natured and reasonable. She and I were in line at the counter, chatting away, when into the salon there stormed, I say without exaggeration, a group of black-robed and black-gloved and black-masked women. They came like a black wave through the tables, and for a second I thought they were coming to get me. I jumped to one side to let them pass. After they'd bought ice creams and surged away (having skipped the queue, pursuant to the relevant unwritten local rule), I said to Lynn, "Jesus, they gave me a fright."

Lynn laughed. "They're only mums," she said. "Just imagine them with no clothes on."

I forced out a culpable little laugh. More than once I've had pipedreams involving women precisely like these women (i.e., dressed in attire designed as a powerful antidote to nudity but counterproductively causing in me precisely the effect of mentally undressing them), and I had the crazy thought that Lynn had X-ray powers that had opened a window onto my revolting inner life. "Yeah, good idea, I might try that," I said. Mildly risqué banter is not what I'm best at, which is a handicap in Dubai, where the nudge and the wink are vital social tools. According to Ollie, Lynn loves it here. In common with many expat mothers, however, she runs away from the summer heat and humidity and goes with the little boy (and, on a tourist visa, the Filipina nanny) to her parents' house in Lancashire, England, for a couple of months of rain. In her absence, Ollie gets bored. This is when he becomes a prankster.

There was the famous time when, under the impression that I was getting what Ollie had termed "a really cutting-edge preventive ungual treatment," I unwittingly allowed one of Ollie's technicians to paint my toenails pink. When the lady technician removed the cucumber slices from my eyes and showed me her handiwork, I let out a shout of dismay that I immediately regretted because it seemed to upset the technician, who clearly was not in on the joke and plainly was worried that she'd done something wrong and was in big trouble. Ollie, of course, was laughing his head off.

This isn't my favorite side of him. Our friendship was made underwater, where the scope for dicking around is zero. Quite frankly, I don't share his taste for mischief and high jinks. One story he told about a night out in Moscow still haunts me. Evidently, Ollie emerged alone from a nightclub in the early hours. (What he was doing in a Moscow nightclub isn't for me to understand or misunderstand.) There was fresh snow on the streets, and the snow in combination with the hour's lateness and darkness had produced a vacant and hushed and newly ominous city—a city somehow connected to one's childhood, if I may gloss the story. Ollie phoned for his car. He was waiting on the sidewalk when along came a horse, pale and jingling and clouded; and in the saddle was a beautiful young woman wearing a fur coat and a fur Cossack's hat. As Ollie stood there, of course bewitched, a zooming BMW Z4 came down the street and, at a short distance beyond the horse, braked hard. The driver rolled down his window and leaned out to take a look at the horsewoman of mystery. As she drew level with the BMW, this man reached out of the car window and fired a pistol into the air. The horse skidded sideways, regained its balance, and bolted. The gunman sprang laughing out of the car, gun in hand. He hooted and slapped his thigh and jumped up and down as he watched the runaway going away with the woman hanging on for her life. Somehow she was not unseated; but the man slipped on ice and violently toppled backward into the snow like a clown overthrown by a banana peel. This caused him to accidentally shoot. It didn't put an end to his joy. Laughing more loudly than ever, he kicked his legs in the air and helplessly rolled and rolled in the snow.

Let's acknowledge right away that Ollie played no part in what happened. He was an onlooker. What bothers me is that he didn't tell his story as if he'd found himself in the wrong place at the wrong time, which is what I take to be the standard reaction of the eyewitness to a dangerous crime. To hear it from Ollie, he'd lucked into an amazing show. I accept that almost every element of the incident—Moscow, a make-believe night, a horse, gunfire, the randomness at the heart of everything—

places what he saw beyond the frontier of the normal and invites a corresponding displacement of sensitivities. But it's not obligatory to accept the invitation. I am the last person to propose an answer to the problem of determining what portion of the world may be treated as a pure amusement and what portion may not; I just know that I see nothing funny about a woman fighting for her life. And who can say if she succeeded? How do we know a car didn't run her down? Isn't it in any case certain that she was in terror? And even if one were to learn that she made it home safely and now viewed the episode as the most fun she ever had, Ollie's story still cannot be removed from the complication of schadenfreude.

Oh, lighten up, for fuck's sake, says a voice in my ear.

Fair enough. It's very possible I'm being oversensitive—that I'm like those thin-skinned smoke detectors that screech at the presence of the slightest cooking fume and, if life is to go on, must be shut down.

When our homes were warm even when air-conditioned and Lynn and son and nanny in due course migrated north, Ollie dragged me out for a drink at Buddha-Bar. It's in the Grosvenor House hotel, five minutes by taxi from The Situation, and so difficult for me to duck out of going to. The only time I'd been there, three sharp-looking anglophone businessmen, intently discussing what I took to be an important commercial opportunity, occupied the neighboring table. When I eavesdropped, I learned that they were in a conversation about world travel in which they authoritatively misinformed one another about Minorca and Majorca. In this sense, I found Buddha-Bar unchanged. There was a supercar (a Lamborghini Gallardo) stationed at the hotel entrance; there was a velvet rope, to my mind an archaism of late-twentieth-century New York and its dream of VIPs and in-crowds; there was a pointlessly hushed ambience; and, scattered in the calculated gloom, there was a clientele of very made-up and dressed-up older British tourists who looked as if they actually believed that they'd passed a test of selectness and, when I entered, stared intently at me as if I might turn out to be Hulk Hogan or Henry Kissinger.

And there was Ollie, signaling to me from a shadowy booth. A blond woman was with him, and I realized right away that he'd sprung another one of his little surprises—a blind date. When I drew closer, I saw that my date wasn't as blind as I'd thought, indeed wasn't my date. She was Mrs. Ted Wilson.

WHAT HAPPENED NEXT IS inexplicably preceded, in my mind, by what happened one evening years ago, in Union Square, New York, when Jenn and I were walking home from the movies. We became separated in the crowd. I stopped on the busy sidewalk and turned with an extended left hand and said, I'm over here, darling, and reached for her. Instead of Jenn I found myself eye to eye with a beautiful dark-haired woman in her early thirties, herself holding the hand of a man not at all amused by the accidental offer to his girlfriend of another man's hand. The couple moved on; Jenn, I'm assuming, took my hand for a little while. Whatever the exact nature of our physical contact, I walked next to her in surreptitious anguish, because in that instant of misidentification a fantasy of distressing power and implication had been released—in which the dark-haired beauty drops the hand of her boyfriend and takes my hand with a smile, and together we stroll into a Union Square filled, as always on summer evenings, with young romancing couples, and we walk on through a steaming urban night, laughing and talking as everything and everyone converts into lights and vapor; and we, my dark-haired woman friend and I, jump into an old but reliable jalopy and drive out across George Washington Bridge, and drive and drive into the green deep of the continent, an adventure of gas station snacks and motel sex and maxed-out credit cards, driving onward through forests and farmland until, on a remote highway that pursues a twisting river—in

Montana, maybe, or Durango, or Manitoba—a small, solid town catches us, and we stop there, and we take refreshments in a friendly little coffee shop, and we spontaneously begin our lives again for good there, among good neighbors. We befriend the lonely, pretty doctor and the gentle judge. We hold small, rewarding jobs, and we make two clever girls who hopscotch in the springtime. I have always wanted daughters. A chronicle of my awareness of my unhappiness would start with this banal, upsetting daydream, which, as I say, serves as a prologue to that moment in Buddha-Bar, when it was too late to make a run for it and there was nothing to be done except to stand there and wait for the unfortunate Mrs. Ted Wilson to be, entirely reasonably, not nice to me.

Ollie made the introductions—and she didn't recognize me!

My first thought was that this was more trickery—that they had conferred about the lentil-throwing incident and decided that to leave me like this, in a suspenseful limbo of non-identification, would be a fitting comic punishment. Then, as the two of them continued with their discussion—I'd taken a seat next to Ollie and was sort of trying to hide behind him—it became clear that my presence wasn't a source of disturbance, or even of interest. This permitted me to conclude that, amazingly, who I was had not registered with Mrs. Ted Wilson; and when I paid attention to what they were talking about and understood that Ollie was sympathizing with her about her traumatic discovery, apparently made only a day or two before, that the rumors were true and there was indeed a second, Dubai-based Mrs. Ted Wilson (who was herself searching for Ted), I guessed that this Mrs. Ted Wilson was in that state of perceptual impairment that I personally know to be a symptom of vital confusion and distress. In those first several months of the Jenn-me split, more than once I stepped off a subway train at a perfectly familiar station only to find myself at a loss as to where I was, a lostness referable in part to my temporary insanity, in part to the real-world derangement that had placed me not only in an unforeseen Lincoln Tunnel luxury rental but in a life populated by a new and unwelcome dramatis personae, chief among them oneself. I am certain that Mrs. Ted Wilson must at some point that evening have asked herself, What am I doing here? Who the hell are these guys? How did it come to this?

I was meanwhile asking myself: How do I get out of here? By getting up and exiting Buddha-Bar, was the answer—and at most five minutes passed between my arrival at the table and (on the pretext of having to take a phone call) my departure. Outwardly, all was straightforward. Inwardly, things were complex. Among the thoughts and feelings that formed part, during those few minutes at Buddha-Bar, of the catastrophe known as my subjectivity, were: (1) I will be exposed. (2) What does [(1)] mean? What or who would be the content of the exposure? (3) Ollie and I are jackals feasting on another person's suffering. (4) What has Mrs. Wilson done with her hair? She seems to have a Pre-Raphaelite thing going on. (5) If I stay, I'll have to walk Mrs. Wilson home. And then . . . ? (6) Might I be a little in love with Mrs. Wilson? (7) Wow, [(6)] is nuts. I'm really out of control. (8) Ollie is preying on Mrs. Wilson *and* helping her. Whereas I'm keeping my nose clean and being of no use. Paradox. (9) I ought to give my full attention to Mrs. Wilson in order to gain an understanding of her experience and offer her the empathy that is called for. Out of the question, as a practical matter. Must leave. (10) Who is Mrs. Wilson, anyway? And who is Mrs. Wilson II? (11) So is Ted Wilson alive or dead? (12) Buddha-Bar really, really is not my scene. (13) Is Ollie going to sleep with her? No. (14) Am I going to sleep with her? No. (15) I'd like to sleep with her/take her into my protection—it comes down to the same thing. Not. (16) She wouldn't want me, in any case. (17) I have to go. Now. (18) Those are nice breasts, as far as one can tell. You never know until you know. Nice shoulders, definitely. Augurs well re everything else—although again, no necessary correlation. (19) Oh shit, did she just catch me looking? (20) Go, now. *Go, Dog. Go!* (21) Night after night, Maman read that book to me. When we moved to the States, I found it embarrassing to call her that. Mom, she became. *Pardonne-moi, Maman.* (22) OK, that's it, now I'm going.

This is the kind of thing that passes for my moment-to-moment inner life. It's discouraging.

On the walk back to The Situation, I initiated the following exchange of texts with Ollie:

Can't do this. Pls convey my apologies.

?

Poor woman. Let her be.

??

He called me the next day. "You all right? What were those texts about?"

I told him the whole setup had made me feel uncomfortable. "Uncomfortable?" "Yeah, it did." After quite a pause, he said, "Fair enough, mate." The conversation pretty much ended there. I could tell he was hurt/pissed off by what he deemed, not wrongly, to be my holier-than-him stance. Of course, this wasn't a subject for feelings-sharing. We handled the matter the way we handle all of our (very rare) disagreements: a week or two goes by, and then I phone him and ask to buy him lunch, and he assents. Or vice versa. I bought lunch, this time; we ate at the Lime Tree Café (the Jumeira branch); and no mention was made of our difference of opinion about the correctness of the evening out with Mrs. Ted Wilson. That's what friends do: they forgive and forget. They let bygones be bygones. They move on.

It's in this forward-leaning spirit that I've written off, perhaps I should say written down, the irrecoverable opportunity costs of time and happiness attributable to the unhappy Jenn years. As for her aggressive behavior in connection with the breakup, I don't blame her. Note that this isn't a case of forgiveness: I don't hold her responsible, period, on the grounds that during this difficult time she was not herself. I'm not asserting *crime passionnel*: I assert that the "Jenn" behaving badly was not Jenn. This opens the question of who it was, exactly, who (lawfully but immorally) withdrew all the funds credited to our joint checking and savings accounts (72,000.98 USD and 244,346.17 USD respectively (incidentally, Jenn's (much larger) salary, for a reason I must have forgotten, always went into an account in her sole name, whereas the money I earned went into our joint accounts and was used for our joint expenditures)) and left me with a net worth of 11,945.00 USD (the salary payment that I just managed to withdraw); who it was who took sole possession of the apartment and all of its furniture and threw into the garbage my family photographs, clothes, books (including my childhood books (including *Go, Dog. Go!*)); etc., etc. I take the view that these were the deeds of a not-Jenn, not Jenn, and that to a large extent I'm the Victor Frankenstein responsible for the bringing forth of the not- or un-Jenn who, as I realized too late and with an astonishment that has never quite left me, did not have my interests at heart. There remains the conundrum, in this analysis, of the whereabouts, during the time of wrongdoing, of Jenn herself, and of the nature of the relationship between submerged true Jenn and emergent false Jenn, in particular—persistent question—: How come true Jenn, when she resurfaced, as one must assume she in due course did, didn't make good the damage to me done in her absence by her malfeasant alter ego? I'm not suggesting that she was responsible for the actions of the other Jenn, but I do note that it would have been the easiest thing in the world, as a practicality, for her to reimburse me. The matter can be put this way: X, a good person, is subject to episodes of somnambulism. During one of these episodes she unconsciously takes possession of an envelope belonging to V, her friend. X wakes up and finds the envelope. It is marked "V's Life Savings," and it contains 100,000 USD. V asks X for the return of the envelope. X—who is, incidentally, a rich woman with no financial obligations or ambitions that she cannot very easily satisfy, whereas V is hard up—refuses. She keeps V's money. Question: Why would X, a good person, do this? Answer: I don't know. It's incomprehensible.

I can think of a few people who might say: Your hypothetical case, as stated, omits important facts. X's behavior becomes highly explicable if you disclose that V was X's long-term partner and (in X's eyes) "dumped" her and "betrayed" her. Hell hath no fury like a woman scorned.

With respect, this misses the point. Never mind that plenty of "scorned" women don't get into a fury; or get into a fury but don't want to destroy the "scorner"; or want to destroy the scorner but don't, because it would be wrong. Never mind that the whole "hell hath no fury" racket (historically justifiable, I'm theorizing, as a way of granting profoundly oppressed womankind some measure of power and justice and psychological ventilation in epochs marked by the prevalence of crudely retributive ideas) in this day and age represents a tacit prolongation of the supposedly discontinued treatment of women as persons with less-developed moral and rational faculties akin to those we associate with young children and (in the inoffensive technical sense) idiots, an act of gender condescension whose inherent unacceptability is moreover combined with an anachronistic dangerousness, by which I mean that the modern legal and social and economic power enjoyed by many women in Western societies (the female entitlement to which power is, I underline for the avoidance of doubt, of course absolutely beyond question or qualification and not for me or anyone else to allow or tolerate or oversee or bless), when exercised wrathfully pursuant to the outdated "hell hath no fury" license, is a dangerous weapon. To put it another way, it's one thing for a helplessly vulnerable quasi-servant to be madder than hell; it's something else if the infuriated party acting with impunity is a rich partner in a law firm who is practically one's domestic and professional ruler. But, as I say, never mind. It's all good. My point is that the Jenn I lived with, or next to, though by no means a saint (why should she have been? I certainly wasn't), would not have done the things done by the non- or un-Jenn on the hellish fury basis. That's why I can't explain why she decided, in effect, to wear the latter's bloodstained shoes.

I don't want to be detained further by this stuff, because life's too short. YOLO. But one last item makes a demand on the attention. It will be noted that our famous maxim doesn't go "Hell hath no fury like a woman in a state of severe romantic disappointment." Rather, it makes express reference to an action attributed to her (ex-) partner—the one who is deemed to have committed an act of "scorning." I have inputted "scorn" in the Free Dictionary. To scorn someone means to treat that person with disdain or contempt; to mock. I have looked up "disdain" in the Online Etymology Dictionary: it is negatively derived, as one might expect, from the Old French *deignier,* to deem worthy or fit, which in turn comes from the Latin *dignus,* worthy, proper, or fitting, which in turn is rooted (as is "decent," I see) in the Proto-Indo-European (i.e., over-five-thousand-year-old) *dek,* to accept, receive, greet, be suitable. I've also looked up "mock." Though it obviously arrives immediately from *mocquer* (Old French), beyond that it is of uncertain origin (though there is a suggestion that the word may have to do with the Vulgar Latin *muccare,* to blow the nose (in a gesture of derision), which is itself the offspring of *mucus,* slime or snot). These investigations confirm that the evocation of the figure of the "scorned woman" contains within it an automatic characterization of the male (or female: I am not aware that the "hell hath" maxim is of only heterosexual application) as actively snotty, derisive, and contemptuous. This blanket judgment, precisely because it is the nature of a judgment, in turn contains a grotesque rumor of the judicial— of a procedurally verified finding.

Was I a scorner? A looker-down? As I recall, this was a very lowly time for me, and I cannot think how I would have been able to look down on anyone, let alone high-up Jenn. Was I an oaf? Yes. Did I culpably cause damage? For sure. Did I fail her? Guilty as charged. It's all somewhat foggy at this point, but certain memories are clear. Jenn had bravely done her bit— taken the follicle-stimulating hormones, gone every second day to follicle-measuring appointments, and above all taken on the chin the emotional agony that the dismal saga of artificial fertilization inflicts. All that remained, in order to try to make the baby we agreed we would try to have, was for me to do my part. The IVF calendar had produced an insemination date on which I'd be traveling for work, and this meant that I had to produce a semen sample in advance: the fluid would be frozen and used in my absence. I duly took myself to the clinic, or facility, which was in the basement of a brownstone in the East Twenties or Thirties. It was a strange little place. A sadness of masturbators, as I will collectively name them, sat around on gray chairs, each waiting his turn. A human voice was heard only when someone had dealings with the cheerful nurse-like woman who sat at a desk behind an open hatch. She gave me a form that required me, as I recall, to be specific about the number of days I'd been "abstinent." I shamefully provided this and other information, and took a seat. The semen production took place in a separate area, the entrance to which was closed by a shut door. Once in a while, a guy went in and a guy came out. I did my best to not monitor the amount of time anybody took in there. Jenn texted,

Good luck.

A different nurse-like worker entered the waiting room. She called out a name that did not sound like a name at all. Everybody looked around. She tried again, with a different articulation. I realized she was trying to summon me, by my first, horrifying name. When I stood up, everyone looked at me with, I'm sure, a kind of revulsion. In I went. A short corridor gave on to the two chambers where masturbation happened. I entered one of these, on my own naturally, though I recall that I was nonetheless taken aback to find myself alone in this little room. There was a surprisingly cheap armchair—maybe I'd been half-expecting some kind of special custom-made jack-off lounger—a few worn pornographic magazines, and a tiny piece-of-shit non-flat-screen TV that must have been about twenty years old. Onan himself would have found the setup a challenge. I studied the laminated instruction card and wrote my name on the receptacle label and stuck the label on the receptacle. I activated the shit TV. There was a scene of a male repetitively fucking some featureless moaning blonde. I hit Fast Forward. Now some other dude was banging a woman from behind while she gave his or her buddy head. I watched for a few more seconds, hoping for some contagious performance of desire on the part of the woman actor, because surely that is the core fantasy—that one is desired. I was already distracted about how much time this was taking. What was normal? Five minutes? Ten? The question of volume worried me, too: I wanted audio, but I didn't want it to be overheard by anyone. Fuck it, just do it, I said to myself. I dropped my pants and got started—standing up, because there was no way I was going to sit on that chair. A minute or two passed. My dick was inert as a sock. I turned off the TV and tried with closed eyes. When that didn't work, I turned off the light, which was a bad idea, because I needed to capture the ejaculate in the receptacle and I couldn't see a damn thing. I tried to relax; I breathed deeply; I recalled certain erotic triumphs of my youth; and I began to get a response. But every time I thought I might be getting close to producing something, the climactic sensation dissipated. I kept working at it. By the time I finally gave up, half an hour had passed, and the guys out there were surely wondering what the hell I was up to. "I'm having a problem," I said to the nurse, actually hanging my head. She looked at my information sheet. "You live nearby, right?" I said I did. She said, "Why don't you take the vessel home with you, honey, and then just bring it back here right away when you're done."

Meanwhile, another text from Jenn:

Done?

I was done, all right—as of that moment. I walked to the rent-stabilized one-bedroom in a chill of nausea. I waited there. When she came through the door, I told her I needed to talk to her. She went off into the bedroom, and when eventually I went in there after her, she went back out into the living room. "Could you please stop moving around?" I said. "I want to say something."

"I'm really, really tired."

I was very clear in my mind what I wanted to say. I did not want to start a discussion. The time for discussion had come and gone. I made sure to use very plain sentences. I told her I'd tried and failed to produce a semen sample. I told her I did not intend to try again.

She said, "You mean you're breaking up with me?" As usual, she'd gone straight to the pith.

I expressed no disagreement.

Next, I remember, she said, "I need a drink." Later she said, "OK, this isn't happening. Let's just go to bed and see where we are tomorrow." Later still, in tears, she said, "You can't do this to me. I want a baby—you give me a baby! You owe me. You owe me my baby!" At some other point she said, "You can't back out now. It's not right. It's not fair. What am I supposed to do? Start dating? Find someone else? I'm thirty-five years old!"

She made further statements, including the statement that I was the murderer of her marriage. She said, "OK, look, just give me the sperm. I'll have the baby myself. I'll take care of the baby. I don't need you. I can do this. I'm strong." And, "I'm going to be a laughingstock." And, "You wait until I'm having fertility treatment, and then you quit? Oh, boy. It's like you've done this on purpose. Is that it? I'm right, aren't I? You've done this on purpose." And, "My God. You're a monster. A monster. A narcissistic psychopath. My God. That's it. That explains everything." She tore off her clothes and bent over and spread her ass cheeks, and said, "Fuck me! Go on! Fuck me! Can you do that? Get your cock out like a man! You fucking asshole! You coward! You had to wait until now? What's the matter? You don't like pussy? You fucking psychopathic asshole." This was when she went for me, when she was naked, lunging at me with a terrible scream and clawing at my crotch and face. I fended her off and ran to my usual retreat, the bathroom, and locked the door. Leave me alone, I said. Please leave me alone. She started to punch and kick the door, which she had never done before, and there was the terrifying new sound of wood splitting. "Open up. Let me in, you coward," she said. "Be a man. Face up to what you've done." I stayed where I was, leaning against the door, panting. A very long time went by, as I experienced it, in which I stayed in the bathroom and she stood at the door and screamed obscenities and threats. Then she began weeping loudly, and the barrier I'd rightly or wrongly put up to defend myself against her agony crumbled, and as she sobbed I opened the door, hoping maybe to be of some comfort or at least to bear witness to her pain, of which I was the cause. I'd opened the door no more than three inches when I felt the crash as she tried, with another terrible cry, to push her way into the bathroom. The sobbing had been a ruse. I was only just able to heave back and lock the door once more.

Then came a quiet. I could hear movements. There was a

longer period of quiet. I didn't dare move. I was well aware that
this was a perilous situation—one of those moments of extrem-
ity when, the statistics show, the otherwise nonviolent can kill
or seriously injure. I heard the front door shut. I waited. After
a few minutes, I turned off the bathroom light and saw no light
coming through at the door's edges. She had left the apartment
and hit the light switches on her way out, as was her habit. I
opened the door. My intention was to pack a suitcase right
away and get out.

I saw her sitting on the sofa in the darkness. I shouted with
fright. "Sit down," she said. "I want you to listen. You owe it
to me." I didn't sit down, but I listened. She had put on clothes.
The lights were still off. She said, "Sit down, please." I did. She
turned on the lights. She began to speak in a monologue. Now
and then I tried to say something and wasn't able to, because
she kept talking so as not to permit an interruption. The gist of
what she said was that I had a choice to make. I could choose
to be a good man or choose to be a bad man. If I wanted to be
a good man, a man of substance, a serious man, I would stay
the course. If I wanted to be a small man, a scrap of a man, a
nothing man, I would leave. These were the two paths. There
was no third way. Either I would be a man who had stood by
his life partner and made a family with her and lived a valuable
and serious life, or I would be a man who would have nothing
to show for himself but the ruination of another human being.
Trying to speak, I made it as far as "—," because Jenn did not
relent. I could, Jenn said, choose to be a real man, an honorable
man, or a mediocre, second-rate man. That was the nature of
the election I faced: this, or that. It was a fateful moment, she
said. The determination that was mine to make was a determination as to whether I wanted to be a whole person or a
broken and scattered person. If I chose the path of wrong, I
would never be able to piece myself together again. I would be
a broken man, without integrity. That was how life worked.

You made choices, and your choices had consequences. For years it had been her understanding that my choice had already been made, namely to commit to a life with her and to start a family with her. Now I wanted to unchoose, or rechoose. You couldn't. There was no such thing. I had chosen, and she had placed reliance on my choice. She had set up her life on it. To now go back on that choice would be to break and scatter not only me but her, too. That was the reality. I held her fate in my hands.

"___"

She said she believed that I was good, not bad. She said she understood that I believed that I was unhappy. But I wasn't unhappy. My feelings of unhappiness were false. I did not understand this because there was a delusion at the center of my life. It was my job to recognize and overcome this delusion. My superficial feelings of unhappiness masked deeper states of truth. In any case, being happy or unhappy did not consist in having feelings as I understood them, superficially. It consisted in the giving of oneself to someone else. The feelings associated with the giving, these were the feelings of true happiness. Because I was a good person, not a bad person, on reflection I would understand all of this. I would overcome my delusion. I would recover the sense of reality that I had lost. To live without reality would certainly have made me unhappy. My unhappiness was the unhappiness of someone who had lost his sense of reality.

Before or since, I've never felt what I felt as Jenn spoke to me in that room. I felt I was being interred from within. Each assertion she made was another shovelful. I couldn't breathe. My lungs were filling up. I couldn't take it. I got to my feet.

"No, you will not leave," Jenn said. "You will stay, darling. You will stay in this room with me until I'm finished. You have had your say . . ."

"___"

" . . . you have had your say, and now I am having my say."

"—"

"Please sit down. Thank you."

She resumed in the same calm tone. There was no saying anything. She would not halt or even hesitate in her talking, and her speech only quickened whenever I opened my mouth or gave some other sign of wanting to speak. She went on and on, irresistibly shoveling words into me, stopping every cavity of my being. I felt numb. I felt cold. I began to tremble. She was right. There were no options. There was no going. There was only staying. She was in the right. What I wanted put me in the wrong. I had to stay here with her. It was my duty to be in rooms I did not want to be in, to have a life I did not want to have, to have a life in which I would not be present. That was the effect of my duty. That was what was owed to her. I owed her an existence lacking the characteristics of being alive, a life as an apparatus of outcomes that were not mine. There was no alternative. It was my duty. I had to accept a posthumous life.

OK, I told her. OK, you're right. I understand. I will stay. Now please stop.

She went on. When I began to drop off, she said I could not. It was my duty to stay awake and to listen. She went on talking, until finally, finally, she had no more to say, and she left the room. I stayed in the room.

The next morning, we got dressed and went to work together. We parted company on the tenth floor of the office building, where I got out of the elevator and Jenn kept going up. I walked to my desk. Then I went to the emergency staircase and ran down fifteen floors. I left the building and got a taxi to the one-bedroom rent-stabilized apartment. All this happened automatically, or so it felt. I found the suitcase I'd been dreaming of and I stuffed it full of clothes and toiletries and personal documents. During the stuffing I became conscious of what I was doing and again became very frightened, maybe because all my life I had been obedient and good, or had tried to be, and now was being bad, maybe because Jenn was more frightening than ever before. I found a hotel room, in Jersey City, close to the PATH train, and I went there directly from the one-bedroom and, once I had checked in under a false name and put up the Do Not Disturb sign and double-locked the door, I felt relatively safe, because apart from anything there was no way Jenn would want to set foot in Jersey City, which I knew she regarded as an extension of the Lehigh Valley, to which she had sworn she would never return. I was right. She didn't follow me into New Jersey. Three weeks later, I moved into the luxury rental by the Lincoln Tunnel.

Those are (in my recollection) the principal events of the breakup. I would argue that they do not disclose evidence of scorn on my part. They do disclose the destruction by me of Jenn. The facts definitely point toward that conclusion. Since I cannot be Jenn, I am not in a position to say how much damage I caused her. I can say that I do not ever again want to be in the situation of seeing someone in the amount of pain and upset suffered by Jenn that was visible to me—and definitely not in the position of again seeing such a person in such a state from the vantage point of the one who has inflicted the pain and done the upsetting (i.e., me). Hence my decision: never again. Never again me-woman.

This must be doable. It may be that most lives add up, in the end, to the sum of the mistakes that cannot be corrected. But I have to believe there's a way for the everyman (the masculine includes the feminine) to avoid the following epitaph:

HERE LIES [EVERYMAN].
ON BALANCE, HE DID HARM.

EASIER SAID THAN DONE, the not doing of harm. Take the Alain/Ali problem. To mention Alain's extortion to Sandro is to put

Ali at risk. To let sleeping dogs lie for Ali's benefit is to put the kid at risk, since clearly he needs to learn to not extort. Whom do I hold harmless—Ali or Alain?

Here's what I've done: seeing as the kid's internship is for just one more week, I've told Ali to take the week off, on full pay. That puts a floor under the situation. In the meantime, I've taken the kid under my proactive supervision to see if I can exert a neutral-to-positive influence on him. It's only for a few days, after all. If, during this time, he chooses to talk to me about his behavior vis-à-vis Ali, I will listen, and decide what to do next. Otherwise the subject is closed. What I don't want to happen is to find Ali or myself in the middle of a storm of accusations, counteraccusations, inquiries, blaming, etc. It seems improbable that that would end well.

The kid's job, this week, is to write a report for his school titled "My Summer Holiday." That is a really uninspiring assignment, in my opinion, but the kid's going to have to suck it up. I'll occupy myself stamping and embossing and signing documents, answering/deleting e-mails, and trying to think of ways to pass the time without betraying my boredom and dread to the kid. I too have to suck it up, in short. The good news is that, however miserable I may feel, no one else has to pay for it. Not that I'm miserable as a rule—I'm doing pretty much OK, all things considered, and I'd like to think that, in spite of everything, in spite of all that I've renounced, I'm a manageably at large, happy-go-lucky type of guy. But I do have my ups and downs, especially in the office, where often there's a disjunction between being and doing—i.e., not enough work to keep me busy, but not so little work as to enable me to take the day off—and I can, especially if Sandro is pushing my buttons, get into an awful rage (when I'm as bad as the Incredible Hulk, with the difference that I become monstrously enfeebled and have to lie down), and in these instances I'm again relieved that I'm single, because it means that only I am connected to my ill humor and unhappiness, and mine is the only parade that's rained on, and I'm not going home to yell at the wife and kids.

I did, once, furtively interview for another job. Ollie was the go-between. He told me there was another Lebanese family, maybe even richer than the Batroses, looking for a man like me. This happened last year, when I was having a particularly infuriating time of it with Sandro. The job interview was to take place at the personal quarters of the head of the family. I say "personal quarters" because this location, which took up the entirety of floor twenty-five of perhaps the Marina's then most exclusive tower, was neither the office nor the home of the paterfamilias but, one gathered, a venue for his more heart-felt activities—he parked his cars there (in his sky garage), he bowled in his private bowling alley, and, according to a silly rumor, he kept a suite occupied by a pair of Kazakh mistresses. The appointment was scheduled for eleven o'clock. I arrived on time. It was noon before I was taken from the first reception area into a second reception area, from where, after another wait of exactly an hour, I was led by a woman with red perfect fingernails into a third room of reception. Each of these three stations was windowless and smaller than its predecessor and situated progressively deeper in the building's interior, so that I began to feel the uneasiness, admittedly rare, of the one who finds himself involuntarily caving. In the last room there was nothing of note but a glass table with a bowl of fruit. It was the fruit that came to preoccupy the other man in the room.

"Can we eat these, do you think?" he asked me easily, even though these were the first words between us. Evidently our shared occupancy of this empty room—five minutes earlier, he, too, had been escorted in—had created a relation. I guess it doesn't take much.

Under consideration was a stack of apples and grapes, the whole perfectly wrapped in transparent plastic film. Apparently the film was the problem, because it gave rise to the question, at least in the mind of this individual, of whether we were looking at food to eat or at something else. The man leaned forward to take a closer look. He was sweating. He experimented with lifting part of the cling wrap, but seeing that he was about to disturb the integrity of this whole, he sat back. "I didn't eat breakfast," he said with a sorry laugh.

I laughed back, but I had myself been thrown into a mild crisis that was not about the ambiguity of the fruit object but about what to do in relation to this perplexing individual. Who was he? Obviously there was no right or wrong way forward in the matter of the fruit display, and clearly the considerate thing to do would be to tear off the cling wrap, help myself to a Granny Smith by way of example, and put the guy out of his inexplicable misery. But I refrained. This man was very possibly an applicant for the position I was after. It suited my purpose to have him starving and flustered.

After I'd thought about it some more, I got up, wished my rival well, and left. I couldn't take the job from him; I hadn't come all the way to Dubai to get into a mano-a-mano; and to tell the truth, after waiting around for a couple of hours I had a not-good feeling about this family/business. I went back to Batrosia.

There is one big hitch with the status quo: with Ali absent, I am the one who must weigh the kid.

"OK, Al, it's that time," I say. "Let's do this thing."

"I don't want to. There's no point."

The kid's right. I've seen the numbers. They don't add up to a Spider Veloce.

"Yeah, well," I say, "you got to do what you got to do."

He is drooping forward on his desk as if an arrow were sticking out of his back. I have a strong urge to forget all about it and make up a number. That's a nonstarter. I can't conspire with the kid to create a fraudulent document.

"OK," I say, "how about you handle this yourself. I'll stay out of it."

He swipes violently at the pens on his desk and they fly to the floor.

> Yo Sandro—"Man hands on misery to man. /It deepens
> like a coastal shelf." Read the poem, dude.

I put the scale in front of Alain and pat him on the shoulder. I say, "Hang in there." I say, "I know, it's a bummer," and I go back to my desk. Later, he comes to me with a note on which he's written his weight. This slovenly rebellious scribble asks me to believe he's lost a couple of pounds over the weekend. Am I to gainsay him? Am I to eyeball the kid and look him up and down? Like fuck I am. I treat the data point as legit, and graph it.

This thing has put me in a bitter mood that isn't helped by the obligation, no longer avoidable, to face my correspondence. I have some paper mail today: junk mail and mail that, though not strictly junk, can also be tossed into the wastepaper basket in the corner. Shoot first, ask questions later, is my approach. For example, the last of this morning's paper basketballs purports to be a Joint Notice from the Dubai Financial Services Authority and the International Humanitarian City Authority, which informs me that I am expected at the FSA office on a certain date in order to discuss unspecified "compliance issues." The term "compliance" is an orange light, signaling as it does a glitch about some arcane local regulation. I crumple up the Joint Notice. Experience teaches, first, that nuisances often go away of their own accord; and second, that without proof of service, letters of a legal nature belong in the garbage. I shoot from downtown. Nothing but net.

My bitterness persists. When I deal with my electronic inbox, I'm more dismissive than I'd like to be.

Hi. Thx for this. No idea. Sorry.

L——, Your inquiry defeats me grammatically. Cheers.

I delete most of the e-mails en masse: I check a bunch of
them and send them to the trash with one deadly click. That
is a significant satisfaction. I'm busy checking away, when I
see that I'm about to delete a personal message from an unexpected source—New York.

When I left the U.S., I gave my new e-mail address to a select
few, and then I guess I sort of sat back to wait and see who
would write. Not many, was the answer. Discounting automatically generated mail (friending requests, etc.), we're talking
about a few college buddies who've cc'd me in on some stuff,
usually announcements about newborns and other accomplish-
ments. I'm not criticizing anyone here, except possibly myself.
I'm bad about writing e-mails, and I did suddenly and almost
completely absent myself from my social circle (which was
a pretty small one to begin with), you could even say went
into hiding, and I understand that most of those who were
my friends have entered that phase of healthy egoism associated with having a young family and trying really hard to not
get fired and not jump off the Verrazano Bridge, and I don't
participate in social media, and I have no first-person news to
declare, so I cannot be thunderstruck that it has all gone quiet
on the old-friend front. Yet I am thunderstruck, it seems.

The e-mail is from Bob Bell.

> Hi! Hope all is well in the land of black gold. Just doing
> a deal with some Saudis. Very nice people. Bob

I would never have predicted that Bob Bell would be the one
to stay in touch, mainly because we were never really in touch
to begin with. He was once a client of mine and, quite frankly,

not an important one. I advised his company—he didn't own it, he worked for it—on a small restructuring matter, and I can't have met Bob, a small gentleman of my age who lives with his wife and daughter in Ronkonkoma, more than three times, including the one time we went out for a (business) drink, when he told me at length about his love of the Rangers. Bob Bell will drop me a line if something Arabian has caught his attention. This happens once or twice a year. I can only think that he is a believer in the value of networking. You know what? I'll take it.

I write back,

> All well here, Bob. Very good to hear from you. Let's hope the Rangers get it together for next season. Must have been a tough winter for you!

Although I'm grateful for the disembodied low-stakes amiability of Bob Bell, it's not salvation. I appreciate actual pals as much as the next man, and this is where Ollie Christakos comes in. I'm on affable terms with quite a few people here, but I'd be in a tight spot if my friendship with Ollie were perchance to end. When we met up at the Lime Tree, I wasn't just happy to see him but very glad to find that the Buddha-Bar/Mrs. Ted Wilson misunderstanding was water under the bridge.

That said, his first words were "So, I suppose you'll be wanting to hear all about it."

I laughed guiltily. He was right. I wanted him to spill the beans. Apparently, I didn't much care if he would be gossiping or slandering anyone or betraying confidences. I was interested. No doubt as a result of genetically successful instinctually nosy and pilfering ancestral primates, we itch to know, and the more disallowed the knowledge, the stronger the itch. It comes down, as maybe everything does, unfortunately, to getting an edge at the expense of the other guy. I well understood that I was taking a theftuous interest in the Wilsons' lives. Then again, it felt to me as if Ollie had information relevant to the mystery of the wreck of my own life.

Ollie told me that Mrs. Ted Wilson had received confirmation from the authorities that her husband had bigamously married a Dubai resident of Filipino nationality and fathered a child with this second wife, who predictably claimed to have no knowledge of a pre-existing wife, and no knowledge whatsoever of what had happened to him, Ted Wilson, of whom there was still no sign. Mrs. Ted Wilson had flown back to Chicago to seek a divorce.

I said, "How sad."

Yes, Ollie said.

We were drinking limeades in the shadow of the great canopies that stretch above the café courtyard and make it possible, if not necessarily pleasant, to sit outdoors in the summer heat. It's one of my favorite spots in Dubai. One could be in Los Angeles.

"What I'd like to know," I said, "is where he got the time. Half the day he's posting online, the other half he's diving, and on top of that he's working round the clock. And the guy's got two families? You've got to hand it to him."

"Love makes time," Ollie said.

"Yeah, I guess so," I said.

His statement had sounded wise and maybe for this reason worn out, and I didn't give it much thought. Yet Ollie's hypothesis has stuck with me, and I have to ask myself if he did not put his finger on something of great importance. My impression is that he spoke from the heart—the inmost island. Of the Ollie who is there, the Robinson Ollie, naturally I know next to nothing.

"Just imagine," he said. "Flying back on that plane alone. Talking to the kids about the father who's just not there anymore. Bloody hell. It doesn't bear thinking about."

Therefore we didn't bear it. A waitress from New Zealand took our orders. We ate lunch and had a few laughs.

At four o'clock, Alain's driver shows up. Before he is taken away, the kid enters my work space, holding his summer assignment. He leaves it on my desk, as if I'm his teacher.

"Good job," I tell him.

Alain's essay can wait till the morning. I'm done. I'm going to head home, take a shower, hit the Pasha, eat take-out Thai, jerk off, take a sleeping pill. Then it's lights out and sweet dreams, Charlie Brown.

NOT SO FAST.

I discover, when I get back to The Situation, that because I no longer have it in me to look at porn, I no longer have it in me to jerk off. I'm going to assume that my erotic circuitry is capable of rebooting and that this impairment will sooner or later fix itself and before long I'll rejoin the ranks of men and women who self-touch in the time-honored way, naturally and self-sufficiently. Until that happy day arrives, I'll have to make the best of it. This means texting Mila to ask if she or one of her friends might be able to meet up real soon for a drink, cough, cough.

Meanwhile it's still too early for bed, so it's back to my computer and my digital vagabondage. The true meaning of humiliation is to be discovered here, I suspect. To "surf" even non-pornographically is to ride one two-foot wave of imbecility after another. Even if one refuses to "drop in" on stories about The Real Bodies of Mothers or Ten Things You Need to Know Today or Yoga Poses You Can Do Without Leaving Your Bed, and one actually "catches" a self-respecting attempt to inform, entertain, or enlighten—even in that eventuality, the readers' comments, by their inanity and mean-spiritedness, are almost certain to bring about one's "wipeout." I think it's the phenomenon of these commenters—who must be taken to represent the masses, a body from which nobody is excluded—in combination with my new intercontinental perspective, that has left me with a most unfortunate impression that my fatherland—inescapably, the United States of America—is, or has become, a strange, gigantically foolish place that sooner or later will be undone by the calamitous mental life of its population, whose bizarre domination by misconceptions is all too well incorporated by its representatives in Washington, D.C. It didn't take long before I gave up trying to follow my countrywomen's (the feminine includes the masculine) political dramas. The election of Barack Obama was very interesting, but his presidency coincided from the outset with the *Finanzkrise* (and thereafter with the Great Recession/Lower Depression), and the opacity of the latter was superimposed on the former. The most pressing responsibility of citizenship, it seemed, was to quickly acquire competence in economic and financial theory, an onerous requirement made worse by the obvious cluelessness and/or bad faith of the governing or controlling theorizers and, speaking for myself, by a strange feeling that even these would-be controllers or governors were ruled by an undetectable legislature whose existence could be deduced from the existence of overwhelming laws of money the content of which was unknown to, or beyond the control of, our overwhelmed ostensible governors or controllers. Who knows. It cannot end well; dolts thrive; one senses an eventual crash of crashes. The only chink of light is that my despair about human stupidity—a commonplace—is almost certainly itself stupid; and fortunately there are few signs that meta-fools like me have the power to direct the affairs of mankind.

The trouble with chinks of light is their connotation of a wall of darkness. Nowhere is the wall darker than at Ted Wilson's Wall. Unmodified since his total disappearance, it is still open to visits and messages from whom it may or may not concern. If ever I should suspect myself of undue optimism, I can visit this electronic relic and refresh my sense of the baseness of our natures. What can to this day be seen on Wilson's Wall, which I shall name a disgrace, began with the return of Mrs. Ted Wilson to Chicago and the attendant public confirmation of Ted Wilson's bigamy. Somebody posted,

You are such an asshole Ted.

This message, in and of itself not too bad, served as the as it were first sign of nightfall in a land of ghouls, and out of the dark came evil spirits, goblins, bogeys, and bloodsuckers. Very quickly the Wall was covered with messages such as

What whore are you fucking now Ted?

I've heard all about your love of underage fuck bud-dies, you rapist.

Hey Ted—terrific job abandoning three kids and two wives.

are you getting your new bitch to shit on you Ted? are you getting what you always wanted? are you happy now?

Psychopath.

douche

I hope you're dead you cheating piece of slime.

I'm sure he is dead. Suicide is the most selfish act in the world and he seems like a pretty selfish guy :(

There were many more. This vile aggression went on for months, and my bewilderment only grew as the vilification intensified and nobody did or said anything about it. Who were these people? Where were his friends or the people he had friended? Where was his well-wishing Facebook community? Was nobody thinking of Mrs. Ted Wilson and her college-age children, who must have visited the Wall and witnessed the public stoning and gang shaming of their (late?) ex-husband/father? I remember worrying if there was something I could and should do, whether, specifically, I ought to join Facebook for the purpose of posting a message of my own, not only in order to come to Wilson's defense, if that is the right word, but to rescue myself from the culpable helplessness into which I had been dragooned by this turn of events. Yes, I felt as if violence was being done to me, who was unknown to these verbal thugs; I felt under attack. Under attack from what? From the peristalsis of circumstance, which forces one forward as a turd is forced. I remember thinking that I had to "speak out," if not to effect change, if not to rebuff the hooligans, then at least to put on the record where I actually stood in the Wilson matter rather than where, against my will, I had been made to stand, i.e., to stand by.

(The record! I've always found it a hoot, this mythic tabula on which our deeds are inscribed and preserved. Where is this record? Who is the recorder? Who are the readers of the record? Egocentricity! Superstition! Anthropocentricity! (One understands the metaphysical origins of the error, of course, it being an almost unacceptable and unbelievable proposition that we exist in an adjudicatory emptiness, and arguably a definition of the human must refer to our distinguishing if babyish sense of (and/or need for) being kept under observation or lorded over. (The fantasy of the record is closely preceded, surely, by the fantasy of the forum—the ideal if invisible fact-finding or listening body to which one mutters one's arguments, sometimes audibly. I do it all the time. It's consternating, really.)) Yet here, it appeared, *was* a record: the eternal, ineffaceable webpage of a disused but still functional Facebook Wall.)

I resolved to do nothing—resolved to not "speak out." I

couldn't work out what my speech would be, and I didn't want the mob to turn on me. I was cowed, it cannot be denied, and filled with the shame of the cowed one. In the time that has passed, my silence has continued, and my shame has deepened. It is open to me this very evening to join Facebook and say my piece on Wilson's Wall. I won't, though. It would rouse the virtual beast—a frightening creature, even if these days it gives off only an occasional hiss of poisonous nostril steam:

I know you're out there Ted. So do your children.

DON'T THINK YOU'VE BEEN FORGIVEN YOU TWO-TIMING MANIAC

In fairness, nothing I might post on the Wall would make a difference to the injustice done to Wilson. When Wilson disappeared, so did the very idea of Wilson's facts, and with them the very idea of justice. I'm not in possession of corrective new information, and, even if I were, it would be non-information, because the factual component of the case is the property of the accusers, who, by virtue of being the de facto fact owners, have unlimited powers of assertion and denial and making shit up. This makes my blood boil, to be honest. Take the last-mentioned accusation: Ted Wilson is a "two-timing maniac." I don't take this to mean that he's insane—which, if true, would remove him from the realm of responsibility to the realm of illness—but to mean that he is a villain of the most conscience-less sort. Maybe he is; it's entirely possible; but there are other possibilities. Maybe something other than maniacal two-timing is going on. In order to investigate this—an investigation I insist on, it seems—we must ignore the frenzy of incrimination by which Wilson is already in the stocks, his face dripping with old tomatoes and rotten eggs. (Where do people find eggs that are rotten? Do they keep them in store, in anticipation of the opportunity to throw them?) We must undertake our inquiry neutrally and methodically, beginning with the basic situation, a man and woman in a marriage, and with the basic acknowledgment that because marital relations are transacted in private, we cannot know what experiences they involve. We begin with a mystery, in short.

(It's a mystery that cannot be dispelled by a couple's self-presentation. I'd guess that nobody at the firm had an inkling about where the Jenn-me deal really stood, behind closed doors. I didn't go around leaking how I was doing (i.e., not well; the line between my being alive and my being dead had faded almost to the point of unimportance), and Jenn—well, she was outwardly sunny because inwardly she was, I believe, in the main OK with the outcomes produced by the her-me undertaking. I'm making no criticism at all here, just adverting to the fact that Jenn drew sustenance from stable-partnership products—a residence, financial pooling, professional assistance, social status, and, in due course, a reproductive and parenting cooperative—rather than from a partner qua partner. She wasn't really a great fan of the whole person-to-person *Liebe an sich* thing, if such a thing actually exists. (She was a wonderfully devoted and even emotional advocate for her clients, and a terrific colleague at work. (On the phone, I always knew when she was with workmates because she would speak to me in a considerate, upbeat tone that in all honesty I very rarely met with if we were talking privately, when she could be a little ratty, if I may say so. (This gave rise, in my mind, to one of those distinctions that seemed important for a while but which, over time, I've come to see as another low point in my personal history of thinking, namely the difference between rattiness *in rem* (innate rattiness, or rattiness toward the world) and rattiness *in personam* (rattiness toward a certain person). I held it against Jenn that she was quite capable of non-rattiness at work yet found it a challenge to not be ratty at home, when

face-to-face with me. This wasn't fair to her, because she could
well have been innately ratty while being, at work, pleasant
in personam. Or, she could have been naturally pleasant but
when at home made grumpy by me through no fault of her
own. Even by my standards, this line of thinking is unusually
futile.)))

So:

1. This was a geographically strange marriage. The Ted Wilsons had long lived in different countries, with no end in sight
to their separation. That they opted for this arrangement does
not diminish its strangeness. On the contrary, arguably. (It's
as if an owner of a pair of socks decided to keep one sock at
home and its match in the country. (We all know what eventually happens to pairs of socks: one of them disappears, or gets
a hole in it, and they are separated permanently. (Although in
my case the retained sock will often live on alone, and be mis-
matched with a leftover sock from a different pair.)))

2. This, the above, puts the marital case in the category of
the exceptional: there is no need to spell out the implications
of a couple living apart, at least to anyone who believes that,
unlike cats, most of us are not solitary creatures with no need
for close companionship.

3. We are concerned, then, with the case of a married person's inability to abide forever by promises whose presuppo-
sitions (of proximity and intimacy) have evaporated. If this
inability is a flaw, very many of us are similarly flawed. It follows that the flaw is non-pathological.

4. Accordingly, one can hardly state with confidence, of either
Mr. or Mrs. Ted Wilson, that it would have been maniacal or
psychopathic of them, over the course of years of apartness,
to seek from a third party the subject-matter of an abstracted
marital monopoly, i.e., the humanly essential flesh-and-blood
tenderness that comprehends, but is not exhausted or defined
by, sexual pleasure. (It pains me to say it, and I'm not sug-

gesting anything, but we have no information as to whether
Mrs. Ted Wilson did or didn't herself take a lover or paramour,
to use decorous language I associate with young ladies in the
court of Louis XIV who've been entered into wedlock with
a romantically unsuitable (much older) man in order to further extra-personal diplomatic/financial objectives, and who
are deemed to be entitled to a discreet liaison with a younger,
more personally compatible gentleman. (Interestingly, men are
not typically said to "take a lover," and I'm not aware that
our language provides them with an equivalent euphemism.
This may be another anachronistic disjuncture, especially as
it's no longer the case that a husband is permitted to sexually
have his way with his wife whether or not she is agreeable.
The spousal rapist no longer goes scot-free, in theory. (This
may be the moment to mention what I think is an important
prevalent confusion about the promise of fidelity, i.e., faithful monogamy. The essence of monogamy does not consist in
abstention from third-party sexual relations but in the dedication of sexual activity to a single person. In other words, the
willfully sexually inactive spouse is not being monogamous: he/
she is being celibate. Those who are in doubt as to the conjugal
significance of celibacy are referred to its historic synonymity
with the Latin source word, *caelibatus*: "state of being unmarried." Properly understood, then, the intentional celibate, in
his/her contravention of the vow of fidelity, is in the same boat
of transgression as the intentional adulterer. (Maybe this is all
by way of a prologue to a confession: Jenn and I "cheated"
(word beloved by the online barbarians) on each other. What
little sex we had was clearly a disturbance of a celibate status
quo rather than an enactment of a monogamous one. The most
erotic episode of our last few years came when, tweezers in
hand, I carefully removed a wasp's stinger from the sole of her
foot and, in the weeks that followed, scratched the bite mark
at her request. She practically swooned with toxical ecstasy.

(Since I'm looking back, I have to rub my eyes and ask where we got the idea that it was somehow sensible and coherent and *reasonably practicable* to pay a woeful price of eternal intimate isolation in order to be "with" each other. Likewise, who or what put it into the heads of the Wilsons that they could pull off an international union that wasn't actually a union? What are they teaching in schools these days? Which planet are we all on? (Nowadays the more unremarkable or self-evident something is, the harder and longer I'll be rubbing my eyes. That's not how it's supposed to work.))))))

5. OK, so Ted Wilson and Mrs. Ted Wilson II (as she isn't, yet) are having a non-maniacal adulterous relationship. Then, she gets accidentally pregnant (it happens to the best of us) and she decides to keep the baby (again, by no means an outlandish decision). This gives rise to a problem. This is Dubai, remember, where it's illegal and unacceptable for an unmarried woman to be with child. So Wilson marries her—not for his sake but for her sake and the child's. He falls on the sword of bigamy. How do we feel about Ted Wilson now? (I'm not saying *tout comprendre, c'est tout pardonner*. I'm just asking the question. (To be clear, we don't know the facts. We'd need to see the certificates of marriage and birth and do the prurient math. But I'll bet that my scenario isn't far from what happened. It certainly cannot be ruled out.))

6. We have answered, in the negative, the charge that Ted Wilson, insofar as he had relations of a worldly and criminally matrimonial nature with a woman other than Mrs. Ted Wilson, must necessarily have been a "two-timing *maniac*." I want to quickly go back to the question of *two-timing*. An overlooked feature of the case against Wilson is the absence of any suggestion that he took action that was wrong *as such*. So far as one is aware, he led two "good" lives—one with Mrs. Ted Wilson, one with Mrs. Ted Wilson II. (Debatably, until it all fell apart, he was twice as virtuous as the next guy, seeing as he was dis-

charging the responsibilities and producing the good outcomes associated with meeting the needs of two women. (I'm just dipping my toe in the water, here. I'm also asking if, as someone who is currently neither betraying anyone nor providing for anyone, i.e., as a zero-timer, I'm not actually worse than Ted Wilson.)) Wilson's wrongdoing lay in the simultaneity of his two lives. Again, no value judgment here. I'm just putting out there that we begin to see a link between morality and chronology. The link becomes clearer if we remember that serial romantic involvement is not generally deplored, so that if Wilson had taken up with Mrs. TW II after his relationship with Mrs. TW had ended, all would have been OK. The accusation of "two-timing" is therefore more apt than the Wall accuser knew: Wilson's crime was essentially temporal. His *timing* was bad. (The rebutter will impatiently say: No, no, no, his crime was his dishonesty: he acted with wrongful secrecy, in breach of trust. The rebuttal has great force. I wonder, though, if it's dispositive. What if both the Mrs. Ted Wilsons had expressly consented to their mutual husband having concurrent relationships in Dubai and Chicago: would this arrangement have met with general approval? I doubt it. Leaving aside the disapprobation excited by polygamy (which I can attest to, having heard the nasty comments made about Emirati families), it seems to me that the very doubleness of Wilson's life would be outrageous. Hold on—he gets two bites at the cherry? Correction— he gets *two cherries*? We're stuck with one life and he gets two? Unfair! We're stuck with the tyranny of the linear and he isn't? He gets a double helping and we don't? He gets to take *both* forks in the road and we're stuck with the path not taken and the false consolation that alternativity is a spiritual splendor? Not on my watch, buddy. Not if I have anything to do with it. (As it happens, I see things differently. I think two lives would be unendurable and unnatural. Oneness may be hard— but twoness? It has a diabolical dimension, to my mind. How would you split yourself? How would you do justice to both your selves and to both your others? (Then again, there's Ollie's revolutionary conjecture: love makes time. (It certainly seems true that lovelessness shrinks time. Jenn and I always seemed squeezed. Always we were in agreement that certain practical things needed to be done right away. Always it was first things first. Always we were in the hurry that postpones the second thing, the good stuff, whatever that was supposed to be. (I now see that our idea of the good stuff wasn't having a good *time* together, or a good that was stuff-like, but having a good situation, i.e., the circumstance, rather than the substance, was the good, and vital to the good was the displacement of time and its replacement by activity. This was a category error, but what did we know? It was all new to us, every second of it. (There's your problem with experience, right there: it's inapplicable, going forward.)))))) (On one view, which I share, I was guilty too, and above all, of causing the most serious chronological damage: I failed to tell Jenn that I didn't want to have a baby with her *earlier*, so as to give her a reasonable period of time in which to mate with someone else. (I'm aware that I have a defense open to me, namely that Jenn specifically asserted that she didn't want a child. The defense doesn't hold up. There was always the chance she'd change her mind, and there was nothing to stop me from telling her that *come what may* I would not have a child with her because our quasi-marriage was a living death for me—surely a pretty significant piece of information that is absolutely one's obligation to communicate to one's partner in a timely fashion. Jenn, I'm so sorry.))

MY MORNING STARTS with a glitch: the office has not been cleaned overnight. I'm not going to complain to the building administration, because I'm guessing that the cleaning crew (whoever they are; they never swim into my ken; they are substantiated

only by newly empty trash containers and a lemony after-smell)
really don't need more shit in their lives; and, let's face it, we're
only talking about carrying two small, light wastepaper baskets to the utility area in the hallway, tipping their contents into
a larger container, and walking the baskets back to the office.
Normally, Ali would take care of this without my even having
to think about it; but he's on enforced leave. It isn't an ill wind,
though: the chore is perfect for the kid.

I say to him, "Hey, Alain, do me a favor. Can you take these
out?" I'm standing by his desk, tendering the little baskets.

"I døn't think sø," I hear him say.

This makes me curious. "How come?" I say.

"How come what?" he says, so lethargically it comes out as
a moan. I get it. His time here is coming to an end, and he feels
he can experiment with insubordination and insolence. I'm just
grateful he didn't have this thought earlier.

How come he doesn't think he should take out the trash? I
answer.

"It's not my job," he says.

Funny. As if the kid had a job. "And whose job is it?"

The kid is sitting at his desk, face resting on one hand. He is
contemplating his next move.

"Oh, fuck off," he murmurs very quietly at the wall.

That's a bold play—a power play. He's pushing me into the
corner of truculence. Or so he thinks. I still have my best move
to come.

"Listen," I say. "You're hurting my feelings when you say
something like that." (I learned about this communication technique in the days when I searched online for expert emotional
guidance. Apparently the vulnerable announcement of one's
suffering will almost certainly give pause to one's interlocutor
and awaken in him/her a measure of receptiveness to oneself
that would certainly not be forthcoming if one proceeded the
usual way, by complaint and criticism.)

The kid sniggers.

Now, that snigger bothers me. Vulgar abuse and childish f-bombs are water off a duck's back. But this snigger is directed at the very notion of fellow feeling.

I take out the trash myself. Then I retreat behind the partition. The kid and I stew in our respective juices.

I hope you're happy with your handiwork, Sandro. Your son is unresponsive to the most basic appeal to his humanity.

S—You know what? Forget that last message. It's not my funeral.

I fight off a bitter urge to take the brat into the bathroom and weigh him.

To cool off, I go online, onto the Dubai Police website. One of the more civilized aspects of the Dubaian way of doing things, in my opinion, is that cameras and radars, not traffic cops, control speeding. If you're electronically caught, you get an electronic ticket that you don't know about until you've checked the police website. I'm not against this system. It's true that there's something fundamentally unsettling about machine-based justice, but I prefer it to the delay, dishonor, and terror inflicted by a flashing, squawking American patrol car. The street-parking situation here is crystal clear: either you feed a meter or you get a ticket. You are spared the cruel enigmas and triple meanings of the parking signs of midtown New York City, which rise like strange totems up the sign poles and gave me great trouble during my stay in the Lincoln Tunnel luxury rental, when I leased a car to cheer myself up. Three times I got towed. I found out that the fleet of the police tow trucks was based a block away and those flatbed-driving fuckers would essentially fill their daily quota in the neighborhood, where the lowest hanging fruit in the city—tourists, commercial drivers, and me—was most densely concentrated. On the other hand, the car pound was right next door, and I won't say that it didn't occur to me to skip the whole parking and ticketing and towing production and drive directly to the pound and leave the car right there.

(Each time I went to the pound, I'd get a police document stamped REDEEMED. One day, looking more closely at this police-blue piece of paper, I noticed this notice:

!!! WARNING !!!
THE SCOFFLAW STATUS IS UNDETERMINED

What? I was maybe a scofflaw? I had that hanging over my head too? *Even though I wasn't a scofflaw?* I made phone calls. I mailed registered letters to the New York City Department of Finance with copy receipts of the parking fines I had paid. I sent faxes and e-mails. Several times over I demonstrated my innocence. It made no difference. There was never an official response. My scofflaw status remains to be determined.)

I see that I have no Dubai speeding tickets. Excellent. Phew. Since I'm logged in, I check on Sandro's status. This is one of those borderline responsibilities I've had to accept. I'd love to be able to dine out on stories of Sandro's motoring excesses, but of course that would be a breach of confidence and not even Ollie can be told about the roughly ten thousand USD worth of traffic violation tickets that Sandro annually picks up. It's not that funny, to be honest. Periodically, his license is suspended and he gets one of the guys at Fort Batros to serve as his full-time driver. Even if there's no rush whatsoever, he yells at the driver to speed up, with the consequence that this unlucky individual soon has *his* license suspended, which of course is a calamity for him. This has been the subject of much real and imaginary mail to Sandro, who, I know for a fact, makes no provision for the loss suffered by his drivers on his behalf. I have had to take it upon myself to make unofficial hardship payments to these unfortunates (out of the Family Office operational budget).

Using my corporate card, I pay Sandro's fines.

His son's writing assignment is on my desk. To get rid of it, I read it.

My Summer Holiday

This year I spent my summer holiday in Dubai because I had to get a job and work. Usually I spend my summer holidays in Beirut. My grandfather lives there and we hang out on his yacht. Dubai is a lot of fun though. But its very hot. There are lots of malls to go to. I had a lot of fun. I swam a lot and listened to a lot of music. I like waterskiing and we did a lot of that. Usually I drove the motorboat and my friends skiied. I have a lot of friends here. My job was really boring though I have to say. I got pretty good at Sudoko though. I'm a brown belt. I'm going to make sure I get a better job when I leave my education. I don't want to loose my time on this earth.

Not too bad, I guess, given the limitations of the genre and the author. He really is not super-mature. (It would be nice if he'd use some of the high-value words I've taught him, but I don't want to get dragged into an editorial or pedagogic or hands-on role here.) Next paragraph:

I got into trouble with my Dad because I tried to take money out of the cashpoint that my family has. He caught me out, aaa! I was not trying to steal though. My Mum asked me to get it out for her. Its complicated!

Well, well, well. The kid took the fall for the mother. This essay is a cry for help. My duty is clear.

I send Sandro a text advising him to read my e-mail ASAP. The e-mail reads:

> Hi Sandro—please see the attachment. This is a scan of Alain's summer essay assignment, which I've just read. You'll see that Alain suggests that Mireille played a role in his attempt to withdraw cash from the ATM.
>
> If Alain is being truthful—I have no opinion about that—it might explain another matter I need to raise with you. It seems that Alain has been attempting to pressure my assistant, Ali, into giving him (Alain) money. Young people can act uncharacteristically when they are in difficulty, and I would guess that Alain may be "acting out" because of the ATM incident.

I feel a lot better. Everything is out in the open. I've done what was needed, and done it in a way that is, I believe, sensitive to all parties. Now it's up to the parents and their child to figure things out. My work here is done.

Meanwhile there's the problem of what to do with the kid for the rest of the day. We can't just sit around fuming and licking our wounds. In any case, my wounds have healed.

I go into his part of the room. "OK," I say. "Let's go. Field trip." I jingle the keys to the Autobiography.

"Where we going?"

We are going to the Al Fahidi Fort, which I've always wanted to visit. It has stood for two centuries and is the real deal, if by realness we mean oldness. These days the fortress is hemmed in by car traffic and by dense, disheveled Bur Dubai, and the old magnificence—towers looming on white sands, warriors approaching on horseback—must be fantasized. For me, that's not a problem: I can't look up at those pale stone battlements without catching a glimpse of Beau Geste and, on the inland horizon, the gangsters of the sands. The fort now houses the Dubai Museum and, we are promised, artifacts from the bygone days. With luck, the kid and I will learn something. I've taken the precaution to not utter the word "museum." At his age, just hearing the word knocked me into the stupor I associate with being clubbed on the head.

And with stepping into the Dubai heat. Our summer sun is a goon. We cannot linger in the fort's large courtyard. We dash past cannons, a dhow, and a hut with walls made of dried palm fronds. We make it indoors.

What can I say about what happens next? We go down a staircase and are confronted with stuffed flamingos hanging midair on strings. There is a soundtrack of waves and bleating birds, and there's a panoramic maquette of the desert featuring the Creek and some trees, all on a ridiculously minuscule scale that presumably replicates the flying flamingo viewpoint. The kid gives me a WTF look. I start to explain that the museum dates back to 1971 and even think about bullshitting him about the interestingness of the technological gap that separates the now from the then. I can't keep a straight face, however. I say, "OK, you're right. This place is weird." From that moment on, we're in a comedy. We have a chuckle at a wood platform used as an outdoor bed, we feign awe at a goatskin drum, we stand in actual awe before a waxworks of life-sized Arab men drinking tea and puffing on shisha pipes. "It's so bad it's good," Alain says, and I can see he's proud of this comment. When he watches some film footage of long-gone fishermen dancing and chanting, the youngster, who let's not forget is sizable as John Candy, if a little shorter, does a funny shimmy. We're having a great time—and, I must insist, not at the expense of the good people who worked hard on these exhibits forty years ago, or out of disrespect for the local traditions honored here. There's room in the world for a bit of innocuous, good-natured irony. It's not anybody's fault that, until very recently, this has always been an uneventful, materially poor, culturally static corner of the world, with inhabitants who did not prioritize their own future prestige or devote themselves to producing deathless *objets* for their museological self-representation in posterity. I find this refreshing. One detects, in the as it were whiteness of the pages of the history of Arabia Deserta, a conformity with ideals of modesty that contrasts favorably, in my book, with the vainglorious agendas of certain other nations. (Ted Wilson (I recall from my YouTubing of a conference talk he gave) thought that Dubai's blank past was a great "storytelling" opportunity. This shocked me a little. I hadn't understood that it's no longer officially denied that history is cooked up. I'm fully aware that country branding is as old as Genesis, but have we become so despairing that we openly boast of our frauds on the facts? Jeepers creepers, whatever happened to lip service and the ceremony of innocence? Do we no longer require of our governors that at the very least they dissemble their motives and spare us, if nothing else, shame? Evidently not. Evidently we live in a world in which deep thinkers or investigative journalists are no longer required to bring to light the mechanisms by which our world, and our sense of it, is controlled. The controllers, like those buildings that wallow in their pipes and ducts, now jubilantly disclose their inner workings. (In this sense, the Ruler is behind the times. He'll learn soon enough, I'll bet. It won't be long before we'll be deafened by the screeches of whistles being blown by whistle-blowers blowing the whistle on themselves.))

The most striking exhibit is the diorama of the pearl diver in action. He wears an ancient diving suit and a makeshift breathing apparatus, and reaches down to the seabed he will never reach. The display commemorates Dubai's claim to notability as a former pearl-diving center. I don't doubt that there used to be some pearl-related activity, but it's odd that I haven't heard a whisper about pearls since I got here. (Where are these famous pearl beds that were once so important? How come I've never seen an oyster?) I'm not sure, in any case, that it's such a terrific idea to lay claim, in memory, to the courage of these swimmers and the supposed glamour of underwater treasure hunting. I may of course have been misinformed, but I think I remember reading that the divers were essentially in the ownership of the pearl merchants/boat owners and needless to say didn't get to keep the pearls they defied death to find. (I'm not saying they were blood pearls, counterparts of today's blood diamonds. I don't have the evidence to support this grave charge. (We should be wary of applying the noun adjunct "blood" to everything and anything that comes to us with the taint of exploited labor. It would devalue the usefulness of the term; there would be no end to it. One cannot live in a world of blood pants, blood bread, blood spoons, blood saltshakers, blood water, and blood air.))

I'm minded to say something to the kid about the historic context of this diver. It's a lost cause, however, because one doesn't know what the cause is. Who can really know what actually happened and what one is to make of it all?

We drive back to the office in silence. The good cheer fades. How could it not?

It's back to business. Alain hits the number puzzles, I hit the stamps and bosses. Very little is said, either in the office or afterward, when I drive the kid home. I make no mention of weighing him. I will have nothing more to do with this boy's body.

NOTWITHSTANDING THE OCCASIONAL COMMENT posted on Ted Wilson's Wall, interest in the Ted Wilsons passed quickly enough. Other scandals occupied us. Let's see: there was the English couple from Emirates Hills, the W——s, whose Sudanese help, hours after she was fired, was found dead on the golf course. There was the saga of the marriage of B. and M. C——, whose union survived revelations of B.'s cross-dressing, M.'s prescription-drug abuse, and certain colorful claims made by their neighbors. And there was that sad story of the Dubai-based American, a gentle soul by all accounts, who bred falcons in Kazakhstan for sale in Saudi Arabia and was fatally stabbed with a screwdriver out there, in the Chu Valley, and presumably died a lonely death. The Wilsons were no longer talked about because they were no longer around. In Dubai, like anywhere else, we focus on our own.

(I don't want to attempt a taxonomy of expat chatter, but some distinctions should be made. Scandalized gossip is not to be confused with other modes of chitchat or outraged discussion:

- *Stories of drunken antics:* doing dumb, dangerous things *while intoxicated* is considered amusing, not scandalous.
- Nobody has much to say about *Western tourists getting into official trouble* (for making out in public, wearing too-skimpy clothes, being caught at the airport with microscopic traces of drugs on their shoes, etc.). People overseas may be interested; we're not. The view here is that visitors should respect and inform themselves about Emirati laws and customs. If they don't, that's their lookout.
- Although a person's *financial failure/employment termination* is always carefully analyzed, very few take talkative pleasure from it. There but for the grace of God goes one.
- *Official injustices done to high-net-worth expats* are discussed with sobriety. Take the story of Karl V——, who was arrested, imprisoned for a year, then deported—all because of alleged homosexual acts in a parked car. That got the attention even of straight people. Why? Because all of our heads are on one kind of chopping block or another. (This isn't to diminish the special and inexcusable perils faced by the LGBT community here.)
- *Misfortunes or injustices suffered by low-net-worth expats* are simultaneously in our field of awareness and not on our

conversational radar. (For example, Karl V.'s lover was a workman from India. He wasn't talked about, even though his unjust punishment was indistinguishable from Karl's.)

- *Tragedies.* We remain sensitive to death, serious illness, the suffering of children, etc., within the expat community.
- We don't talk about *injustices done to Emiratis by Emiratis.* We don't care.
- When it comes to the *judicial mistreatment of raped women,* we are affronted; and our affront has no communal limitation. Take the story of the young Emirati teenager who was abducted from her home and driven out into the desert, where she was raped, beaten, and left for dead. No asterisk of nationality is placed next to our sympathy for her experience or our horror at the fact that, after she somehow made it home, the rapists were exonerated and their victim, on account of her alleged failure to wear sufficiently modest attire in her own garden (into which the two rapists had furtively peeped), was officially blamed and disgraced for her alleged provocation of the rapists. This is no less appalling to us than (for example) the story of the French woman who was raped by three men (Christian foreigners, note well) and was charged with adultery after she reported the facts to the police. (The overseas press picked up both these stories, and there was a furor without borders. International outrage has no effect on our domestic outrage, except maybe to reduce it, because we disidentify with the fingering holier-than-thou crowd who look down their noses on Dubaians of every stripe, always unaware, in their anxiety to piss on us from a great height, that they have forgotten to wipe the shit from their shoes. (That's not to question anyone's freedom of speech or opinion. I'm just saying.)))

Nor should it be forgotten that, of the people who might have been interested in the Wilsons' miseries, at least half left

Dubai within a year. Yes—we have had a lot to brood over, starting with the near-bankruptcy of the emirate and the great economic paralysis that befell the land. (This development, so ruinous to so many, prompted a lot of gloating in the foreign media (British, in particular), where opinionators delightedly recognized a case of "hubris," an intensely annoying word only used, in my opinion, by a nose-in-the-air jerk who is about to stride into a manhole. (These criticizers—who denounce our carbon footprint from their own catastrophically deforested, coal-built countries—not satisfied with characterizing the Emiratis as until-recently-illiterate camel-jockeying upstarts who have finally been taught a good lesson; not content with repeating unverified scare stories (the taps at the Atlantis give forth cockroaches; The Palm is sinking; The World is dissolving); and not sufficiently gratified by their "exposés" of the "dark side" of the "desert playground," also attacked us, the expats. Apparently we were fleeing the "suddenly bankrupt" "sheikh-dom" in "droves" (i.e., mindlessly, like driven cattle) or in "a Gadarene rush" (i.e., like the demoniac pigs who ran into the sea). I don't let this stuff get to me. I do, however, look forward to the day Dubai has bounced back and the hubris experts, down in their manholes, are begging for a helping hand.))

So I've had a lot on my mind; a thousand and one troubles have kept me awake at night; and yet for some reason I have continued to think about the Wilsons.

Initially my thoughts followed Mrs. Ted Wilson; that is, in my mind's eye I traveled to Chicago and omnisciently followed her into her own home, and into her bedroom, and into the shower, and watched her doing all the things associated with those places. These crimes of fantasy were of course perpetrated in secret, and with impunity. One's thoughts are not yet searchable, thank God. Let me say, if I'm allowed to, that it's not as if in these scenarios I was interacting with Mrs. Ted Wilson or doing gross stuff that would be wrong; and it's interesting that increasingly I have watched her doing everyday, out-in-the-open stuff—shopping, driving around, drinking coffee. I think what I've wanted, most of all, is someone nice and safe to hang out with. Evenings in The Situation can get awfully long.

I have not Googled Mrs. Ted Wilson. The Jenn Rule applies.

(The Jenn Rule provides: It is wrong to Google a person who does not want to be Googled by you. As its name implies, the Rule was promulgated by me to me, in response to my incessant Googling of Jenn, an exhausting but irrepressible habit that did nothing to advance my understanding of how she was doing, if that was in fact my purpose. It dawned on me, after about a year of banging my head against a rigid superficies of data, that Jenn would not want me peering into and sniffing around her life; and it followed that I shouldn't. I would not want her to shadow me online, that's for sure. Once I had established, or discovered, the Jenn Rule, I saw no valid reason to limit its scope to Jenn. Thus, it applied to Mrs. Wilson because she would likewise not want me to Google her. (Note, however, that the Rule does not apply to cases where A, the searcher, is unknown to B, the searchee, who by definition cannot want to not be Googled by A. (Confession: my observation of the Jenn Rule is not really attributable to any uprightness in my character. I broke the Rule many times. It was only when a "Jennifer Horschel" search consistently yielded only third-party Jennifer Horschels (a few do exist) and it came to me that my Jenn had become unsearchable by me—it was only then that I stopped Googling her and found myself in compliance with the Rule. (I was of course terrified by Jenn's sudden virtual absence, but I calmed down when I saw that nothing online or anywhere else pointed to her death. I could and can only conclude that she broke her own rule against getting married and in the process completely shed her maiden name, for which she also had no great fondness, I suspect, especially after some prick at the office thought it would be smart to dub her

J-Ho. Although the tag didn't stick and Jenn claimed to see a funny side, I have to think her feelings were hurt. (I did briefly re-break the Rule in order to track her down under her new identity, and I found out, by viewing the relevant photographs, that none of the Jennifers still working at my old firm was Jenn. Clearly she had also made a professional move. (I stopped my prying there, which again was hardly laudable. To refrain from making investigative phone calls is not exactly a triumph of abnegation. (Is Jenn a mother now? I hope so. Is she happy? I hope so.))))))

While as it were haunting Mrs. Wilson, I'd "see" her raging and weeping about her ex-husband, and it was this, I suppose, that eventually turned my own thoughts to the *disparu*. What happened to him? Where is he now? There was and is no information to be had, not even by way of a rumor. Ted Wilson has never been sighted again in Dubai or, as far as I know, anywhere else. Nowadays it's he, rather than his beautiful first ex-wife, who loiters most often in my thoughts. I locate him fantastically. He is always somewhere in the East. At first I saw him in Bangkok and in Hong Kong, in Kuala Lumpur and Jakarta, and then, as I considered his position more carefully and understood that these places would be too exposed, that he would be able to survive there only by surfacing into identification, I saw him in smaller, still more remote places such as Balikpapan and Makassar and Davao City. I came up with these last-named ports by drifting always eastward on the online atlas, whereupon I'd image-search these specks on the map and understand that they were large, roaring, self-involved cities with refineries and airports and mature economies that likely would not make special deferential provision for the random incoming white man, and I—I mean Ted Wilson, of course—would have to move on still farther, in search of somewhere still smaller and more receptive to a stranger of dislocated competence who must remain incognito and yet keep his head above water. Is such a destiny still possible? It must be; there must be countless Lord Jims out there, bearded beyond recognition, every once in a while glimpsing with horror a face they know. And it may even be possible, I dream out of sympathy with Ted Wilson, that somewhere out there in the isles of the East, in the Sulu Sea or the Banda Sea or the Timor Sea, there is a neglected little port where honorary consuls drink sundowners on verandas, and ceiling fans whir almost in vain, and sinecures are not extinct, and the long call of the orangutan may yet be heard, a green and placid little harbor where an older white man of indefinite occupation may yet, without further inquiry, be received as a gentleman. This is what I imagine, in relation to Ted Wilson.

But here's the thing: the fate of Mrs. Ted Wilson II went undiscussed. It was beyond our pale. It became known, or said, that she had avoided deportation and continued to work as a singer at the Arabian Courtyard, in Bur Dubai. No more was offered, and I made no inquiries. There wasn't anything I could single-handedly do about the general neglect of Mrs. Ted Wilson II, if "neglect" is even the right word. Yet I came to be bothered by the disparity in the attention paid to the Wilson wives, not least by me. I felt ashamed—specifically ashamed, that is, which is to say, filled with a shame additional to the general ignominy that is the corollary of insight, i.e., the ignominy of having thus far lived in error, of having failed, until the moment of so-called insight, to understand what could have been understood earlier, an ignominy only deepened by prospective shame, because the moment of insight serves as a reminder that more such moments lie ahead, and that one always goes forward in error.

Some months ago, I was startled by a phone call from the past. Don Sanchez, the vertical athlete, was in town, and staying at the Arabian Courtyard. I had no memory of giving Don my contact details and had no wish to see him again, decent man though he is, and I really, really didn't want to paint the town red with the guy. It was only because I couldn't resist the possibility of laying eyes on Mrs. Ted Wilson II that I agreed to meet him at the Arabian Courtyard's Sherlock Holmes English Pub. Don wanted to meet "somewhere more adventurous," but I twisted his arm. That wasn't very nice of me, I know, but those were my terms.

The Sherlock Holmes is like so many of the British-themed pubs that have spread all over the planet, a gloomy, friendly, wood-everywhere bar with dark Victorian-style wallpaper and a scattering of TV monitors showing "live" broadcasts of defunct soccer matches. It's a fine establishment, in other words. Don and I ate hamburgers and French fries and drank pints of Foster's. Don explained that this was his "one drinking night": the inaugural Burj Khalifa tower race, which was the reason he'd flown over, was four days away, and his "hydration schedule" allowed for the consumption of his "four last pre-race units" of alcohol that evening. Don needed no prompting to tell me about the physical preparations he'd made for the race, which he said was the "most severe challenge" he'd ever "accepted." He told me he had left the Lincoln Tunnel luxury rental ("I felt I'd gone as far as I could with the setup there") and moved into a fortieth-floor abode on the Upper East Side ("which was lucky timing, because I had no way of knowing that I'd be running the Burj, and frankly the forty-floor track is a superb amenity"). I was hearing all about his nutrition goals and training routine and run plan when the entertainers—two female singers and a male keyboardist—appeared, to the loud clapping of a bunch of Indian dudes who occupied the table next to the little stage.

I was excited myself. While Don shared his recent performance stats and detailed the changes he was making to his stride pattern, I studied the two singers. I'm not an ethnicities expert, but they looked like Filipinas to me—small, brown-skinned, dark-eyed young women with glossy black hair that fell straight to their shoulders. Which one, then, was Mrs. TW2? Reproductive logic suggested that it had to be the older of the two—I assessed her to be in her early thirties—who wore a tight-fitting but entirely respectable very short black dress and high heels, and not the younger one, who looked to be in her early twenties and wore a short, sexy red dress and even higher heels and was the prettier of the two ladies, I guess most people would say, though personally I'm not one to start pitting women against each other in a competition of beauty.

The keyboardist hit the keys, and, before an audience of nine men and a woman, Mrs. TW2 began to sing "Jolene." What a sweet voice! The nightingale of Dubai! She sang the song exactly and effortlessly in Dolly Parton's voice, which is saying something, in my opinion. I further tuned out poor old Don, who was so to speak verbally ascending a tower of data of concern only to himself, ordered another drink, and fell into an ecstatic, inebriated appreciation of Mrs. TW2's artistic abilities. The young singer may have been the object of the Indian dudes' admiration, but I was rooting for the single mother and maritally wronged lead vocalist, who sang with great spirit at a venue whose league she was way out of. When Don suggested we go elsewhere, I bought him another drink and stayed right where I was. When Mrs. TW2 sang "Islands in the Stream," my cup overflowed.

Except that I'd developed a dislike of the keyboardist, a—what, fifty-five-year-old?—white guy in a black shirt and a pair of John Lennon shades. His very long gray hair occasionally fell in front of his gaunt face, and as he played, he would pull the hair back into place with a cruel-looking little finger. From time to time, Mrs. TW2 gave him a frightened glance and received in return an indecipherable signal. The more I studied the onstage dynamic, the stronger grew my conviction that this repellent individual was a Svengali under whose invisible rule these two women, Mrs. TW2 especially, found themselves. You could be sure that he controlled the ensemble's finances and kept for himself the vast bulk of its earnings, a regime he certainly enforced by the malign use of his physical and/or mental powers. What a douche. I felt like going over there and pushing him off his little stool.

There was a break in the music. The Indians confidently called over the younger singer, and she went to join them as if she knew them well—which may have been the case. Acting under the inspiration of their example, and ignoring another request by Don to "make tracks," I waved an inviting hand at Mrs. TW2. She beamed at me but didn't move, ostensibly preferring to drink a glass of Coke with Svengali.

I got to my feet and went to her.

"Hi," I said to her. "Me and my friend"—I gestured toward Don, who appeared to be taking his own pulse—"we were wondering if we could buy you a drink. You're a wonderful singer."

Mrs. TW2 beamed again. "I'm glad you're enjoying the show."

I smiled right back, making sure to blank Svengali, who was right there next to her, in order to demonstrate to Mrs. TW2 that he wasn't all-powerful. Very amiable and harmless, I said, "Where are you from? The Philippines?"

She beamed.

"I'm from the U.S.A.," I said. I said something about "my buddy over there" being in town for the Burj race. "Is that a Coke?" I said.

Now Svengali leaned over to her, and they exchanged words. "I have to sing now," Mrs. TW2 said very happily.

"OK, great," I said, I think. That's when I gave her my card and said something innocuous, along the lines of "If you ever want to get in touch."

Svengali spoke up. "My friend," he said. "This is my wife. Please be respecting."

That got under my skin—the ironic "my friend." I was going

to say something about it, when the "wife" assertion registered. Mrs. Ted Wilson II was now Mrs. Svengali.

"Hey, sorry, man, whatever," I said.

Don Sanchez said, "Well, I'm hitting the hay. It's past my bedtime."

"Me, too," I said. A week or two later, Don e-mailed me a picture of himself in running apparel, arms raised skyward. He'd made it to the top.

Naturally, the incident in the Sherlock Holmes is mortifying to recall. I had too much to drink. I misread the situation. I embarrassed everyone concerned.

Ollie was of the opinion that my blundering was even greater than I thought. When I told him about meeting Mrs. TW2, he said, "How do you even know it was her?"

"I can't be sure," I admitted.

We were having a sundowner at the Code of Hammurabi, which is one of the Unique's six bars/eateries.

Ollie said, "Well, let's hope you're right. Good to know she's landed on her feet."

He was trying to be kind to me, which made me feel a little foolish. I decided to drop the subject, which was, as I've said, by that point regarded as ancient history. Nor was it the occasion to mention that Mrs. TW2, or the person I'd believed, rightly or wrongly, to be Mrs. TW2, was now a Mrs. Svengali, outwardly smiling and singing and inwardly robotic. (I believe that the conjecture retains its validity even if the woman I met was someone other than Mrs. TW2. I saw what I saw.) Ollie doesn't go in for that kind of thinking.

"I might be leaving town," he said.

"Oh? Where to this time?"

"I mean leaving for good. There's this opportunity opening up in Shanghai."

"Oh," I said.

"Yeah, we'll know a bit more in a few months. It depends on a few things falling into place."

"Shanghai," I said. "Cool."

"Yeah. Lynn is pretty psyched. I think she's ready for something new."

"Cool," I said.

Ollie went on to say that although Dubai was a "great market," China was a "truly exceptional market," even allowing for widely expected drops in its GDP growth rates. Ollie said it would be a super place to "headquarter" going forward, although he would of course retain a "strong presence" in the Gulf.

"That makes a lot of sense," I said.

"It'll be an adventure," Ollie said.

This was some months ago. I've heard nothing more about it. Don't go, Ollie. Don't leave me stranded.

Hello, here's the cavalry—Mila. I should get a special bugle tone for her texts.

You want two friends tonight? You can handle???

THE THREESOME. The trio with brio. I'm well aware of the appeal. I've done the porn.

It's not for me. A sexual encounter should retain at least the structure of the real thing, i.e., the one-on-one. The two-on-one, or the one-on-two, or the one-on-one-on-one—these are in formal contradiction, in my opinion, of the raison d'être of the coming together in closeness of persons. The problem of the third person is not the problem of the third wheel, which was solved once and for all, one would think, by the invention of the tricycle. It is the problem of the third as the third. His/her presence abolishes the bilateral relation of the first and the second—already fraught with difficulty—and installs in its place a trilaterality that, by its very multiplication of the possibilities for pleasurable physical interaction, by its generation of a beast with three backs and six arms and six legs and eight holes and one cock, involves the sexual participants in a meta-morphosis in which they are turned into organs of an organism seeking only its sensual organization. Gone is the great promise of mutual caring enabled by one special other, whereby the carers together eliminate the terrible problem of space. (By "space," I don't just mean the isolating sea of interpersonal separation. I also mean the cosmic sea.) Even a fiction of this caring (of the kind I happily settle for in my semi-pro pairings) is impossible. In its place comes a nonfiction of meat and bones, of blow jobs and hand jobs and you-name-it jobs, of stick-that-in-here and my-turn-your-turn-her-turn, of you-do-this-while-he-does-that-and-I-do-this. The falcon cannot hear the falconer. Everything turns to crap.

> One friend please

is my reply to Mila.

I've showered, shaved, and shat, and am all set to head out, when a doorman calls: Mr. Ali is here.

I meet the great man in the lobby. "Well, Ali, how are you keeping? Everything OK?" We shake hands. I tell him, "One more day. Then Alain will be gone."

Ali smiles. "I have information for you, boss," he says. During his brief sabbatical, this most diligent of assistants has made it his business to repeatedly visit the Project X site. "Today, I speak to a man there," he says. "He is American. I ask him, 'What is this building?' He tells me, it is a 'mah-kp.'"

I ask Ali to repeat that last word.

"Mah-kp," Ali repeats. "This is what he says. They are building a very big tower somewhere else. This is the mah-kp."

"A mah-kp? What does that mean?"

Ali cannot tell me. He is relaying what the man told him.

"OK," I say. "That's very helpful. Thank you very much." I'll get to the bottom of this later. "Anything else?"

Ali shakes his head. I give him taxi money and send him on

his merry way. I/Godfrey Pardew also go on our merry way, to the Unique Luxury Resort and Hotel.

I valet-park the Autobiography and brace for the Nubians. They're nowhere to be seen. I breeze unseen past the front desk: a first. It's exhilarating. The childhood dream of invisibility has come to pass.

My hostess is Oksana. She has an amazingly high forehead, very black hair in a ponytail, and small, decidedly elliptical eyes. (Where is she from? I'm guessing Novosibirsk.) The good-time girls I've had dealings with are usually dressed up, and made up, semi-formally and semi-glamorously, as if en route to the commercial attaché's reception. Some even look as though they're about to ice-dance. Oksana looks like she's come back from the gym. She *has* come back from the gym: her discarded gym shoes are over there by the TV.

Good for her, I say.

She lights a cigarette. "You want to fuck?" she says. "You want to drink something?"

"Maybe a drink," I say.

Oksana responds with an eye roll toward the minibar.

I'm getting disdain? I'm being put in touch with my unworthiness? Here? By her? I don't want to sink to the contractual level, but submitting to a personal assessment by Oksana isn't part of the deal. I insist only on niceness, and this isn't being nice. If she doesn't want to be in this room, neither do I.

I'm about say something when I see, on the bedside table, something extraordinary: a Martial Arts Sudoku book, Black Belt.

I ask her, "May I look?"

She sucks on her cigarette. We'll call that a yes.

My God, over half of the puzzles have been solved. The numbers are written down in a flawless, invariable hand. There isn't a correction or marginal notation in sight. These solutions are totally clean.

Oksana is a Black Belt?

"Bravo," I say. "These are very difficult. You must be very intelligent," I say. (Clumsy, I know, but it's incumbent on me to speak to Oksana as if English were a foreign language for me, too.) All I get out of her is more smoke. Very shy, I hold out the book. "Can you teach me? How you do it?"

Oksana is beautiful, I realize. How wonderful it would be to lie on this bed with her doing Sudoku puzzles, laughing and sharing and solving. And then a breakfast of fava beans, and then a car journey on sand flats and corniches, and then a trip by speedboat to an island, and there a small cabin build of clay and wattles made.

Oksana terminates her cigarette. Sitting on the edge of the bed, she begins to remove her clothing, starting with the white socks. Then it's off with the leggings and the T-shirt. In her underwear—sports bra and regular panties—she goes into the bathroom. She locks the door.

Oh, woe is me. Oh, woe is she.

She comes out a few minutes later, wearing a towel-turban and a hotel bathrobe. "OK," she says, lighting up again. "First, money. Then we fuck."

Clearly, Oksana isn't aware of the protocol. I explain to her that I pay Mila and Mila pays her.

"Mila will not pay me," Oksana says. "My friends tell me this."

I didn't come here to argue and bargain and transact.

"How much?" I say. The evening has now been spoiled.

"Two hundred American," she says. "This is what Mila promise."

Two hundred? Out of five hundred? Mila gets to keep three hundred bucks plus tip? I've never heard of a booking agent taking 60 percent plus. It's unconscionable. I cannot be party to such an arrangement. The Mila connection can no longer be.

I'm carrying cash. I pay two hundred dollars and make an announcement. "I'm sorry, but I have a headache. I will go home now."

Her eyes narrow even more; one glimpses the steppe, wild horses, the Great Khan. "You are angry? You make problem for me?"

"No problem," I say. "I'm happy, really. I just have a head-ache." I smile. "It was nice meeting you."

I see myself to the door. It's bye-bye, my Black Belt, and it's farewell and adieu, Godfrey Pardew.

Another solo celibate night in The Situation it is.

I get in, or on, the Pasha for a twenty-minute session. After three hundred seconds, I can't take one more rub of the roller. Off, or out, I get.

Night has fallen, and it's safe for me to approach the windows and look out. When I try this in daylight, I keep re-seeing that shadow, or bird, or dropping thing, out of the corner of my eye, and I find myself jerking my head leftward time and again, always too late to catch sight of it. It's uncontrollable. It does no good to remind myself that in all probability I saw nothing in the first place and my post-traumatic flashbacks, if that's what we're talking about, are founded on a trauma that never occurred. The falling shadow nonetheless appears; my head nonetheless jerks over my shoulder. This has been going on for a few days, and it's not getting any better, i.e., it's getting worse. It's got to the point where I can't take in the view from my apartment until the sun has set and all is dark. Is this what I've come to? Nocturnality? I have to keep a vampire's hours?

What with the moonlight and the lunar/man-made glow of the Marina, I have no problem discerning the pale X of Project X—the "mah-kp."

I permutate the vowels: "make-up"; "mark-up"; "mock-up."

Mock-up. Let's consult the sum of all human knowledge. Let's Wiki it.

In manufacturing and design, a mockup, or mock-up, is a scale or full-size model of a design or device, used for teaching, demonstration, design evaluation, promotion, and other purposes.

No mention of the construction of buildings. I Google "mockup + building." Here we go: a "pre-construction mockup" is not uncommon, it seems. It seems that "scale representations" of "exterior wall systems" and "other structures" may be useful to builders, engineers, and architects, for a variety of purposes.

It follows that Project X is a scale representation of part of another building. It is, if I correctly recall what Ali told me, a representation of part of the "very big tower" they're building "somewhere else."

So Project X isn't a project at all. It's a dummy run. It's a mock-up. There's no actual residential proposition going up down there. The action has moved somewhere else. Privilege Bay is toast and The Situation is fucked. The Uncompromising Few and the Pioneers of Luxury™ and the Dreamers of New Dreams must be re-named.

I'm going to bed.

And in the morning, immediately on waking up, I am jolted by gladness as I see blue sky through the window, and spontaneously I get out of bed and empty my bladder. The joy of this routine—invariably, the happiest time of my day—is, unfortunately, a simple matter of oblivious recurrence: in the drowsiness of renewed consciousness, the current blue morning is indistinguishable from the blue mornings of yore. I forget where I am and where things stand and what lies ahead. Then I remember.

It's the kid's last day. I'll get through it. Then Ali and I will regroup.

There's no sign of Alain at the office, though. His driver usually deposits him at 11:00 a.m. sharp. It's not till an hour later that a Batros shows—and it's Sandro. He makes straight for my chair.

"OK, so who is this guy—Ali," he says.

"What do you mean, who is he?"

"That's what I mean: who is he? Why's he here?"

"He's my assistant. He's worked in this office for a long time. You've seen him a million times."

Sandro says, "What are his qualifications? Where'd he go to college? Where're his references?"

What is he talking about? "Sandro, he's an office boy. He gets paid peanuts. I don't need references. He's a superb worker. I trust him totally."

Sandro nods. "You trust him. Right."

"Yeah, I do. He's one hundred percent honest."

"More honest than my son?"

"What?"

"You're saying he's more honest than my son?"

"I don't understand the question," I say, even though I do understand that this is big trouble.

He smiles at me like a mafioso. "Alain says he didn't shake your guy down. He says your guy is making it up."

"Why would he make it up?"

"You tell me," Sandro says. Oh no—he's spotted my rubber stamps. He takes one and bangs it on my blotter. "Why would my son lie?"

I say, "Alain's a terrific kid, but he's a kid. Kids are always making stuff up, saying stuff that's not accurate, denying stuff. They're kids. They screw up."

"These things are really great," Sandro says. He's trying out another stamp, pressing it into the wrong ink pad. *Bang.* "You made Alain go with this guy to the bathroom?" *Bang.*

Very carefully, like a lawyer, I say, "You requested that Alain be weighed. Alain wished to be weighed in the bathroom, which was entirely appropriate. I asked Ali to accompany Alain to the bathroom to take note of the weight readings. He did not accompany Alain into the stall. Alain was in the stall by himself. When Alain stood on the scale, Ali could see the reading through the gap at the bottom of the stall. All he ever saw of Alain was his feet. If you recall, you oversaw the procedure the first day it happened."

"Don't tell me what I recall and what I don't recall," Sandro says. *Bang.* "You let this guy, this stranger, take my son to the bathroom and be alone with him there."

I'm trained for these situations. You have to push back, firmly and calmly. "I put in place, with your approval, an appropriate procedure for carrying out your instructions."

He grabs another stamp. *Bang. Bang.* "I asked Alain if he was comfortable with the arrangement. He told me he wasn't. I said, Why not? No answer. I asked him did this guy, Ali, did this guy try anything funny. You know what he said? Nothing. I'm like, Did he or didn't he? He didn't want to talk about it."

He's building a case out of a non-answer to a leading question? Has he gone mad?

"He told me something else," Sandro says. Now he's handling one of my embossers. "Your friend is an illegal. That right?"

"He's a bidoon. I e-mailed you about it a long time ago. What about it?"

"You know what? I'll be the judge of what you e-mailed me, OK?"

"I'll send you a copy, to refresh your memory," I say.

"Don't worry about it, he's fired," Sandro says. "I don't want to see his face again." He says, "How does this thing work?" He's put a sheet of paper in the embosser's jaws. "Do I just . . . ?" *Crump.* "That's neat."

"If you fire Ali, I'm quitting." I say this serenely, because I've thought through and fantasized this scenario many times. I am ninety-nine percent sure Eddie will be in my corner. He's not going to lose a high-value asset (me) on account of his crazy brother's whims.

Sandro says, "*If* I fire him? I just did."

"In that case, I quit."

"In that case, I'm calling security."

Another line borrowed from TV. Or maybe Sandro, too, has often dreamed of this moment and knows his script backward. I get the cardboard box I've set aside for just this eventuality, and I rapidly box my personal embossers and stamps and the other possessions I keep here, which are very few. "Here," I say, and with great satisfaction I toss Sandro my Batros employee's I.D. card and credit card.

"The car keys," Sandro says, wiggling his fingers. I almost forgot. The Autobiography is his, not mine. I hand over the keys.

Back at The Situation, the first thing I do is e-mail Eddie.

I'm sorry to inform you that, with effect from 12:36 PM today, I am no longer serving as the Batros Family Officer and related positions. Earlier this morning, Sandro capriciously and in bad faith terminated the employment of Ali, my assistant. This action, along with various actions taken and statements made by Sandro on this and on other occasions, makes it impossible for me to discharge my responsibilities and/or remain in my job. I will happily provide you with more details, if you wish. Please note that I have not resigned. I have accepted the unlawful repudiation of my contract of service and am entitled to compensation on that basis.

I look forward to receiving your proposal of financial settlement.

Eddie responds within the hour:

Your resignation is not accepted old amigo. I'm in New York. Why don't you fly over tonight and we'll talk it over.

I knew it. When backs are against the wall, Eddie will come out shooting.

FROM THE BELT PARKWAY, the city looks ragged. Manhattan shows in distant dribs and drabs. The three-quarters-built Freedom Tower, if that's still its name, looks—I'm afraid there is no other word for it—unintelligent. I saw the Burj Khalifa at a comparable stage of completion. The Arabian spire had the natural inwit of a blade of grass. Its American counterpart, for all its massiveness, looks like a stump—a gargantuan remnant. From my inspection through the taxi window, I actually find it hard to accept that this protrusion is indeed the so-called Freedom Tower. The building seems, as I say, not without nationalistic embarrassment, dumb—a meathead tower. It's not even that tall. Mistrustful as I am of the first impression; conscious as I am of my limitations as a critic of architecture; wary though I may be of the personal ruling: I cannot hold back a thumbs-down.

This is my first time back in New York since I left, four years ago/yesterday; it's the first time I've set foot in the land of President Obama. My basic reaction is one of unaccountable infuriation. It gets under my skin that the Belt is as worn-down as ever, with the same potholes and, I'm almost prepared to swear, the very same orange-striped traffic cones marking off the same dormant roadworks. The same battered NYPD saloons lurk roadside with the same lethargic and dangerous cops inside them; and the proud, industrious *Volk* still drives around as if the Rockaways mark the end of the factual world. I'm being irrational, I recognize. To interpret is to misinterpret, never more so than when one is gripped by the prejudicial dismay that's typical, so I've gathered, of the expatriate on his or her return home from brand-new Dubai, who must acclimatize to the older, stick-in-the-mud society of origin, and must be careful neither to overprize nor to overestimate her new knowledge, and of course must reconcile himself to the subtle pigheadedness of his native country, which will withhold from her any interest in, let alone understanding of or esteem for, her overseas experience and the value-adding perspective it has granted, and will not give an inch, and will force the returner from Dubai into one more contemplation of his inefficiency. So it's not surprising that I'm exasperated as my taxi edges toward downtown Brooklyn and its Marriott hotel, and offended by everything, even the poor old sun, modestly falling into New Jersey. It holds itself out as a bright cloud, and does nothing wrong.

The psychologizer will say that something is afoot, and the psychologizer will be correct. This is J-Town, and I'm having Jenn-jitters. Even though I have no information as to her current whereabouts, I'm very afraid of running into her. I'm well aware that, in terms of probabilities, this is like worrying about being waylaid by Jerry Seinfeld—but guess what, I once walked right by Jerry Seinfeld, on Broadway at Seventy-Seventh Street. That's why I'm spending the night in a Brooklyn hotel, because Brooklyn, in Jenn's mind, is another extension of the Lehigh Valley, and a borough of shame. And it's not only to avoid road traffic that I travel by subway to my meeting with Eddie: in Jenn's mind, the subway is a zone of shame.

I don't want to make her out to be a snob. She isn't, or wasn't; she was prepared to live in a rent-stabilized one-bedroom, after all. It's just that she was involved in a quest for metropolitan dignity. This plucky, meritorious girl from ABE was trying make good, and my job was to cheer her on and, when the going got tough, as it will, to cheer her up, i.e., to run out into the rain for DVDs, and open a bottle of wine, and lay me down like a bridge over troubled water. Talk about cluelessness. Talk about underestimating the loneliness of the viaduct. But what was the clued-in alternative? One still has no idea. One's heart goes out to this young couple on the A train who drowsily lean on each other as they hurtle toward Manhattan and who knows what else.

He rudely shoves her: she has accidentally drooled on his shoulder. He's very upset. He likes his jacket, and now his jacket has drool on it. He calls her a name. The train stops, and he gets up. She sort of screams at him to stay, and follows him. She's pregnant, I see, this nineteen- or twenty-year-old Hispanic girl who wears very high platforms. The train lurches into motion, and she loses her balance and begins to topple over. Instinctively, I move to one side and catch her.

She shouts at me—Get the fuck away from me, asshole.

I've got my hands up as if it's a stickup. I'm looking around the carriage for confirmation that this criticism is outrageous and I'm without blame and in point of fact saved the day. I get nothing but blank faces. Now here comes the knight in shining armor, the boyfriend, all fuck this and fuck that, and getting in my face, pointing and gesturing and threatening, and bitch this and cracker that.

"What did you call me?" I say. "Cracker?" Now my face is right up against his. "Say it one more time. Call me that one more time."

The girl is still shouting at me and making accusations.

I call you what I like, bitch cracker, the boy says.

Everyone's watching now. Everyone's waiting to see what I'm going to do next.

I've made a mistake. I'm looking at a lose-lose-lose-lose-lose-lose.

The train brakes: West Fourth Street. I get out, as if it's my stop. The boy is yelling and laughing at me from the door of the train. His girlfriend is next to him, screaming with laughter and pride, hanging out of the door, standing by her man. I have brought them together. As they are pulled away, they mouth more insults at me and bang on the train windows. This will be one of the great stories of their romance.

I walk toward the station exit, sweating and shaking. I have to take care to not mutter audibly, because I'm thinking of things to say to the kid. Then another A train roars into the station. I can board it and be in the clear. Nobody on this train knows me: a new train is a new beginning and a clean slate. Not quite. I'm still in New York, where I am ignominious. I remember all too well how it began.

This was during the awful period when Jenn and I were co-workers but no longer involved. My office interactions were getting stranger. Colleagues had started to act with the weirdly chirpy and compliant standoffishness that is usually reserved for crazy neighbors, bores, people with halitosis, etc. When I engaged them in conversation, they'd say, "Got it," or "Absolutely," or "You bet, X.," and then they'd be out of there.

(Almost immediately after its aggressive introduction by Human Resources, my first initial became my office handle: everybody called me X., even clients. (Even Jenn, even after I told her I didn't like it. "Please," I eventually insisted, "can you not call me that?" "It's alluring," she said. "It makes you kind of mysterious. How many other X.s do you know?" "I don't like it," I said. "It's not my name. It's not me." (To her credit, she did as I asked. But she was right: that goddamned X. made my name unique and that much easier to drag through the mud. If I state that John Smith is a coward, no John Smith will lose sleep. John Smiths have safety in numbers, like the gnus of the savannah. If I state that Q. John Smith is a coward, a gnu is separated from the herd. The predators are in business.)))

I was in my Lincoln Tunnel luxury rental, drinking and Googling my evenings away, when I decided, maybe guided by some sixth sense, to search an unusual person—me; that is, I Googled the professional name that was, as I say, thanks to the accursed X., distinctively mine. As I typed, the Autocomplete function spontaneously offered search suggestions. The following appeared in the search box next to my name:

attorney
sexual harassment

embezzlement
tiny cock

Naturally, I was horrified. Anyone who Googled me—as clients and professional colleagues did, all the time—would see this list. They would think less of me. It would make no difference if they followed the search suggestions and duly discovered that there was no actual Web content connecting me to sexual harassment, or embezzlement, or a tiny cock, and/or if they understood that these Autocomplete suggestions were not the results of multiple arm's-length searches by disinterested parties but had been generated by a malicious person or persons Googling me again and again and again in conjunction with the words suggested by Autocomplete in order to create the defamatory and false impression that I was somehow infamously involved in scandals of money-related dishonesty and inappropriate workplace behavior toward subordinates, and on top of it all was notorious for being meagerly endowed. Even if the Googler understood all of this—understood that I was the victim of a fiendish new form of defamatory publishing that one might term "search libel"—I would still be lowered in his/her estimation for the simple, unfair reason that whoever is (whether rightly or wrongly or inaccurately or correctly) publicly ridiculed or embarrassed automatically suffers a loss of reputation and respect. Nor would it change anything if I were to make some sort of public announcement making clear that I was not, and had never been, implicated in any kind of financial or sexual wrongdoing. That would only aggravate the publicity. A fortiori if I were to post online a photograph that would quash beyond peradventure the nonsense about my being not well hung.

There was nothing to be done. I consulted, in the strictest confidence and professional privilege, an attorney who specialized in verbal torts. She expressed the opinion that this was a very interesting case. She advised that the absence of any express statement, whether defamatory or otherwise, made problematic even a defamation claim based on innuendo, since an innuendo was an unstated secondary meaning contingent on the existence of a stated primary meaning. She pointed out that the text originated algorithmically from a computer program, Autocomplete, rendering complex even the basic issue of authorship. She stated that, as a practical matter, there was no reliable way to identify the responsible spiteful human searcher or searchers. She told me, as if in admiration, that whoever had done this was possessed of low legalistic cunning.

"Do you know who it is?" she asked.

I said, "I have no idea."

The lawyer looked curious. "Really? We could always send her a cease and desist."

I felt that conclusions were being jumped to about the gender of the person injuring me. I couldn't say for sure that it was Jenn or some other female in the office or elsewhere. And the world was filled with male malice. Without making any claim to moral rarity, I wasn't about to go down the road of unfairness. "I'm sorry," I said. "I wish I could tell you, but I can't."

"In that case, I'd try not to worry about it," the specialist in speech wrongs said. "It'll go away. Enmity is a lot of work. People get tired. They move on."

I was alarmed by how she'd put it: enmity. The earth contained a person, or persons, with the will to cause me harm. It was hard to grasp. I could understand hatred and rage and pain. I could understand ruthlessness—one person falling under the wheels of another's advance—and I could understand tsunamis and bolts of lightning. What I couldn't understand was acting with a calculated and methodical intent to damage a fellow human for the sake of making that human suffer damage. I still cannot understand it.

In one respect, my adviser was wrong. My enemy did not

tire or move on. The search libel did not go away. When Sandro Batros flew into town to talk to me about Donald Trump, I received him as a savior.

And now I'm meeting Eddie to save me from Sandro.

We're having dinner at Per Se. The maître d' leads me to the best table, by the famous big window, with views of sparkling traffic and the wonderful night-time blackness of Central Park. Eddie is waiting for me, and embraces me. I'm still rattled by the subway altercation and pretty rattled generally, so it feels unusually good to get a big hug out of someone who knows me from way back and, now that I think of it, in Dublin once had lunch with my parents, at the Stag's Head. He may be the only person I'm still in touch with who knew me when I was not yet orphaned. This fills me with emotion.

"Let's get a drink in you," he says.

And we drink, and we eat, and we talk about student days. Over Irish coffees, I say, "Maeve MacMahon—remember her?"

"Maeve MacMahon," Eddie says. He shakes his head, amazed. "Maeve MacMahon." The words make a dark, beautiful sorrow. Eddie says, "Where is she now, I wonder? Maeve MacMahon."

Where, indeed? Where has everyone gone? Where is everybody?

It's time, I feel, to get to the point. "Eddie, about Sandro—"

He stops me with a signal of the hand. *"Ne parlons pas de cette bêtise, mon vieux,"* he states. "Forget it. It never happened. There's something else we need to talk about."

He asks me if I've recently heard from the authorities in Dubai. I'm about to say no, when I remember (because I'm bureaucratically competent) the Joint Notice from the Dubai Financial Services Authority and the International Humanitarian City Authority. I was supposed to meet these jokers the day after tomorrow, Tuesday. I mention this to Eddie, and he says, "Yes, that's what I'm talking about. Now, listen carefully."

I listen carefully, and I really don't like what I'm hearing.

In executive summary: the Dubai authorities are about to formally launch an investigation into possible malfeasance by the Batros Foundation. It is suspected that certain charitable activities of the Foundation—specifically, the provision and operation of health clinics for the African poor—have been used as a vehicle for laundering monies ("Many millions of dollars," Eddie says, when I press him) debited without authority (i.e., stolen) from Libyan banks and transferred, via a series of offshore intermediaries, to the Foundation in Dubai, which has accepted these monies as donations. ("I don't know the details," Eddie claims. "I've got nothing to do with Africa. But what I'd like to know is, how are our people supposed to know if a donation is legit or not?") Apparently there are further questions about the redistribution of these donations to African sub-charities, i.e., whether the money in question was devoted to the Foundation's charitable purposes or whether, in fact, it made its way back to the thieves/donors/money launderers. "It's all very probably a big nothing," Eddie says, "but that's not the point. Apparently the Libyans are pretty steamed up about their missing cash, and Dubai feels it has to do something. This needs careful handling."

"I can see that," I say.

Eddie says, "The problem, from your point of view, is that, as the Foundation Treasurer, your name is all over these transfers to Africa."

I say, "I think you'll find that my role has always been pro forma. I have disclaimers stamped all over the recent transfers. My position is very clear."

Eddie is sympathetic. "I'm sure it is, but they're going to look for accountability. You know that. They're not going to let technicalities get in their way."

Accountability? What's going on?

Eddie says, "What we're hearing from Mahmud, and I can

tell you he's reliable, is they're going to go after you. To make an example of you."

"But I've done nothing wrong."

"I know that. Everybody knows that. But that's not what this is about."

I'm stunned.

"Listen," Eddie says, leaning forward. "You're not going back there. That's what I'm telling you. You're staying right here. You do not go back to Dubai."

"Wait a minute. I've done nothing wrong—and *my* head rolls?"

Eddie makes a dismissive gesture. "We don't know that. We don't know how it's going to pan out. We're getting our lawyers all over it. We've got Mahmud on the case. They're going to raise hell. You're going to come out of this just fine."

I'm spluttering. "It's monstrous. I have to fight this. What's it going to look like if I stay here? I'm going to be a fugitive from justice? Eddie, I'm an attorney. If they do me for money laundering, I'm finished. I'm on the street."

Eddie says, "We'll figure something out. We'll take care of you."

"How are you going to do that? This is my good name we're talking about."

"Your name?" He laughs. "What name? Nobody has a name." He leans forward once more. "Look," he says, "you don't have a job to go back to. As of now. I hereby terminate your employment. Do you understand? There's nothing to go back to."

I'm fired? Again? "Why am I fired? What are the grounds?"

"Come on, now," Eddie says. "Don't be like that. Here," he says, filling my wineglass. He raises his glass, and I'm in such a daze, I do the same. "Land without rent and death in old Ireland," Eddie says, as if this were a toast from the old days, which it isn't.

IT'S NOT JUST BECAUSE I'm half-asleep, blinking stars, and maybe not entirely sober—Eddie and I wound up singing "Dirty Old Town" in a bar near Times Square at three in the morning, and I returned to the Marriott only so as to pick up my suitcase en route to Heathrow—that, when I arrive at Dubai International Airport, Terminal 3, it's as if I'm a dreamer. From the gate, one passes on a moving walkway through an unprecedented forest of silver-colored pillars and then, by the paranormal merger of escalator and floor, one is delivered to the border-control stations, an archipelago of kiosks between which coasting border controllers, their all-white apparel copied in the sheen of the floor, make oneiric white shadows. I sail through their attentions. The dream intensifies. I am in a vast white palace filled with rows of the grandest white columns in the world. These fluted, mysteriously twinkling, enormous uprights, maybe ten feet in diameter, point to a civilization, wiser and more advanced than ours, elsewhere in the cosmos and elsewhere in time, and the sensation of otherworldly transportation— not expected by the air traveler, who has the idea that she has completed her journey—is reinforced by the decorative metal band on the white ceiling above the central concourse, an airy argentine river containing lights and the images of the same lights, reflected from the marble floor, and the images of those images: this overhead reflection of reflections, a pluperfect constellation, is repeated underfoot, where the dots of light on the ceiling, an infinity, are optically doubled; and so there are heavens above and heavens below. This is the realm of the luggage carousels. Gigantic circling coelacanths, their scaly black belts carry suitcases from Manchester and Trivandrum and the Seychelles. It almost feels like an option to hop aboard and go around like a bag for ten minutes and be picked up and towed away on one's little wheels and, in the fullness of time, be taken wherever—Dar es Salaam, Rio de Janeiro, Ho Chi Minh City. A taxi and an elevator move me from the airport to my bed, and I wake up on a Tuesday morning refreshed and clear-eyed—and still it seems as if I'm dreaming.

There is no awaking from the facts. I have no job, no car, and (a futile attempt at online banking confirms) no access to my dirhams: my bank has frozen my accounts, presumably upon being notified, by the Batros Group, that my contract of service has been terminated. I have no right to be here. Unless I promptly find employment—very difficult for anyone, in this economy; very, very difficult, for the tainted job seeker—I will be forced to pack my bags: a foreigner is permitted to live in this country only if, and for so long as, she or he is a worker sponsored by an employer. ("Employer," in this sense, cannot include oneself: the sole contractor or freelancer is a juridical nonentity in Dubai. One cannot be one's own boss.)

And I have no Ali. I'm assuming he, too, has been formally canned. I cannot be sure, because he is not responding to my messages. That isn't illogical. I am no longer his manager; he is free to ignore me. And why wouldn't he? I put him in the way of harm. I failed him.

Yet from a different tributary of feeling come strength and excitement. I'm pumped up as I head off to the DIFC for my encounter with the regulators. They want a piece of me? I'll give them a piece of me.

When I arrive at the FSA office, high up in The Gate, I'm told the rendezvous has been canceled. After waiting around and pushing for answers, I'm informed that the regulators have been made aware that I'm no longer a Batros employee and that consequently they lack jurisdiction to meet with me. It does no good to explain that I offer myself as a volunteer, in order to be of assistance. There will be no encounter.

So be it. My day will come. I will have my say. This will not stand.

"This will not stand," I repeat to Ollie, very importantly. We have convened for an emergency drink, in the afternoon, at Calabar. Our table overlooks the artificial lake that serves as a waterfront for Dubai Mall. I well remember the huge cavity that was here before, and I regret not having witnessed the record-breaking inundation that produced this body of water.

Ollie says, "What won't stand?" When I start to reply, he interrupts with "Yeah, I know all that. I'm just saying, there's nothing to take a stand against. I know they've sacked you, but what you're talking about hasn't happened. Nobody's coming after you—yet."

"You think they won't?"

Ollie says, "I wouldn't stick around to find out. I'd be gone. There's nothing for you here except a shitstorm. Mate, get out while the going's good."

I don't answer him. What Ollie doesn't understand is that I will not be bounced from country to country. I can be pushed only so far and no farther. There comes a point when I draw a line in the sand.

Ollie says, "Are you all right for money? Just say the word."

I'm OK, I tell him. (Although my Dubai cash is inaccessible, I have funds in my New York account—26,455.70 USD—and I have my old New York credit cards. I'm not completely illiquid.) To be honest, I'm a little disappointed with my old buddy of the depths. When I told him about Sandro's despicable conduct, he didn't really react. I'm not expecting Ollie to tell Sandro Batros to go fuck himself and find someone else to take care of his fungal feet; but I think I detect, in his demeanor, evidence of a self-interested computation: he has his commercial interests to consider. This unspoken reckoning of utilities may not be inconsistent with mateship, but neither is it pretty.

"Look, I can't skip town," I tell him. "It's a question of principle."

Ollie takes a swig of pineapple juice and clatters his glass on the table. "Fair enough," he says. "I won't be around to see it all go down, unfortunately."

A cold, cold chill. "Shanghai?" Why is this word, Shanghai, in my life?

"Yeah," Ollie says. He tells me that they've found a great pre-school for Charlie, and an apartment that's "smallish, but fantastic. We're even shipping out Walda, the nanny." Ollie says that he's started to get excited, and I believe him. He's already calling it Shangers.

"Sweet," I say.

A little while later, we part company. The world goes on. It doesn't care—unless it has you in its sights.

I have long had my suspicions about the escape to figuration—the flight to metamorphic representation of which I'm so often guilty. How can A be turned into B? Doesn't A = A? Isn't B really a way to hide A? Yet I'm also aware that the great personages of the history of thinking, to whom I owe my small measure of liberty from ignorance, have seen fit to deploy apparent misrepresentations in order to progress into the unknown. It's in the spirit of the doomed, last-ditch sortie that I embrace the idea of the submarine to attempt to account for the deep element of illusion into which, it feels like, I have been hurled, as if—and here one definitively leaves behind the stockade of the literal—as if at some point in one's past one was thrown unconscious overboard, and one has only now gained an awareness of one's situation, which is that of the human person going downward in water, and one is in a fix, to put it mildly, and heedless fish-people swim by, and a terrible bathyal reality prevails, and one can only go down, and cannot breathe, and one's humanness has no medium. The perils of such a fantasia are evident—what about people who have actually been thrown overboard, for example? Is their experience to be frivolously appropriated? Nonetheless, once I'm restored from my aquatic delirium, I'm left with a new, possibly valuable, clue-like question: when was I tossed into the sea? Because, as I review my history of living without a feeling of insight, I cannot say that it all started yesterday, at Dubai International Airport. I have trouble identifying a moment, if I may flip the question, about which I can say, At that moment, I certainly had not yet gone under; at that moment, I was on the good ship. Indeed it seems to me that every epoch of my life has involved a snorkeler of sorts, a gasper . . . O brightening glance! There must be a way to Wiki this. There must be an answer.

I go to sleep. When I stir, at dawn in The Situation, nothing has changed. The facts are all still there. Tomorrow is not a new day.

Except that sometimes the details are new. Today's new detail is Watson. Watson is the most trusted and put-upon Batros lawyer in Dubai, and all of our dealings have been pleasant and successful. I would not go so far as to call him a friend, but I will say that I like and respect him and have reason to hope he feels the same way about me. "Good morning," he says on the intercom, "I was wondering if I might come up. I've got some paperwork here, I'm afraid."

"Of course," I say.

Watson accepts coffee. He asks for permission to sit at the table, and he waits for me to join him before he reaches for his briefcase, and he asks for permission to place the briefcase on the table. Again, I grant permission. I must say that I warm to this man. He is a compact, reticent Scot. "Please accept this by way of personal service," he says, handing me a document titled "Terms of Settlement."

I read the document. The "Reason for Termination" is stated to be "Gross Misconduct." My "End of Service Benefits" are stated to be "None."

I say, "Right, well, of course I take issue with all of that."

Watson bows his head. "Your countersignature isn't necessary," he says, "but it would make life easier. And I'm going to need your passport," he says. He explains that the company will cancel my employment visa, which will be followed by the cancellation of my residence visa. I will then have thirty days to leave. "In the circumstances," Watson says, the company "declines" to make the customary payment of repatriation expenses.

I say to him, "Tell me about the gross misconduct. I have no idea what I'm supposed to have done."

Watson says, "I'm not able to help you with that today, I'm afraid."

"I'm very, very unhappy about this," I say. "They're making me the fall guy. It's completely unacceptable."

Watson says, "You're aware the Dubai police are taking an interest in this matter?"

"Let them. I've done nothing wrong."

Watson bows. "May I speak unofficially—collegially?" I tell him he may. Wearing the hat of the colleague, Watson says, "My guess is that the authorities will not confine their investigations to your role at the Foundation." He says, "I apprehend there are some question marks about your dealings with Alain Batros. Privately tutoring children is against the law here. For the protection of minors."

"That's ridiculous. He was an intern, for God's sake."

"If you gave him academic help," Watson says, "there may be a perception that you unlawfully acted as his tutor in the privacy of your office. And there's the question"—Watson raises a finger to cut me off—"there's the concern about Mr. Ali's dealings with Alain, and your role in those dealings."

"You've got to be joking," I say.

Watson says, "Your corporate computer would appear to have been put to illegal use. The technicians have found an unauthorized virtual network, and somebody has used your computer to make visits to pornographic websites. That's a problem, obviously."

I deem it best to say nothing.

Watson says, "Does the name Godfrey Pardew mean anything to you?"

So that's how it's going to play out. I'm a fiend. I'm a round-the-clock criminal.

Really, Eddie? You would do this?

"Collegially," I say, "how do you think it would pan out?"

Watson says, "In my experience, someone in your position should have at the forefront of his mind the real possibility of a criminal conviction and a lengthy custodial sentence—five to ten years is by no means out of the question. In any event, you're looking at hostile, complex, expensive, drawn-out legal proceedings: best-case scenario, a lengthy investigation coupled with house arrest. The house arrest could go on for years, as I'm sure you're aware."

Watson is only telling me what everybody here already knows. A handful of men have famously chosen to fight for their honor in Dubai rather than be convicted in absentia of crimes (relating to financial failures, almost invariably) of which they claim to be innocent. By and large, it seems to have not worked out for them, insofar as one receives continuing reports about their suffering and/or mistreatment in prison and/or in the court system and/or while under house arrest for the duration of indefinite "investigations" (i.e., in a halfway house between guilt and innocence in which the compulsorily domesticated party is denied the creditable adversity of being in jail and, simultaneously, the good standing associated with so-called freedom).

I ask Watson straight out: "What do you suggest?"

He gets up, takes his first and only sip of coffee. "I'll come back in a couple of hours to collect your passport. If I were you, I'd think very carefully about whether you want to be here. I understand that I may not be the only visitor you receive this afternoon."

"I see," I say, quite literally, because I'm envisioning Dubai policemen charging in and taking me away.

We shake hands. "Thank you for your hospitality," he says.

No sooner have I closed the door behind Watson than I start packing. Mysteriously, I find myself moving with the efficiency of an assembly-line worker, i.e., someone who has performed my actions thousands of times. I limit myself to that quantity of belongings capable of fitting into one laptop bag and one carry-on case. The decision is easily made, because I have nothing physical I'm attached to, and because to eliminate stuff is a dark, strong joy. There is the temptation to keep going—to eliminate even one's only bag. The temptation must be resisted, arising as it does from a mistaking of actual luggage with that which is dragged around psychically. Ridding oneself for a perfectly wearable pair of underpants solves nothing.

I must not, in my haste, forget my passport. Very good: it's still valid. Mine is the new, so-called biometric edition. A huge bald-eagle head dominates the page above my photograph. The bald eagle would only have to lean over to gobble up my head. These days, the U.S. passport looks like a picture book for children. To flip through it is to contemplate, beneath festive clusters of exit and entry stamps, renderings in pen-and-ink of an alleged American quintessence: a farmer and two oxen plowing the prairie; cowboys riding with cattle; a grizzly bear devouring a salmon; a Mississippi steamboat; a sailing ship off the New England shore; and so on. This folksy, somewhat ominous little graphic paperback ends with an image of North America viewed from space, as if through the eyes of an awed celestial being. The moon is in the picture, too, perhaps to indicate our nation's extraterrestrial reach.

The blue pages put me in mind of the carpets of Zurich, pale-blue fields on which I daily spent hours playing and massacring with the plastic little cowboys and soldiers and Indian braves that served as dolls for small boys of my generation. These battles—G.I.s firing bazookas at the redskins behind the table leg, flamethrowers clearing gladiators out of the deeppile—connected the young me to his rumored fatherland, for which I felt a homesickness that strangely only deepened when I moved there. It is from this era that I retain one of my few ineliminable memories of my mother. She is standing at the sink, washing up in Switzerland.

There are quotations above the pictures, I see:

> Let every nation know, whether it wishes us well or ill, that we shall pay any price, bear any burden, meet any hardship, support any friend, oppose any foe, in order to assure the survival and the success of liberty.
> *John F. Kennedy*

> Let us raise a standard to which the wise and honest can repair.
> *George Washington*

> The cause of freedom is not the cause of a race or a sect, a party or a class—it is the cause of humankind, the very birthright of humanity.
> *Anna Julia Cooper*

My country is now in the sixth grade?

I bear in mind that expatriation is distortive. I accept the proposition that I wrongly see the U.S.A. as a Jenn-land and my feelings about it are accordingly twisted. I quash my rebel's excitement. I factor into my thinking the panic of the fugitive. I reject as unreliable and extraneous to the decision I must make the jolt of abhorrence caused by my passport and my sudden insight that American nationhood is part of an outdated worldwide protection racket and that it should be possible, surely, to live without a state's say-so. I set to one side all theories and systems. Bailiffs, clear the room: Jenn, Don Sanchez, the Batroses, the three Ted Wilsons, the contempible couple from the A train—I want all of them out. I must be left alone. I must deliberate.

I will deliberate in the Pasha. When I take a seat, I shift a little in order to remove my passport from a buttock pocket. The egg-shaped blue marks of the Department of Homeland Security declare ADMITTED and ADMITTED and ADMITTED.

The phone. Ali!

"Ali!" I say, clambering out of the Pasha. "How are you? Are you OK?"

"I am at the airport, boss," Ali says.

He's one step ahead of me, as always. He has foreseen my departure and is in position to wave goodbye.

From what he next tells me, I gather that Ali is about to board a plane. I gather that his application for Emirati citizenship somehow resulted in an unrefusable offer of citizenship of the Union of the Comoros. I gather that he has a wife and two children. I gather he is now about to leave for the Comoro Islands in the company of his wife and two children. I gather he has no option. I gather that, as a Comorian national, he can no longer be in Dubai because he now has another place where he can be.

"I want to say thank you, boss," Ali says. "You have helped me."

"No, I thank you, Ali" is all I can think to say to him. "Good luck to you and your family. Stay in contact," I say, very stupidly, because there is no way that Ali and I will be able to stay in contact. "OK," he says, and he disconnects. My friend is gone.

But gone how? To what effect? Not to devalue Ali's subjectivity, but for me his fate lacks depth. The Comoros?

Surely there's time for one last search.

The top search suggestion is "Comoros crash": the Comoros

are notable, in the first place, as a site of aviation accidents. They constitute a sovereign state and comprise a chain of volcanic islands in the Mozambique Channel, northwest of Madagascar. Since independence from France was achieved in 1975, the islands have seen twenty coups/attempted coups. Comorian and French are the main languages; Arabic is also spoken. The main economic activity is agriculture: vanilla is cultivated there, and the islands are the world's largest producer of ylang-ylang, the oil of which is an ingredient of Chanel No. 5 perfume. Photographs of the Comoros show a lake in a crater, a mongoose lemur perched on the rusted tin roof of a one-roomed residential proposition, and a very run-down little port, Moroni, the capital. Its old colonial warehouses give prettily on to forested uplands; its fishing boats lie prettily at anchor; there is no sign of activity.

Hold the airplane door, Ali, I'm coming.

Let's not be rash. Let's take a closer look.

Unemployment is very high in the Comoros. About half the population lives on less than 1.25 USD a day. People regularly try to "escape" to the nearby island of Mayotte, a French overseas department, and a good number drown in the attempt. As for Moroni, it sits at the foot of a highly active volcano. Moroni is Comorian for "in the heart of the fire."

I will not be joining Ali.

I'm shutting the laptop when, for old times' sake, and for the first time in a long time, and for the last time, I swear, I search myself, X. and all. Autocomplete suggests:

> dubai
> attorney
> forcible touching
> gay

The defamation continues. It's shocking. It's enough to make me want to lie down.

It's back into the Pasha. And it's back, on recollection's ice, to Mar-a-Lago.

The wedding of Melania Knauss and Donald Trump was an unusual event, but I think it may have been especially out of the ordinary for Jenn and me, who in the context of that gathering qualified as so-called "real people" or "civilians." This was in January 2005, in the very early, very successful days of *The Apprentice,* and many well-known NBC "personalities" and stars of reality television were wedding guests, and of course there were celebrities from other walks of life and reality. Jenn and I knew nobody there and yet, by an enchanting paradox, we were able to identify many of those present. These individuals had the charisma and suddenness of fauna. Here was Barbara Walters, startling as a secretary bird; there, like a small upstanding crocodile, was Paul Anka. It was especially outlandish to sight them in the church. The fellow next to me on the pew had a familiar TV-face—Pat O'Brien, I later figured out, the *Access Hollywood* host who afterward had a brush or two with disrepute, poor devil—and I remember that I could not help feeling it odd that he and his ilk should have to squeeze into the hard pews and humble themselves on the kneelers like everybody else. Jenn and I of course were known to nobody, but by virtue of our mere occurrence were understood to possess imperceptible power or renown, and certainly wealth. Almost every net worth present at the wedding was very high, I would say. At dinner, I was seated near two likable, non-famous, not-loaded-looking guys who said they were connected to the bridegroom by business. It was a relief to locate people on my own level, and we were able to talk about this and that. I kind of dried up when they began to exchange details of the résumés of their pilots. This isn't in any way to pooh-pooh them or the occasion.

As the dinner drew to an end, my attention veered to a neighboring table, where a man was eating almost in solitude:

save for a woman who was clearly his wife, the seats around him were vacant. Looking more closely at this forlorn diner, I recognized him from the newspapers: Conrad Black, the newspaper publisher who had given up his Canadian citizenship in order to accept a British peerage. Now Lord Black was an alleged embezzler. The SEC proceedings against him were only several months old and nothing had been proven, yet already a distinct cloud of downfall hung over this man, and apparently one or two of those seated near him had decided to eat somewhere else. I observed all of this unreflectively. I did not feel, stirring within, the organizing of moral faculties. I looked at Black like a boy looking at a duck. In the years since, I've kept half an eye on the Conrad Black story, though not out of any special sympathy for its protagonist, who seems unaccountably to have a Napoleonic idea of himself and, to be honest, rubs me the wrong way with his scornful pronouncements from on high, and absolutely doesn't strike me as the kind of dude I'd like to chill with, not that that's a valid measure of anything. No, I've followed his fate out of the same childish, selfish strain of curiosity that led me to gawk at him in the first place—that yearning to enter the territory where, deep in a forest, a dragon breathes heavily on a hoard of knowledge.

After dinner, there was dancing around the swimming pool. Jenn and I spectated. "The richer you are, the worse you dance," she said. I wanted to dance but I didn't ask her to, because she didn't like to dance, I think because it made her afraid. At a certain point, the Conrad Blacks took to the floor. The wife had eyes only for the husband, and vice versa, and as they swayed and shuffled on the spot, always smiling, they took turns to murmur confidences into the other's ear. For the duration of a song, they were the only ones on the dance floor, and Jenn said, "Who are those two?" I said, "He's Conrad Black. I can't remember her name. Mrs. Conrad Black." "Huh," Jenn said. I imagine that, like me, she was wondering what to make of this performance of amorousness, which I suspect left many feeling by comparison romantically wan. The uncharitable observer—is there another kind?—would say that the flaunting of a supposed connubial superiority was an important part of the fun the Conrad Blacks were having. I say, Maybe so; but subsequent events have shown that, whatever else they may be accused of, they are not guilty of making an insubstantial marriage. It is reported that Mrs. Conrad Black—a personage of independent notoriety, it would seem—has moved full-time to the couple's Palm Beach residence in order to be near her husband in his correctional facility, this even though she suffers from a skin condition that responds poorly to tropical sunlight, and even though she owns a pair of huge guard dogs, of Hungarian provenance, whose thick white fur makes them, too, ill-suited to Florida living.

As is well known, Lord Black's relations with the forces of justice only deteriorated after the Trump wedding, and I haven't kept up with the various convictions, judgments, suits, appeals, and proceedings (including moves to "strip" him of membership of the Order of Canada, to bar him from holding U.S. company directorships, and to discourage him from sitting in the House of Lords) that have engulfed him. I take no sides. I will only say that, if the moves against Black show no sign of ending, neither does Black's strangely joyful struggling. For the time being he remains in prison in Florida. Here, I find myself moved to a certain respect and sympathy—and, is it possible, envy: he has, as it were, surfaced from illusion. He is purely disgraced. He is behind bars. He wears a jumpsuit. His enemies have revealed themselves—as have, I feel sure, his friends. Also, obscurely, he is in the clear. Maybe I'm perverse, but I connect imprisonment to a limit of culpability. It's certainly true that, so long as he's inside, he can hardly be punished more.

The Swedish frictions came to an end some while ago. I have no wish to move. Because of my new phobia or new PTSD, the Pasha now faces away from the windows, and to open my eyes is to see a white wall. In its way, it is a magnificent vista. I could stay where I am, looking at that wall, for a long time— and in fact this is what I do, quite without foreboding. On the contrary: any minute now, Watson, followed soon after by the others, will as it were rat-a-tat-tat on the door.

ACKNOWLEDGMENTS

I am grateful for assistance received from the Dorothy and Lewis B. Cullman Center for Scholars and Writers; the John Simon Guggenheim Memorial Foundation; the National Endowment for the Arts; and the Corporation of Yaddo.

A Note About the Author

Joseph O'Neill was born in Cork, Ireland, and grew up in South Africa, Mozambique, Turkey, Iran, and Holland. His works include the novels *Netherland*, which won the PEN/Faulkner Award for Fiction and the Kerry Group Irish Fiction Award, *The Breezes*, and *This Is the Life*; and a family history, *Blood-Dark Track*. He lives in New York City, and teaches at Bard College.

A Note on the Type

The text of this book was set in Sabon, a typeface designed by Jan Tschichold (1902–1974), the well-known German typographer. Designed in 1966 and based on the original designs by Claude Garamond (ca. 1480–1561), Sabon was named for the punch cutter Jacques Sabon, who brought Garamond's matrices to Frankfurt.

*Composed by North Market Street Graphics,
Lancaster, Pennsylvania*

*Printed and bound by RR Donnelley & Sons,
Harrisonburg, Virginia*

Designed by M. Kristen Bearse